SHARON EDE

MAGE

First paperback edition March 2020

Book cover design & formatting by Damonza
Editing by The Expert Editor

Photo on cover credit to © Frode Bjorshol
https://flickr.com/photos/23391210@N06/23273281972

Thanks to

Joanna Penn, The Creative Penn www.thecreativepenn.com

ISBN 978-0-646-81511-4 (paperback)
ISBN 978-0-646-81663-0 (ebook)

www.magethenovel.com

A catalogue record for this work is available from the National Library of Australia

*To my mother, Irene, my father, Brian, and my
sister, Tanya, who support me in all I do—and
have always wanted to understand what I do!*

*To Professor William Rees and the late Professor Andrew
Wilford, for their work which inspired ideas in this book.*

*To Cherie Hoyle, Paul Downton, and Chris Adams—
friends and mentors whose guidance and generosity with
their time and knowledge have been invaluable to me.*

*Civilisation exists by geological consent,
subject to change without notice.*

—Will Durant

*We are systematically destroying the biosphere
as if we believe this is normal. Why?*

—Mathis Wackernagel

*The real problem of humanity is that we have paleolithic
emotions; medieval institutions; and god-like technology.*

—E.O. Wilson

*When we quit thinking primarily about ourselves
and our own self-preservation, we undergo a
truly heroic transformation of consciousness.*

*—Joseph Campbell, author of The
Hero with a Thousand Faces*

PROLOGUE: THE WAVE

Khao Lak Bay, Thailand, Boxing Day, 26 December 2004

Thirteen-year-old Ambra Lightstone skips across the white sand towards the turquoise sea; the clear water skimming the sand flirts with her feet.

Wearing her new red and silver swimsuit, her most prized Christmas gift from the previous day's festivities, she turns to see if her mother and father are paying attention to her.

In the distance, Robert Lightstone, sitting on the third-floor balcony of the family's holiday villa, is watching, and waves encouragingly.

Ambra sees him nudge her mother. Lillian Lightstone looks up from the book she is engrossed in, waves and smiles at her daughter before returning to her book.

Satisfied, Ambra turns back to play in the rippling shallows. Her older brother Jevon would have joined her in her morning swim, but today he has gone on a motorbike tour up the hills behind their villa. She looks up and beyond the villa, wondering if he will see her from the top of the hills.

Wading into the sea, Ambra revels in sinking her toes into the sand, burying her feet up to her ankles. She goes deeper into the water. The caress of the sea is irresistible. She slips into the water to lie on her back and float, gazing up at the powder-blue sky.

A perfect morning.

After a minute or so, Ambra rights herself, pulling her wet hair back behind her neck, and wringing out the seawater. She squints into the bright sunlight, taking in her surroundings.

Around her are the sights and sounds of carefree bliss. A young couple wading in the ocean are embracing. A family splashes on the shoreline, the smallest child shrieking in delight. An elderly couple are sunbaking on the beach. Out to sea, fishing boats dot the water.

The sun disappears behind one of the few clouds in the sky, casting a shadow across the coast. Ambra's eyes adjust, and she can see further into the distance.

One swimmer is much further out than everyone else. Ambra can just make him out—a young man with jet-black hair. Perhaps a local, used to these waters? Though in contrast to his dark hair, his skin is strangely pale, almost translucent. No one else is with him, and he appears to be intently surveying the coastline.

Then he raises a hand from the water, which Ambra knows is a swimmer's call for aid, and she fears he is in trouble; yet his face wears an incongruous expression of ecstasy. She waves at him to get his attention—he glances at her and then looks away.

She looks about to see if anyone else has noticed the lone swimmer, but everyone in the water in her vicinity is engrossed in their own fun. The sun reappears.

She turns back to look for the swimmer, but he has gone.

Ambra is convinced he is in trouble, and now she must raise the alarm to get help for him. She begins to head back to shore.

Then a most unexpected thing happens.

The sea disappears. Just like that.

In one instant, Ambra is standing waist deep in water on a tropical holiday. The next, the joyful sounds of other holidaymakers have gone quiet, replaced with confused murmurs as wet bathing suits cling to high-and-dry swimmers.

She wonders if the swimmer she had noticed was swept away in the receding water. He is nowhere to be seen. She begins to feel anxious for him—and about the sudden retreat of the sea.

Ambra looks around to see if her parents have noticed this odd incident, but her mother is still buried in her book, and her father appears to be napping behind his sunglasses.

She notices some disturbance along the shore, people gathering, pointing—a shark? Ambra is a surf lifesaver in training at home, and she is well aware sharks are one of the biggest threats in the ocean.

There seems to be some shouting, but she can't make out what is being said. She looks out to sea again, though the shoreline is now far below where it had been all morning and the evening before, when she had celebrated Christmas with her parents and Jevon.

Something is not right.

Then, far in the distance, she sees a concave of blue sitting above the horizon. It is almost imperceptible at first, but as it draws closer, she can see it is clearly racing towards her, and growing larger. The sea is returning—fast and fierce.

'It's a tidal wave!' she shouts, to warn anyone within hearing distance, frantically waving to get the attention of the couple and the family with the child.

'Hey! You have to run as far from the beach as you can—and get up as high as you can!' she screams, shouting and pointing to the horizon, then the shoreline, receiving quizzical looks in return. The older couple who had been sunbaking sit up.

'What are you talking about?' says the woman, with a slight accent. 'Oh—what has happened to the sea?'

'Get up! Get up and run!' yells Ambra.

Her head snaps around to look at the shore, but her parents on the balcony are still unaware. She holds her hands out in front of her. They are shaking uncontrollably. Her legs have turned to jelly.

A millisecond later, Ambra's body explodes with adrenalin, surging through her like fuel that has been set alight, and she turns to run.

She knows the incoming wave is many times her height, and it is moving much faster than she can hope to, despite her athleticism from training in surf and sand. But she has no choice; she must try, or wait to be engulfed by the torrent of water that is racing towards them all.

Her legs are burning with panic as she flies over the sand, wanting to put as much distance as possible between her and the watery wall of death.

She does not look back, but hears a steadily increasing roar behind her, like a thousand planes bearing down on the beach. Over the roar, she can make out faint shouts, but this time not shouts of joy.

Ahead, beyond the beach, she sees tourists, resort staff, and the local Thai people alike reacting—some fleeing, others looking out to sea, transfixed.

Everything goes silent.

Filled with terror and unsure if she will make it to safety, Ambra knows that her family is also in mortal danger. Have they noticed? She must warn them. She cannot get the air into her lungs to cry out—it is as if all of her survival instinct is being channelled to her legs.

Over the fury of the ocean gaining fast on her, she hears her father shouting from the villa ahead of her, two words that seem merged into one long, desperate howl: "AMBRA, RUN!"

Ambra makes it to her family's villa and halfway up the first flight of stairs. Despite the roar of the water, she can hear her father bellowing to her as he runs down to meet her. But he is too late.

The first wave of the tsunami hits. Water surges up the stairs behind her. She grabs onto the railing in the stairwell, but the water is rising too fast, snatching at her legs, then her waist barely a second later. She sees her father's crazed eyes looking down at her as he rounds the stairwell, the moment the water tears her from safety.

Everything goes dark as Ambra is sucked into a black washing machine of debris and filth. Around and around she tumbles, losing all sense of up and down. As the water churns, it vacuums out furniture, appliances, people and their belongings from her building into an artery of dangerous, toxic soup flowing into the streets.

Ambra's head finally breaks the water's surface and she gasps for breath. She tries to grab an approaching tree branch, but the rapidly moving water, coupled with being in shock, thwarts her attempts. The turbulent water slaps her eyes. It is hard to see far enough ahead to grab anything. There is a foul taste in her mouth, and her legs brush past all sorts of unidentifiable and unspeakable things.

Ambra recoils as she bumps into, and pushes away, drowned people and animals. Something sharp cuts her left leg and she knows it is bleeding, but she can only manage a weak cry.

She bumps into something solid and heavy that knocks the wind out of her. A car has become wedged in between a building and a sturdy palm tree. Ambra is able to haul herself out of the clutches of the water and climb onto the roof, which is jutting above the surface. She dares not think about whether anyone is inside—if so, they would already be drowned.

Teeth chattering despite the heat, she surveys the surrounding area from her precarious perch. She does not recognise where she is. She looks away from the sea, up to the hills behind, trying to orient herself, looking for a landmark. Jevon should be up there. She imagines him looking down on the scene below, and her throat tightens. Is he up there, or has he returned to the villa? And what of her mother and father? Have they eluded the watery wall of death, or are they in a situation like hers? Or are they—

Ambra shuts out the thought from her mind.

As she stands shaking on top of the car, gulping in deep lungfuls of air, the water appears to slow, though that could be because of the sheer volume of stuff the tsunami has swept into its path. Chunks of wrecked buildings, shredded boats, lifeless bodies, broken glass, plants and tree branches, souvenirs, shoes, fruit, suitcases—all floating past in a foul parade of destruction.

A call in a tongue she does not understand catches her attention, and she sees a boy floating towards her car, dark head bobbing up and down, his petrified eyes looking at her. For an instant, she wonders if he is the boy whom she saw out in the water earlier, but she can't be sure. Despite her own fear, her instincts kick in.

She gestures for the boy to try to move towards the car. The water level has dropped slightly, and she realises he is not going to wash past within arm's reach. Looking around, she finds nothing to aid her, no lifeline to throw to him. There is only one option, and no time to waste.

Ambra peels off her one-piece swimsuit and—strangely given the circumstances—feels a rush of embarrassment as she stands naked on the car roof. She holds one end of the suit and waits for the right time to cast the other end to the boy to give him the best chance of grasping it.

But the tsunami is not yet done. A second surge is churning on shore and moving inland.

Ambra drops to her hands and knees and flicks the loose end of the suit towards the boy, who grabs at it and manages to hang on. She lies flat on the car and attempts to reel the boy in. He is calling the same words rapidly, over and over, like a mantra.

Ambra doesn't need to understand what they mean to understand their meaning.

She uses all her strength to fight the current and, using her swimsuit rope to draw him closer, is able to grab the boy's wrist. He is wearing a braided leather bracelet on his wrist, which helps her maintain her grip.

Then the second surge hits. The car wobbles ominously. The boy's eyes are large with fright as the force of the surge causes Ambra to lose her grip on his wrist.

Her fingers snag under the bracelet, a tenuous last line of defence.

But the water is too strong. The leather bracelet snaps, and she watches in horror as the water snatches him away, still clutching her swimsuit. In the next moment, he vanishes under the water.

Over the surge, she hears hysterical screaming and looks up to see a Thai woman on the roof of a still-standing building which had been closer to the shoreline. She is pointing to the spot where the young lad vanished, her petrified eyes darting between the last sighting of the boy and Ambra. She fixes her gaze on Ambra, her face contorting with anger and shock as she wails her grief.

Ambra shakes her head, waving her upturned palms towards the woman.

'No, no, no, no, no … I didn't let go of him … he slipped,' she cries.

The woman continues to howl from the building roof. Though her words are incomprehensible to Ambra, every one of them hits her like an arrow.

Ambra collapses on top of the car roof, clutching the boy's bracelet, and bursts into tears—for the boy, and for her parents and brother who could well have met the same fate. She goes into shock, lapsing in and out of consciousness.

She is still lying comatose, curled up on top of the car roof when rescue teams find her five hours later. Devoid of any other effects or clothing that could identify her, her rescuers assume the leather bracelet she has clutched in her hand is hers, and so tie it to her wrist.

❧

It is three days before Ambra is reunited with her family, who are mercifully all alive—Jevon, because of his decision to go on a tour, and her parents because of the height and structural strength of the building they were in when the wave hit.

Her parents have endured an excruciating search of emergency centres and makeshift bulletin boards, all but certain their daughter has been swept to her death. But unlike so many others, their anguish ends when they find Ambra alive.

Ambra, traumatised, bruised and sore, and fighting an infection in her leg where the open wound had been exposed to the polluted water, is repatriated back to Australia, where she fights off bacterial infections with a cocktail of various drugs that make her nauseous.

Her lung function is affected by the amount of mud she has inhaled, which she is still coughing up months later, and her sinuses and ears have to be operated on to clear them of silt.

And every night she is shaken from her sleep, crying out as the wave chases her, and as the black water snatches a small boy from her grasp.

But she has survived.

Almost a quarter of a million other souls—both locals and visitors, in countries from Indonesia to Thailand, from Sri Lanka to India—have not.

THE UMBRELLA MAN

Adelaide, South Australia, ten years later

AMBRA SLIPPED INTO the amusement arcade and held her breath. Had she lost him?

Looking down at her sandy feet, she hoped that the grainy trail would not give her hiding place away. The adoring brown eyes of Casper, her golden retriever, whose leash she dangled from her left wrist, looked up at her.

'Good boy.'

She stroked the dog's downy fur.

Inhaling deeply, she tried to slow her breathing. Her inner voice chided her:

There's nothing to worry about. You're just being stupid!

Ambra's breathing slowed. Around her, various retro arcade games and pinball machines blinked, bleeped, jangled, and sought the attention of damp-haired kids in board shorts.

This old-school arcade had been a favourite place for

Ambra and her friends to hang out during high-school days, and right now it was a safe haven.

Either she was paranoid, or that strange little man was following her.

She had first seen him less than an hour ago, as she walked Casper along the beach.

There was a peculiar sort of paleness about the man, set as he was against the neon blue water and the myriad bright-coloured swimsuits, towels, and sunshades of the beach-goers. His white, Buddhist-style robe was gathered about his slight frame, and he was completely bald. His movements were calm, languid.

No one else seemed to notice him among the swimmers diving into rolling waves, the drone of the shark-spotting plane, squeals of sandcastle-building children, beach cricket cries of 'caaatchiiiit!', and the owners of various dogs ensuring their canine charges were not taking off with the tennis balls *thwacked* by beach cricketers.

That he did not attract attention other than Ambra's was even stranger than the man himself, for to shield his pale skin from the harsh sun, he held aloft an extraordinary umbrella.

It was the most magnificent umbrella Ambra had ever seen, shimmering with all manner of pale pinks, blues, greens, and silver. It was ethereal and looked like it might tear if you so much as touched it with the tip of your finger.

Casper in tow, Ambra ploughed her way through the soft white sand back to the foreshore. She longed for a cool drink herself but stopped to give the panting dog some refreshment before continuing home.

As she emptied the remaining drops from Casper's bowl, out of the corner of her eye, she saw the man making his way up to the foreshore.

Ambra and Casper crossed the street, and had begun to set off in the direction of home, when she noticed the stranger … following them? It was surely a coincidence; after all, paths to the beach for everyone were only at certain access points.

But a niggling unease gripped Ambra.

As she ambled along with Casper, she stole a glance at a shop window across the street and caught the reflection of the curious character, and his umbrella, about fifty paces behind her.

Should she stop and confront him? Or go to the nearest police station? What, and make a fool of herself if it was nothing! Perhaps she should just go home? Then this odd person would know where she lived. Until she was sure, she could not bring herself to go home.

Ambra chewed her lip and weighed up her options. The best way to find out if the pale man was following her was to quicken her pace. To keep her in sight, he would have to increase his pace too, and give his intentions away. Then what? She would worry about that later.

Ambra broke into a run, Casper loping along beside her, her bag—containing Casper's metal bowl, the plastic litter she had collected during her walk, and other beach paraphernalia—banging painfully on her hip. She rounded a corner as soon as she possibly could to break the stranger's line of sight.

She darted through Pete's fruit and veg shop, which had two street frontages, in this one and the next street over. Although Pete and Casper were good friends, dogs were not allowed in his shop. But Ambra and Casper shot through at such speed that they were in and out the other side before a surprised Pete could say a word.

Ambra doubled back towards the beach and bolted towards the amusement arcade on the foreshore. She would wait in here until she was sure the man with the pale umbrella had gone, and she could make her way home.

Casper flopped down on the floor of the arcade, tongue lolling, patiently waiting for Ambra's next game. Five minutes passed. No further sign of the man. Ambra cautiously peered outside. He was nowhere to be seen.

'You alright, love?' came a gentle voice.

Ambra looked around to find Stan, the arcade owner, peering at her over his glasses, a look of concern on his grizzled face.

'Uh—yeah, all good, thanks, Stan. Just playing a game with Casper,' Ambra said, her cheeks flushing further.

'Bit hot for games. Going to be another scorcher tomorrow,' said Stan, taking off his glasses and using the hem of his shirt to wipe the sweat from them. He ruffled the fur behind Casper's ears.

'Yeah—I've got to work tomorrow too,' said Ambra, glad for a chance to change the subject.

'Still, if you have to work on a hot day, an ice-cream shop's not a bad place to be,' chuckled Stan.

Ambra smiled as Stan gave her a wink and then went back to tinkering with the electronic insides of an arcade game.

'Come on, Casper,' Ambra tugged at the leash. Two feet and four paws headed for home.

From under a shimmering umbrella, a pair of pale eyes watched them go.

SEMAPHORE, SOUTH AUSTRALIA

THE BEACH WAS cooling relief for many enjoying their summer holidays. The southern summer had already been breathing its furnace-like heat over Adelaide for a week. Water restrictions were in force, and all that had been soft, lush green during winter was now crispy yellow-brown.

Ambra and Jevon had agreed to housesit while their parents were on extended absences for work, and Ambra had plenty of people-watching opportunities from the second-storey window of her parents' Semaphore home, which was on the Esplanade at the end of Hart Street, across the road from the beach. As a child, she had often sat curled up on the cushioned seat in the bay window, gazing out to sea, or using the telescope to spy sailboats, pelicans, and dolphins.

In the winter, she would watch storms roll in, mesmerised by their epic displays of lightning, as thunder rumbled all around.

In the summer, she would often catch sight of the nippers—junior lifesavers—in their brightly coloured swim shirts and caps, tearing up and down the beach, practising sitting over their boards and paddling through waves. Along with many of her friends, Ambra had been a nipper in her primary-school days. Fascinated with the sea, she had dreamed of becoming a marine scientist.

But since the Boxing Day tsunami, Ambra had been unable to swim in the ocean. She loved the beach; she could even still paddle. But she could not make herself swim.

She could not risk going under the water. And she had long since let go of the notion of a professional career in an underwater environment. Her psychologist had made it clear that she would be suffering lifelong effects as a victim of trauma, and to avoid situations where the trauma could flare up.

Sitting in the upstairs window seat, she absentmindedly twisted the braided leather bracelet on her wrist around and around.

Ambra had never uttered a word to anyone about her experience with the boy lost to the tsunami, and her inability to save him. The bracelet was a constant reminder but, somehow, she couldn't bring herself to get rid of it.

Watching the ocean, and the sunlight reflecting on its layers of aquamarine stretching to the horizon, she went over the afternoon's events in her mind. Should she tell Jevon about her strange experience? She wasn't even sure if the man had been following her.

A call from the lounge room lassoed her mind back to the present.

'Hey, Mum's on the news!'

Ambra barrelled down the stairs and joined her brother in the lounge room where he was sprawled on the couch, his gaming controller tossed to one side, gesturing at the TV screen.

The siblings had been anticipating this. The picture cut from the local newsreader to footage of an instantly recognisable city, half a world away.

The news monologue continued:

Adelaide scientist Lillian Lightstone has arrived in Venice, ahead of the release of her team's groundbreaking work, expected to be announced this week. Lightstone's international team, comprising leading academics, researchers, and practitioners from fields spanning psychology to neurobiology, have been working on a classified project for the last few years.

The screen cut to a shot of their mother, Professor Lillian Lightstone, surrounded by a sea of microphones wrapped in the logos of various international press outlets.

'This research announcement is one of the most significant since scientists revealed that they had succeeded in mapping the human genome,' said Lightstone.

The voiceover continued: *Lightstone's team expect to be demonstrating their research results in the next day or so.*

The screen cut back to the local newsreader, who was promising further coverage with a special report in the coming days.

Brother and sister smiled at each other.

'This is going to be great for her career—she'll end up on magazine covers,' said Jevon.

'And the research could change the world, could change history!' said Ambra.

'Well yeah, that too … shame Dad's not here to see it right now.'

'He'll see it soon enough. You know he's up to his neck in that project of his right now. But yes—he'll miss Mum's announcement,' lamented Ambra.

'That project' was what their father, Robert Lightstone, a computer programmer with the CSIRO, Australia's national science agency, had been working on for months in Canberra. Neither of them was clear on exactly what it was, but then their father had been somewhat vague in explaining it. Since Christmas, he had been on a two-month special assignment in an undisclosed location and unable to communicate with his family.

'Well, he's off-grid for the next few weeks until his work's done, so I don't reckon he's gonna see anything,' said Jevon, who vaulted from the couch as soon as the news turned to announcing a string of car chases, fires, and local crime. With a grin, he thumbed in the direction of his game console. 'I'm off for a run. It'll be too hot to go out tomorrow. That'll give me a chance to get stuck into my two new games.'

Ambra rolled her eyes. 'Such a waste of time. Get a real hobby! What are we doing for dinner?'

'Dunno.'

'Are you hungry yet? It's gone seven. I'm getting hungry.'

'Let's worry about it when I get back,' she heard him call, as the screen door banged shut, and the sound of his footsteps increased in pace, decreased in volume, then disappeared. Ambra was alone in the house.

She flipped through all the TV channels, but eventually gave up, instead gathering up textbooks, notebooks, pens, and her laptop, and settling herself at the dining-room table. Her final year of university was starting in a matter of weeks. She flipped open her *Bachelor of Communication and Media* course guide. It was her second choice for study and career. Though her family had encouraged her to try, she had decided not to pursue marine biology.

The room filled with golden light as the sun followed its path to the horizon. Fifteen minutes later, Ambra was engrossed in her first semester university schedule, unaware that the man with the mother-of-pearl umbrella had arrived at her door.

THE SAND POET

THE UMBRELLA MAN had slipped up the stairs to the verandah, silently opened the screen door, and entered the Lightstones' living room.

Sensing an arrival, Ambra looked up from her university documents, expecting to see Jevon.

Instead, the pale-skinned stranger from the beach was staring back at her, his umbrella tucked under his arm.

Ambra jumped out of her chair.

'Who the hell are you, and what are you doing in my house?' she barked, her eyes darting around the room in a frenetic search for the nearest object she could use as a weapon.

The pale one calmly held up his hands, palms facing her in a conciliatory gesture.

'I, Sand Poet. No afraid.'

Ambra's tense muscles softened slightly.

At that moment, she heard the rapid breathing of Jevon returning from his run. Footsteps up the verandah stairs, the bang of a door, Jevon arrived and stopped short as he discovered an odd-looking stranger in an uneasy situation with his sister.

'What's going on? Who are you?'

The peculiar man began to speak, in a soft, sing-song voice. He put his hand on his heart.

'I, Sand Poet. No afraid. Deliver message for you.'

Jevon looked to Ambra.

She shrugged. 'I don't know who he is, but—I thought he was following me on the beach today.'

'You didn't tell me!'

'I wasn't sure if he was or not. Didn't think it was any big deal.'

The Sand Poet opened his umbrella, which was swirling with different colours—now ice blue, now soft pink, now pale green, now silver.

As Ambra and Jevon watched, mesmerised, the patterns on the umbrella seemed to coalesce and take form. The colours deepened and diversified. Shapes appeared. The picture began to materialise, a silhouette of a person.

The image continued to fill with detail, like a file downloading, its resolution sharpening. Finally, they could make out a familiar face.

Their mother, Lillian Lightstone. The image spoke:

Jevon, Ambra—please listen carefully and do as I say. The authorities here in Venice have made us aware of a threat to our team, from certain interests who don't want our technology made available. We are extremely worried that our loved ones may be tar-geted to coerce us into preventing its release.

I am trying to contact your father, because I will be unable to use any electronic communication shortly, as I cannot risk our exact location being revealed. If you have not heard from Dad by the time you receive this, then you must go with the bearer of this message for your own safety, as we are no longer sure whom we can trust in our world.

I know this must seem strange to you, but please don't worry—this man and his people can be trusted. I'll see you soon. Love you.

The image blew a kiss and then dissolved.

Ambra's eyes filled with tears.

'How do we know she wasn't made to say this? That you don't work for whoever it is she is warning us about?' said Jevon, eyeing the Sand Poet suspiciously.

'Is truth,' said the Sand Poet, his face serene.

'And what did Mum mean by *we're not sure whom we can trust in* our *world?*' cried Ambra.

The Sand Poet glided towards the Lightstones' glass-topped coffee table in the living room. He moved a book and a vase, carefully setting them aside. Then he reached into a bag he had concealed within his robes and scattered several handfuls of fine white sand onto the tabletop.

Murmuring softly as he worked, he began to craft a picture from the grains of sand on the living-room table. His hands shaped what appeared to be a city, a magnificent structure built within a giant sphere that appeared to be floating in, and partly under, the ocean.

'Atlantum,' said the Sand Poet, as he put the finishing touches to the image his hands had crafted.

'This is where you're from?' asked Jevon.

'I, Sand Poet, must bring you to Atlantum, home to Ondans.'

Ambra's face contorted with horror.

'What? You mean—*under* the ocean?'

'No fear. T'will be all right,' murmured the Sand Poet.

Ambra had gone as pale as the Sand Poet's umbrella.

'Who on *earth* are the Ondans?' Jevon demanded.

The Sand Poet chuckled at this, as if it was a clever joke.

He removed a glass vial from within his white tunic, loosened the stopper, and sprinkled a small amount of a powdery substance into his hand. Like his umbrella, the dust shimmered pink, green, blue, and silver.

'Mother-of-pearl dust,' explained the Sand Poet, as the siblings peered at the small pile of fine powder in his pale, smooth hand.

Without another word, without any warning, the Sand Poet swung his arm across his body in a wide arc, casting the dust into Ambra's and Jevon's eyes. A blue-green veil clouded Ambra's vision. Her ears filled with the sound of the roaring ocean, the taste of saltwater on her tongue. She became irresistibly drowsy. She could not fight it.

ATLANTUM: SOUTHERN
PACIFIC OCEAN

AMBRA'S EYES HALF opened.

She propped herself up on her elbows. She was in a circular bed, bundled up in soft, snow-white sheets and pillows. Covering her was a light dove-grey woven blanket into which dozens of tiny pearls had been stitched. It was exquisite, and the most comfortable bed she had ever been in.

But it was not her bed.

Yawning, she rubbed the last of the Sand Poet's dust from her eyes.

The Sand Poet's dust!

Her memory snapped back like a rubber band.

Looking around, she saw she was alone in a small, spherical room that shone blue-green with the light that penetrated its translucent walls and ceiling. There was a mirror on one wall, with a pattern of dozens of tiny seashells engraved around the edge. An ornate silver lamp hung over the centre of the room emitting a soft glow. It was completely quiet.

It was a haven of peace and beauty, yet Ambra's heart was racing.

Where am I? And where is Jevon?

Swinging her legs over the side of the bed, she found she was still fully clothed, but someone had removed her shoes, which were placed neatly under a chair next to the bed. She padded towards what looked like the door to the room—except it wasn't, as there didn't appear to be a handle, just a wall of swirling, spiralling blue and green. Was it even solid?

Ambra gingerly put out her hand to touch it.

The door vanished, revealing a spacious, concave room with a high ceiling. Jevon sat at a long oval table, intricately carved from what looked like white marble. He was speaking in a low voice with a curious-looking man. There were two crystal cups and a matching pitcher on the table.

The Sand Poet was nowhere to be seen.

The two looked up at Ambra's appearance.

'What's happened? Where are we?' blurted Ambra at Jevon, ignoring the stranger. She had not meant to be rude, but was disoriented and had many questions.

Jevon smiled at her as he got up from the table.

'Don't worry, Ambs, Mum's asked these folks to bring us both here, so she doesn't have to worry about our safety—just in case.'

'In case what?'

'There are vested interests - certain governments and corporations - who don't want her team's research released. The team have got security around them, but Mum wanted to make sure no one got to us.'

'What about Casper?' Ambra fretted.

Jevon grasped his sister's shoulders.

'Mum got a message to Ruth before we welcomed our sand-throwing visitor. She'll go get Casper and look after him.'

Ruth was their elderly neighbour. She and Casper adored each other, and Ambra had no doubt she would care well for him. He was probably napping on Ruth's living-room floor under the ceiling fan right now.

'This is the safest place until the announcement. We'll only need to be here a couple of days.'

'Where is "this"? Where exactly are we?' Ambra's voice quaked. 'We're under the bloody ocean, aren't we?'

'Not exactly,' said Jevon.

Ambra began breathing rapidly and shaking.

Oh no! I can't have a panic attack now!

'I can't be here, Jevon! I want to go home!'

Jevon put his arm around his sister, then turned back toward the marble table, gesturing to the man he had been speaking with.

'This is Quill,' he said, introducing the sturdy man who was walking towards Ambra, hand outstretched.

Ambra was quivering. She grasped the man's hand.

As his skin made contact with her, Quill's energy spread through her every muscle, blood vessel, and nerve ending, like liquid light. Her shoulders dropped and her jaw loosened. She exhaled.

Quill was older than both of them, but it was impossible to guess his age. His dark hair was flecked with grey and cut short enough to stop it curling.

He wore a leather work belt that held a variety of different writing instruments in silver cylinder casings; some were elaborate antique pens, others looked modern and high-tech. He had a pleasant face and wore rectangular spectacles, over which he peered at Ambra with kind blue eyes.

'Ambra. I am Quill, Chronicler of the Ondans. I keep and write our history. Would you like a drink?'

'Uh … yes. Yes please. Sorry, I'm still drowsy from … sand …' Ambra shook her head. 'What *was* that?'

Quill went over to the marble table and produced a third crystal cup, into which he poured a pale orange-coloured liquid from the pitcher. Ambra wasn't sure she wanted to drink it, but once she put it to her lips, she discovered it was cool and refreshing, with a delicate floral flavour.

Within moments, she felt a deep sense of relaxation in her body.

'That's lovely! What is it?'

Quill smiled. 'Iced coral tea. It will calm your anxiety

about being here. It was developed especially for Terran guests who felt as you do, then it became a favoured beverage of Ondans too. Its effects should last for several days.'

'Where's the Sand Poet? I didn't know who he was or what was going on—and then without even warning us, he threw some kind of magic dust over us, and *whoosh*!'

Quill's face creased with amusement.

'The Sand Poet is almost mute, at least when it comes to speech—his sand-pictures are how he prefers to communicate,' he explained. 'I apologise if his limited ability to communicate frightened you, but we had to send him, and not only because his magic dust and umbrella were needed to bring you here to Atlantum. Ondan Sottomarans cannot be exposed to direct sunlight, and as fragile as he is under your sun, Sand Poet tolerates the Terran environment a lot better than most of us, as long as he has his umbrella.'

'What's different with him, then?' asked Jevon.

'Many years ago, the Sand Poet's mother had a child who was part Terran. The boy's name was Lyris, but as he grew and became one of Onda's most celebrated artists, he became known as the Sand Poet.'

'So, this is Onda?' Ambra gestured at their surroundings.

'No, this is Atlantum, the capital city of the Ondans, *amphibious submarinis*. We are one of two tribes of ocean dwellers, known as Sottomarans,' explained Quill. '*Onda* means wave, as we live within structures that stay on or just beneath the surface of the waves, depending on both the weather and proximity of Terran ships, planes, and satellites.'

'How do you hide something this big from us … from Terrans?'

'The outer domes of Atlantum, and our other smaller cities, have been specially engineered and built with a reflective coating developed for use in Terran military applications. It makes us invisible to the human eye, and any kind of radar or satellite detection devices.'

'Do you … take this thing under the ocean surface?' asked Ambra.

Quill laid a reassuring hand on her arm.

'Don't worry, you will be perfectly safe. Your brother has told me about your fear of the sea.'

Ambra forced a smile. She didn't like people knowing about it, but there was no choice here.

'What about the other tribe? Do they live in cities like this?' asked Jevon.

'The Nautilans, *nautilus submarinis*, are the other tribe. They inhabit the depths of the ocean and are never above the surface. Unlike Ondans, Nautilans can only last a few minutes on Earth's surface during the day, as they have evolved underwater. Their skin is very pale, almost translucent, and they are highly sensitive to not only the sun, but any natural Terran light including the moon. Exposure to direct sunlight will kill them in less than a minute.'

'*Submarinis* … both tribes share one Latin name—are you from the same family?' asked Ambra.

'We were,' replied Quill.

Ambra noticed a wistful look cross Quill's face.

'Let's not dwell on that,' he said in a brighter tone. 'You've arrived at a special time for Ondans. Tonight, we celebrate one of our most important occasions, a royal birthday, to which you are both invited as a welcome for your arrival in Atlantum! Our host will be Her Majesty, the Queen of Onda.'

'Thank you, we'd be honoured, although I am not exactly dressed for it,' said Ambra, looking down in dismay at her dishevelled clothes.

Quill gave her a wink.

NAUTILA: DEPTHS OF THE NORTHERN INDIAN OCEAN

NECRO, CROWN PRINCE of the Nautilans, strode down the long, darkened corridor towards his mother's court. The felt boots all Nautilans were required to wear in their deep-sea abode masked his footsteps.

His mother couldn't stand unnecessary noise.

The corridor was lined with black light LED strips that emitted a dim glow, reflecting the deep ocean habitat of Nautila, home to the several hundred thousand of their species that remained.

Entering the court, Necro's eyes took a moment to adjust, as the cavernous room was lit with royal-blue light.

A long, wide table dominated the room, decorated with silver flute glasses and platters of food laden with Nautilan culinary delights, and also a bowl of apples and bananas—exotic fruits Necro had brought back from his last voyage to Terra.

At the head of the table, on a raised bed of black rock hewn from the seabed, sat a distinguished older woman on a massive throne carved from the same black rock as the table. Her throne was lined with luxurious purple-and-navy cushions and silks.

'Mother …,' began Necro.

'Your Majesty!' snapped the older woman from her throne.

Necro sighed under his breath, and only just managed to stop himself rolling his eyes.

'Your Majesty.'

His twin brother, Neven, and their younger sister, Nemeia, were seated on either side of the head of the table, directly below their mother's throne. As next in line to the Nautilan crown—by virtue of being born two minutes before Neven—Necro hated being chastised in front of either of his siblings.

Nefaria, Queen of the Nautilans, lifted her chin an inch. Her long silver hair was woven into a thick braid. Her navy eyes bored into her oldest son. Almost imperceptibly, one eyebrow moved, indicating that Necro could speak.

'Nadir is nearly ready to be activated,' he said. 'There is just a bit more technical testing to carry out.'

Neven and Nemeia exchanged glances.

'What do you mean *technical testing*?' his mother demanded.

'Just a few minor tweaks. And I still need to source the superconductor.'

'Oh—you mean the one thing you need to make it

actually work? That is not *technical testing*, it is the essential element to initiating Nadir!'

'I've got people on it.'

Queen Nefaria waited.

'Our Terran contacts,' offered Necro.

'Your climate-denier Terrans, who are happy to see many of their species wiped out? They haven't been able to come up with a thing—not one option for a superconductor of the capacity we need, in two years,' Nefaria replied caustically.

'I'm on it, Mo—Your Majesty,' said Necro through gritted teeth. 'I'm chasing down several promising leads. But you know we have to move carefully—they cannot know its true purpose. They would never provide one if they knew we intend to rid the world of *all* Terrans, including them.'

'It's one of two possibilities: they either genuinely don't have, or know where to access one; or they do, and don't want to deliver it to us, for some reason - perhaps some dissent among their ranks about providing it,' mused Nefaria.

'We need an incentive to unearth whoever can provide us with a superconductor,' said Necro.

'We might be in luck on that front. Lillian Lightstone and her team are in Venice, Italy, about to make a major announcement,' said Nefaria. 'I don't have to tell you why they chose that particular city for a media event. The Terran press are at fever pitch over it. We don't know what the exact details are, something to do with geo-engineering to prevent sea level rise, but we can't allow them to go public until we know more.'

'How is that going to help us find a superconductor?' said Necro.

'We can use Lightstone's research as leverage with the Terrans. There *has* to be a buyer *somewhere* on Terra who knows where to source a superconductor - someone who is prepared to make a deal to give us that information in exchange for the opportunity to interpret this announcement for the mass media.'

'You mean spin it,' interjected Nemeia.

Nefaria turned on her daughter. 'You will stay silent!'

Nemeia's face remained impassive.

'What do you need me to do?' asked Necro.

'Go to Venice. Locate Lightstone's team, remove from them whatever they are about to announce to ensure it is not released as Lightstone intends.'

'The Nerean Kiss, perhaps?' said Necro.

Nefaria's lips formed a faint smile at Necro's suggestion.

'That may be unwise,' said Neven, shifting in his seat.

Nefaria turned slowly to face her second son, considered his words momentarily, and returned her gaze to Necro.

'No—not yet. It is not worth risking our relationship with the Terrans by harming Lightstone, not until we have a superconductor.

Without another word, Necro bowed, turned on his heel and marched out of the court in the direction of the transport dock.

Nefaria watched him go. Nemeia watched her mother.

VENICE

IN WINTER, VENICE was a different creature.

Her hot, crowded tourist high season had long since ended, and the northern winter had crept in along the canals and into the bones of the city. *La Serenissima* was wrapped in grey, white, and pale blue.

Necro had arrived after dark and immediately set about looking for Lightstone and her team in the maze of *calle*, churches, canals, and courtyards that was Venice.

He was unable to pursue his mission during the day. Having evolved in a much deeper and darker ocean environment than their Ondan kin, Nautilans risked literally frying to death within a minute of exposure to the full Terran sun. Even the moon's reflected sunlight, as it waxed and waned, and especially around the time of the full moon, could result in a painful case of moon-burn.

Though his father had been Terran, and Necro could therefore endure limited time on Terra, he was still only able to visit after sunset, and he found the cooler, darker seasons easier to bear than when the sun was at its zenith.

Just before dawn, he returned to his aquapod, a small autonomous submersible, to dive into the depths of the lagoon, where he slept and waited for the sun to slip below the horizon.

Lightstone's team had chosen the week leading up to Carnevale as the time and place to make the announcement about their breakthrough work.

There was an increasing buzz in the city as Venetian society, along with visitors who had arrived from across the globe, prepared for the festivities, buying and fitting costumes, and organising food, music, and decorations for elaborate events.

Necro discreetly enquired at major hotels and restaurants, but no one had noticed the researchers. All attention was on the approaching Carnevale.

For two nights, he roamed the narrow streets and alleys, listening to conversations and talking to shop owners. He rode the *vaporetto* along the Grand Canal, scanning both sides of the main waterway.

On the second night, he was en route from San Marco to San Polo when he happened across two young women on top of the Rialto Bridge, gazing at the lights of the Grand Canal, and the watercraft gliding in both directions under the famous arch. It was well past midnight, and few other people were about.

They are not Venetian.

People don't tend to sightsee in their own city, and

aside from Carnevale, this was the tourist off-season. They weren't wearing or carrying Carnevale masks or costumes.

As he watched, one of the women farewelled her friend with a kiss on the cheek and a wave as she descended the bridge stairs towards San Polo.

Necro climbed to the top of the bridge, stood a few feet away from the remaining woman, and placed his hands on the ledge, breathing in the frosty night air.

Alerted to his presence, she turned and smiled at the striking stranger who had appeared next to her. She was in her thirties, plain, but with a pleasant enough face. Her light brown hair fell in soft waves to just below her chin. A red scarf circled her neck, the ends tucked into a fitted black winter coat.

'*Buona sera*,' said Necro, his voice velvet, his eyes making contact with the young woman's and holding her gaze.

'Hello,' she replied. She was not drunk but had clearly had a few drinks with her friend.

'You're not from here,' Necro said.

'No, I'm from Seattle.'

'Ah, an American. On a tour?'

'I wish. I'm only here for a few days. I'm part of an international research team that's meeting here for the first time. We've got some big news to announce. The press is going to go crazy tomorrow.'

A faint smile flickered across Necro's face.

She turned back to look at the canal with a wistful look.

'A shame it's a business trip. I was just saying to my colleague that Venice is such a romantic city.'

'Indeed, it is. I can never decide which *sestiere* is my favourite part of Venice, so I stay in a different area each time. This time it's San Polo. What part of Venice are you staying in?'

'We're all staying in San Polo too!' she exclaimed. 'We're staying in a gorgeous place that has a breakfast room overlooking the Grand Canal.'

Necro grinned, less at her effusiveness than at how helpful she had been in narrowing the search down. He thought about offering to walk her back to her hotel so he could discover the team's location, but then decided she could give him that information in a different way, and serve a far more powerful purpose.

They spent another few minutes chatting, Necro making her laugh on several occasions. He sensed her warming to him. There was a moment of silence. He took his opportunity.

'You truly are a beautiful woman,' he whispered.

She did not reply and seemed lost for words. He couldn't tell if she was blushing, or if it was the cold night air, or the wine in her cheeks.

He gently took her face in one hand and lifted her lips towards his.

'I don't even know your name,' she murmured, with no further sign of protest.

Necro brushed his lips over her willing mouth.

Then he gave her the Nerean Kiss.

From deep within him, and also out of nowhere, a torrent of seawater regurgitated from Necro's mouth into the woman's. She struggled but he held her fast, the flow filling her lungs in seconds, the overflow spilling onto the Rialto Bridge and down the steps.

Though she choked and tried to break free, he was too strong. There was a dreadful gurgling noise, then she lost consciousness in his arms, and finally went completely limp.

Necro released his grip and her body slid to the ground. He wiped his mouth, gathered his victim's red scarf and threw it over the edge of the Rialto Bridge into the Grand Canal, before slipping quickly and quietly away from the scene.

The city authorities would find the body in the morning—not in the water, where it could be assumed the poor young woman had drowned, but on top of one of Venice's famous landmarks.

The murder would delay the media event of Lightstone and her team, giving him the opportunity to steal the research and technology, and then find a buyer.

His mother had instructed him not to harm Lightstone.

She hadn't said not to harm anyone else.

ATLANTUM

'YOU READY?' CAME Jevon's soft voice from outside her door.

Ambra had already bathed and dressed, relieved to find clothes befitting the occasion laid out on the bed in her room, courtesy of Quill—a simple but elegant white sleeveless top, a pair of soft, loose pants in pale green, and an Indian sari-like garment in royal blue, with tiny silver stars embroidered through it—and was now slipping her feet into strappy silver sandals.

There was a mother-of-pearl clip on the dressing table, which she used to loosely pin up her wavy, shoulder-length hair. A coral-coloured lip gloss had also been provided, and she swiped a dab of it over her lips before emerging from her quarters.

Jevon was waiting, dressed in a fitted royal-blue shirt and white pants, the colours setting off his tanned skin and wavy, dark hair. Ambra had often wished that she, too, had inherited her mother's olive skin and dark hair, and not her father's light skin and auburn hair.

As the siblings stepped out from the windowless blue-green domed rooms where they had arrived in Atlantum, they found themselves on a balcony overlooking an entire city. Ambra's mouth formed an 'o'. She turned to look at Jevon, whose eyes were struggling to take it all in.

The majority of the buildings wore cloaks of green vegetation, the hanging gardens scattered with splashes of colour where various plants were flowering or bearing fruit.

Ambra inhaled lungfuls of sweet, cool air.

A grand, white, onion-domed building gleaming in the centre of the city caught her attention.

'That has to be the Royal Palace,' she said, pointing.

'Incredible,' whispered Jevon, 'there must be half a million of them living here.'

Atlantum was constructed across several layers. The lower layer was aquatic, with some of the buildings half-submerged, water lapping at their walls. A series of canals ferried watercraft of all kinds, some with cargo, throughout the city. A separate system of water canals enabled the amphibious Ondans to traverse their city by swimming instead of walking if they preferred.

Ambra watched as an Ondan with a young child on his back emerged from the water, climbing up a short flight of steps and onto a footpath. At first, he and his child were dripping wet, but by the time he was at the top of the steps, their clothes and hair had dried.

The central layer from which Ambra and Jevon surveyed the city was a series of narrow roads and narrower walkways connected by arched bridges over the waterways.

The Ondan roads were not roads in the Terran sense, as there were no motorised vehicles, but there were all kinds of wheeled devices from hand-pulled carts to what appeared to be cousins of the Terran bicycle.

Looking up, Ambra realised there was an aerial layer to the city, its structures connected by sky bridges and walkways, and even a few ziplines.

She was glad that she would be able to get about the city without having to use the canals, and tried not to think about the entire structure being in the ocean.

Above her, a vast, transparent dome let in the sun and the blue sky overhead. It was well after midday right now, which by Ambra's reckoning meant they were in a time zone, and therefore a location, not far from home.

As she scanned the dome, she spied something that caused her breath to catch in her throat.

Despite being enclosed, the city's atmosphere was fresh ocean air, as the dome was fitted with multiple vents that could be opened or closed as needed.

Ambra clutched Jevon's arm, pointing to the vents.

'Why would they need vents that *close*? They don't seriously take this thing ... *under* the water—do they?'

'Hello!' came a call from below them, saving Jevon from having to answer.

Quill was beckoning them down the stairs that led down to the street from their quarters.

The siblings joined Quill, following him along the streets and paths of Atlantum.

'All the street and building signs are in both English and Ondan. Everyone in Onda speaks English, and many of us speak two or more Terran languages.'

'Hang on—if Ondans can't visit Terra for any length of time, how'd you learn our languages?' asked Jevon.

'We have had researchers and scientists from many countries spend time here over the years, including your mother,' said Quill. 'She has been learning from our scientists who have developed an advanced technique related to her field. And we are as keen to learn from Terrans as they are to learn from us, though a condition of such visits was that they were sworn to secrecy, a promise they were prepared to keep in order to protect us—and to enable their return visits to Atlantum.'

Crossing a narrow footbridge that spanned a canal, they emerged into a square where groups of Ondans were enjoying lunch, relaxing, and socialising under leafy trees.

Ambra inhaled the scent of orange blossom, and the garden beds full of flowers that were dotted throughout the square. A fountain played at the far edge of the square, the water cooling and moistening the air.

At the centre of the square was a tall obelisk of white marble, carved with Ondan characters. At the top of the structure was embedded a timepiece fashioned from burnished steel and precious metals.

'Wow—what is this? Some kind of artwork?' asked Ambra.

'It is certainly a work of art, but its function is a

long-range clock, designed to keep accurate time for ten thousand years. Rather than measuring time hour by hour, it ticks once a year. The century hand moves forward once every hundred years. And on the millennium, a cuckoo comes out,' explained Quill.

Ambra laughed. 'That's a long time to wait for a cuckoo! Why would anyone build such a strange clock?'

'One of the Terrans who visited built it in conjunction with our craftspeople. It is called the Clock of the Long Now, and it is intended to stretch out our short-term thinking. Just as the Terran astronauts took a picture of our Earth from space and unleashed an idea of a bigger "here", this clock encourages us to think about a longer "now"—longer than the next week, next quarter, next year, even the next generation.'

'What are those other things, besides the numbers? Those orbs, and—are those stars?' asked Jevon.

'This clock keeps track of time not in only in our current cultural sense, but also natural time—the solar and lunar cycles, and the precession of the equinoxes through the zodiac, which is a cycle of about twenty-six thousand years.'

Ambra gazed upwards at the clock, trying to imagine life on Earth that far into the future.

Exiting through the square, they ascended a staircase that wound around the outside of a tower, arriving on a rooftop with a shaded balcony where they stopped to admire the view over the city.

Ambra craned her neck and waved towards the top of the dome.

'How can you have the sunlight coming into the city if you can't be out in the sun?'

'We are surface-dwellers, so we can tolerate the light, to some extent. And our dome protects us from direct sunlight—the intensity of sunlight in Atlantum is much less than actually being under the sun. See how it is more of a glow, instead of a bright light that makes you squint? No Ondan needs sunglasses.' Quill smiled.

He pointed at the dome. 'It's made of material that filters out harmful ultraviolet light, which is the main problem—especially after the Terrans thinned out the ozone layer and created a hole over the South Pole in the summer. Yet we prefer to stay in the southern hemisphere, where there is much more ocean and much less chance of being detected.'

Climbing down from the tower, they passed a small shop where stacked copies of the main Ondan newspaper, *The Raw Prawn*, were on display. Ambra could not read the Ondan characters, but Quill stopped to pick up a copy.

'Two teztels please,' said the shopkeeper pleasantly, as Quill fumbled in the small purse he kept strung about his neck. He handed over two tiny gold coins, then flipped the folded paper out.

He frowned at the headline.

'What is it?' asked Jevon.

Though she couldn't make out what the article was

about, Ambra saw the accompanying photograph. An ornate stone bridge over a river in a city somewhere. She felt sure she had seen it before, perhaps in a book, but couldn't quite place it.

'Nothing to worry about,' said Quill, his frown dissolving into a smile as he folded the paper. 'Let me show you around the Royal Palace before the banquet tonight.'

TOKYO

Umiko Satoshi burst into the eighteenth-floor meeting room of the True Illusion Agency's Tokyo office. On any other day, she would stop to take in the view over the grounds of the Imperial Palace. Through the frosty windows, she caught a glimpse of the palace, dusted in white, but did not stop to admire it.

'We know where he is!'

Her boss, Onmitsu Kaito, glared at her, but motioned her to a chair across the table from him. Several of her colleagues shuffled down the table to make room for her.

Umiko tabled a copy of *La Stampa*, and a handful of photographs she had printed from the electronic shots sent by the TIA's office in Rome, concerning a strange drowning of a young American woman on the Rialto Bridge.

Kaito gathered up the Italian newspaper and photographs and spent what seemed like an endless minute assessing them. Umiko could barely sit still. Finally, Kaito looked up.

'In Venice. It can only have been him,' he said.

'Yes! We can deploy inside three hours. If I leave now, I can get there in, say, fourteen hours, maybe by late afternoon tomorrow. When—'

'Hold on,' said Kaito quietly.

'What do you mean, "hold on"? We've been looking for this character for over ten years! We know what he's up to.'

'Umiko, we are the TIA. Our mission is very specific—to create the illusion of environmental crises before they occur, so that the public demand for change is well ahead of the actual anticipated crisis. Not to pursue individuals who may or may not be terrorists.'

'I know our mission, but unlike us, this character doesn't want to create the *appearance* of anything—he actually is looking for a way to *do* it!' cried Umiko. 'And if we don't stop him, even if he half-succeeds, we will get the blame if our agency and its work are ever revealed.'

'You overestimate his capability. There is no proof of your suspicions. In any case, there are other intelligence agencies who can deal with him.'

'But the other intelligence agencies have *not* dealt with him,' Umiko pointed out. 'If I can find him, I can find out more about what he's planning, and how to stop him.'

'What is he doing in Venice?' enquired Kaito.

'An international team of researchers has convened in Venice to release the results of some top-secret research. He's after it, but I don't know what it is or what he plans to do with it. That's why I need to go there. I don't know what this research is about, but if he wants it, then it is probably something we wouldn't want him to have.'

'Where are you at with your work program?'

Umiko's face flushed. 'I'm – er – in between projects right now.'

Kaito fixed his gaze on her. 'You mean you've been off tracking Necro.'

Umiko pressed her lips together and did not reply.

Kaito sighed. 'Very well. Go to Venice. That research is due to be released imminently, so by the time you get there, you will have only a small window of opportunity to find him.'

'*Arigato!*'

Umiko Satoshi, Special Operations Officer of the Eurasian Branch of the TIA, was on the next flight out of Narita, en route to Marco Polo Airport, Venice.

ATLANTUM

THE GRAND BALLROOM of Atlantum was lit with the golden glow of the setting sun, yet the air was pleasantly cool.

A thousand guests were expected for the banquet to celebrate the birthday of Lumina, the Ondan Queen's daughter.

Long tables with pale-green tablecloths were set with white plates, gold cutlery, and crystal glassware. Fresh flowers scented the air with jasmine. A five-piece string orchestra filled the vast room with a gentle melody.

Ambra and Jevon were seated with Quill, near the raised platform on which the royal table was set, where Queen Cresence of Onda and the rest of her party would shortly take their places.

Platters of pre-dinner treats were already laid out. Ambra spied pieces of what looked like finely spun toffee, shimmering with all the pale cool colours of the Sand Poet's umbrella. They were irresistible, and she reached out to take one.

'Featherlight sweets,' a new voice said, as Ambra placed

one of the pieces in her mouth. It melted like sherbet, the flavour changing from violet to lavender to rose.

'This is Aroz—he's our Chancellor.' Quill indicated the newcomer to Ambra's right. 'Aroz, this is Ambra and Jevon, from Terra, the children of Professor Lightstone—this is their first visit to Atlantum.'

Aroz was a tall, slender man, with a shock of spiky grey hair and a pointy nose. He was dressed in a tailored suit of royal blue and a silver-and-white silk scarf.

'Oho! Terras!' noted Aroz, his nose and one eyebrow lifting.

'Terrans,' corrected Quill.

'It's funny that you call us Terrans,' said Ambra. 'We're used to thinking of ourselves from whatever country we're from. And now you see us as just from Earth.'

'Earth—pah!' scoffed Aroz. 'Human beings are so self-absorbed. Of course, you Terras would call this blue orb Earth, when clearly its surface is three-quarters H_2O and $NaCl$!'

'It's *what*?' said Jevon.

'H_2O—water, and $NaCl$—sodium chloride, also known as salt. Don't they teach you anything of chemistry in your Terran schools? Saltwater, it's a beautiful yet paradoxical concoction—on the one hand, a sustainer of so much life, but also potentially toxic to any human who ingests too much of it.'

'Sounds like Ambra's cooking,' muttered Jevon, receiving a jab in the ribs from his sister in response.

Aroz waved his hands in the air. 'Tell me: what in Terra's name does your tribe think it is *doing*? Climate change! Mass extinction of species! Polluting land, air, and ocean!'

'It's a mess, isn't it?' admitted Jevon.

'Imagine,' continued Aroz, 'if this continues and you trigger ecosystem collapse. All of your human history could be lost. Every great work of art. Every literary masterpiece. Every reality TV show episode—'

'A lot of people on Earth—on Terra—are trying to change those things,' argued Ambra. 'But, of course, there are many who are resisting, or who don't see a need to change.'

'Resisting? It looks to us like a war between the human tribes,' sniffed Aroz. 'In fact, we call it *The War on Terra*.'

'Now, Aroz,' chided Quill, refilling the Chancellor's glass, 'the Terrans are not the only species in conflict with each other.'

Quill turned to Ambra and Jevon. 'We Sottomarans have our own conflicts.'

'What do you mean?' asked Ambra.

'Remember I told you about the second group of Sottomarans—the Nautilans? Once we were one. We'd evolved differently, yes—Ondans near the surface, Nautilans as the depth-dwellers—but we co-existed peacefully.'

'But not now?' prompted Jevon.

Quill shook his head.

'What happened?'

'Things changed when the Nautilan ruling family produced a queen who has some beliefs and values that are alien to even most Nautilans,' said Aroz.

'When Queen Nefaria came to the throne, she sought to consolidate her power by expanding Nautilan influence and ideology. The Nautilan elite see both Ondans and Terrans as inferior. Nautilans believe that because sea creatures are older than land creatures, they are evolution's preference,' explained Quill.

'Well, that makes zero sense—evolution's preference was for creatures to come out of the sea, onto land,' pointed out Ambra.

'We Ondans, however, evolved differently to the Nautilans in how we lived and adapted. As we have evolved closer to the surface and the shore, we have more in common with Terrans, and share the goal of stopping the Nautilans' destructive plans.'

'What destructive plans?' asked Ambra warily.

'The Nautilans refer to "Earth" as "Oceanus" because it is mostly water. To the Nautilans, more ocean means more territory and resources for them, which will allow them to expand and increase their numbers. They literally seek to "unearth the Terrans". They want the whole planet to become ocean once again, returning Earth to its watery origins.'

'What?' gasped Ambra. 'Can they even do that?'

'They don't expect they will have to. Nefaria and her eldest son and heir, Necro, have been pursuing their ideology by conspiring with Terrans who are attempting to block efforts to address climate change,' said Quill. 'The Nautilan royal family figure that by playing on the short-sightedness, foolishness, and inaction of these people that the Terrans will do their work for them. Simply by doing nothing, and staying on their current trajectory, Terrans will bring about a world in which the ocean reclaims the land, or at least a good part of it.'

'Wait—I'm trying to get my head around this,' said Jevon.

'So even though your people also live in the ocean, you're trying to stop these Nautilans?'

Quill nodded.

'From the Ondan point of view, the last thing our people want is for climate-induced sea-level rise. It will send untold volumes of Terran waste, pollution, and poison into the sea, fouling our homes and wiping out our food stocks, something that will not affect the Nautilan dwellers of the deep to anywhere near the same extent. That's why we are secretly working with key Terrans to help them tackle climate change, and to neutralise the influence of those the Terrans call *deniers*.'

Ambra winced as she thought of the tidal wave of muck that she had been swept up in by the tsunami and imagined what it would be like magnified many thousands of times.

Before she could properly take in Quill's revelations, a fanfare announced the arrival of the Ondan royal family. Along with everyone in the Grand Ballroom, she stood as Queen Cresence and her entourage entered.

VENICE

Umiko was the first one off the train when it arrived at Venice's Santa Lucia railway station from the airport.

Her phone pinged—it was a message from Kaito, conveying intelligence from the TIA's Rome office.

'LEAD RESEARCHER LIGHTSTONE STAYING NEAR SAN POLO, EXACT LOCATION UNKNOWN. CURRENTLY MEETING WITH ITALIAN AUTHORITIES.'

She took a *vaporetto* to the San Polo district and looked for accommodation. It was after sunset when she finally found and settled into a bed and breakfast, as most available rooms had been taken by visitors converging on the city for Carnevale.

While she was having a light supper in Campo San Polo late that evening, she spotted a man she had never before laid eyes on—but who was at the same time very familiar—slinking through the square in the direction of the Rialto Bridge, the scene of the previous night's killing.

It was Necro, without a doubt. After years of tracking

him virtually and learning everything she could about him, every detail of his physical appearance was etched in her mind's eye.

Leaving money on the table, Umiko abandoned her half-eaten meal, and followed her quarry out of Campo San Polo and under Sotoportego de la Madoneta, until she saw him slip quietly off the Ponte de la Madoneta into the freezing water, heading back towards the Grand Canal.

Umiko thought she had lost him, until she peered off the bridge. She could just make out a figure re-surfacing a short distance away, slithering up a drainpipe and unlatching a window before disappearing inside.

Crossing the bridge, she estimated where the associated street entrance was for the building Necro had slipped into and began weaving her way through the streets towards the Grand Canal—right on Calle del Forno, then right again, following the narrow street around until she glanced through the rails of a wrought-iron fence into the forecourt of a building. There was a small garden, the silhouette of a cat sitting on a ledge, and something unusual for Venice moving about in the yellow interior glow of the lobby—armed security guards.

There was no commotion from inside the premises, so it was unlikely Necro had been discovered by the security guards. He was waiting for Lightstone.

Umiko weighed up her options. Rather than engaging heavily armed security, which would risk alerting Necro to her presence, she decided to wait for the professor's return and prevent her from walking straight into him.

She melted back into the shadows. All was quiet, apart from the sound of a water taxi on the Grand Canal nearby.

Ten minutes went by. Her phone was on silent but buzzed in her pocket. Kaito.

'LIGHTSTONE HAS RETURNED TO HER ACCOMMODATION.'

Umiko's mouth opened slightly. How was that possible? No one had arrived or left. No one had arrived or left, *via the street entrance.*

She glanced to her left and followed the path down to the water at the canal's edge. Peering to the right, she saw a small dock, and a water taxi further up the Grand Canal, heading away from the dock, towards the Rialto Bridge.

Dammit!

&

Necro had swiftly discovered where Lightstone's team were staying in San Polo. All he had to do was wait till the next evening when the colleagues of his victim came to grieve and leave flowers at the spot where she had been found.

In their distracted state, it was very easy for him to tail them back to their accommodation without being seen. He was hours away from securing the leverage to demand a superconductor from the Terrans. With what he would soon have to offer, they would fall over themselves to make a deal.

The research team were in a series of apartments right on the Grand Canal, with many of the rooms featuring windows that opened onto a smaller waterway leading off the Grand Canal.

Instead of attempting to get past a number of security guards and cameras that had been put in place to protect the team, he had determined that it would be easier to swim up the side canal in the dark and climb up through the window.

A quick search of Lightstone's apartment unearthed nothing. Finding the safe empty, Necro concluded she must have the material for the press conference on her person.

It was just before midnight as he lay in wait for Professor Lillian Lightstone to return.

A key turned in the lock, and Lillian Lightstone flicked an entry light on. Her face was drawn. She had spent the day liaising with the Venetian authorities, the media, calling the young woman's family, consoling her team, and shoring up security arrangements. The changed security procedures meant the team would now be accessing their accommodation by private water taxi only, not via the street entrance.

'Hello, Professor Lightstone.' A lamp was switched on, casting a low light into the room.

Lightstone jumped. She turned to see a strikingly beautiful young man with cropped dark hair reclining casually on the couch, one leg crossed over the other.

'I'm here for your announcement assets, professor. And you'll give them to me one way or another, because you've seen what happened to your colleague,' said Necro, as he got up from the couch.

Lightstone took a step backward. Adrenalin flooded her body, but she kept her voice even.

'You will pay for what you did to that young woman. And you know you won't touch me—it will open too many questions into why I was killed. Anything you might use our material for will lack credibility.'

Necro grabbed Lightstone's arm and twisted it behind her back.

'Give it to me—now. You must have it with you, for tomorrow's press conference.'

'The press conference has been delayed because of the murder you committed!' seethed Lightstone.

Caught in Necro's grip, she glanced across the room to see that the safe had already been opened.

Necro's hands began to frisk her, searching for an electronic storage device. Jacket pockets, pant pockets. Lightstone struggled, but Necro was too strong, and held her fast.

He pulled aside her shirt and put his hand inside the Professor's bra, finding a custom-made memory stick inside a specially sewn pocket in her left cup. One end of the stick held a tiny capsule enclosed in a clear case.

He released Lightstone, whose face was blazing with anger and humiliation. He turned the stick over and over in his hand.

'So, just out of curiosity, what was your announcement going to be? Before we tell the world what the announcement is,' said Necro, as he tucked the stick and its capsule into a waterproof pouch and stuffed it inside his jacket pocket.

Lightstone glared at him. She undertook some quick mental calculations. If she shouted for help, Necro could well make her his next target for the Nerean Kiss, and in less time than it would take security to run up the stairs.

Since he already had the memory stick and capsule, she decided to tell him, partly as a way of stalling him, but also to see if she could learn anything about his next move from his response.

'Throughout much of human history, people have struggled to survive. But now there are eight billion of us, with a quarter of that population enjoying a material standard of living most people who have ever lived could not have dreamed of, and many more aspiring to the same life. Yet our indicators for human consumption and ongoing ability of Earth to support this tell us it's not possible even now, let alone into the future.'

Necro nodded. 'The Terran conundrum. What a pity for all of you that most of this planet is not land, but sea.'

'The same genetic traits that have been assets in our evolutionary success—including expanding into every available biological niche and becoming the biggest consumers of resources in Earth's history—have become a dangerous liability, and now threaten our survival.'

'Nautilans would agree—Terrans have become a pest species,' said Necro.

Lightstone ignored Necro's jibes.

'Yet, though the evidence of our detrimental activity is all around us, we cannot seem to find the "off" switch for this evolutionary momentum. In short, the Rapa Nui Gene is real—we have identified it. We have a genetic predisposition to bring about our own demise, as a species,' said Lightstone.

Necro's eyebrows rose.

'Genes, however, are only one factor, a tendency that will play out in the absence of cultural inhibitors to behaviours. Since we can't seem to develop such inhibitors, and don't have an inbuilt switch that trips when we reach sufficiency, we need to edit our genes. The complementary part of the research is that we are capable of overriding our genetic predisposition with our gene-editing technology and process, and this is the critical part of the findings,' Lightstone continued. 'We have developed a way to edit the Rapa Nui Gene using cutting-edge nanotechnology, which makes it safer, more accurate and possible to scale deployment of a process that will "switch off" the gene in human DNA. It is also germline gene therapy, which means this change will be passed on to subsequent generations.'

'You surprise me, professor. All the rumours and speculation I was hearing was that there would be an announcement of some type of geo-engineering technology,' said Necro. 'The Terrans have been talking for some time about everything from sun shields in space, to developing artificial leaves, to building walls under ice shelves to stop them melting.'

'Our Rapa Nui Gene is what is driving our *current* forms of destructive geo-engineering,' said Lightstone. 'You could think of this as a form of geo-engineering, in that it is a process that changes the geo-engineers themselves.'

'And so, when I take these discoveries to my contacts in the "climate denier" mass media, as you call it, they will tell the world the truth. Just not the whole truth,' said Necro.

The Nautilan's plan dawned on Lightstone, and she saw Necro smile at the realisation on her face.

'This is one of the biggest announcements in your field since the sequencing of the human genome was completed in 2000,' said Necro. 'We'll have the attention of the world, and we are going to tell the human race that the gene has been identified, which shows their civilisation is destined to collapse, like so many other examples of civilisations through history. But we're just going to tweak the truth about rewriting their genetic programming. We might even use the word "eugenics". That should turn people against the idea of editing.'

'You bastard!' spat Lightstone. 'This is nothing of the kind! We have the proof to show otherwise, and I will personally be live-edited during our press announcement.'

'What is that Terran saying, professor? A lie can get halfway around the world before the truth has its pants on. The retraction, the clarification, never gets the same focus as the first headline. This will be enough to sow despair and a widespread belief that humanity may as well resign itself to its inevitable fate.'

The door was kicked open.

'Put your hands behind your head, *now!*'

The slight frame of Umiko Satoshi was backlit in the doorway. Her gun was drawn and pointed at Necro. Close behind her was a black-clad security guard, his gun raised.

Momentarily, everything stopped. Then Necro bolted across the room to the open window.

Without looking back, he dove from the ledge into the canal. Umiko was not able to make the shot without risking hitting Lightstone, who had been too close to the line of fire. She raced to the window and peered into the darkened lagoon.

Aside from a ripple, there was no sign of Necro, who had no need to stay near the surface in order to breathe. Both the direction of his dive and the movement of the water told her he had headed for the Grand Canal. But had he gone left or right at the junction connecting to the Grand Canal? There was an even-odds chance of guessing correctly.

Umiko cursed in Japanese as she reholstered her firearm. Lillian Lightstone slid to the floor.

Umiko turned and darted over to the professor.

'Are you alright, ma'am?' she asked, putting her hand on the professor's shoulder.

Lightstone let out a long breath. 'I'm alright, physically,' she said. 'But he's just stolen technology and years' worth of research that is of vital importance. And I've just had a pretty rough 24 hours—that man killed one of my colleagues last night.'

'I'm sorry about your colleague. But you have copies of your work, yes?'

'Of course,' said Lightstone wearily, as one of the security guards appeared in the doorway. 'But due to the security risk, it needs to be brought from a place far from here, and the announcement has to be made before Necro releases the information in an unintended way. Within the next day, it will be announced to the world, but not by those who did the work. It will be misused and misrepresented by that thief, in collusion with certain powerful influencers in broadcast media.'

Umiko frowned. 'I don't understand.'

'Selective release of the findings will undermine efforts to tackle climate change, which puts at risk billions of dollars in infrastructure from sea-level rise, will exacerbate mass loss of species, lead to spikes in deaths from both pandemics and everyday illnesses, and reduce our capacity to produce food, among other critical concerns.'

'He is much more dangerous than even that, professor,' said Umiko. 'I'm sorry, I don't have time to explain right now.'

Umiko turned to the armed security guards, who had let her up to the room when she had approached them and shown them a badge identifying her as an officer of Japan's Public Security Intelligence Agency, and who had now come to investigate the altercation.

Switching to Italian, she instructed the guards to look after the professor before disappearing down the stairs and out into the labyrinth of the Venetian night.

MENLO PARK, CALIFORNIA

ALF ORTELIUS, HEAD of the US Geological Survey's California office, was poring over reports when his senior seismologist, Leith Williams, rapped on the open door of his office.

'What do you make of this?' asked Williams, thrusting a series of files with cover sheets pinned to the front under his chief's nose.

Ortelius frowned as he flipped through the files and examined the data, his eyebrows raising as its meaning emerged.

He leaned back in his chair, clasped his hands behind his head, and looked at Williams.

'Seems like we have some activity ramping up in a few spots of concern.'

He sat forward again and gathered up the files to double check.

What was going on? he wondered.

The fault lines in the Ring of Fire that stretched around the Pacific were reasonably predictable.

This activity was well out of the ordinary.

As he read, his fingers traced the areas of the Pacific Ocean the data were pointing to on the accompanying maps.

There were anomalies in ocean-floor trenches off the coast of Japan and, equally disturbing, along the San Andreas fault line, which ran the length of the west coast of North America.

The USGS and the Japanese authorities had been particularly nervous since the magnitude 9 earthquake that had hit Japan in 2011, and the devastating tsunami it had unleashed, causing catastrophic loss of life and a level 7 meltdown of a nuclear facility, leaving thousands displaced as it wreaked havoc in coastal communities.

Debris from that disaster was still washing up on North American shores years later.

Ortelius, who had been alerted in the small hours, US time, had witnessed that tsunami unfold live on television, watching in horror as the brown wave consumed the countryside, swallowing houses and people and cars that could not outrun the water. Tens of thousands had died, many swept away and never found.

That day haunted him, but the quake had been so powerful, and so close to land, that there was little lead time to issue any warning.

'I don't like the look of this,' he said to Williams. 'Get

me some intel on whatever might explain this—military exercises, fibre optic cables, mining—whatever. I don't care what or who, just that there's an explanation.'

Williams gave his boss a nod and disappeared from the doorway.

Ortelius rummaged through his address book and found the card for his contact in the Japan Meteorological Agency.

For all the technology he used in his job, he was old school with his communication. He reached for the phone.

VENICE

Necro emerged from the freezing Venetian lagoon onto the platform of the San Silvestro *vaporetto* stop.

It was late at night in the depths of winter, and there were only a few people about. No one noticed him emerging from the icy water. He shivered momentarily, but it soon passed, as he was dry in under thirty seconds.

The moon was almost full, but it was obscured in an overcast sky of slow-moving grey clouds, which was a relief. It meant he would not be in too much pain or need to move about under cover.

Lightstone's stick was safe in his waterproof pouch. He began making his way towards the less-visited edge of the watery city, where he had left his aquapod.

Remaining in the lagoon would have been better for staying unobserved; however, the icy water was barely tolerable, and to cross from this part of Venice to where he had docked the aquapod was quicker on foot than swimming around the city.

He slipped along Calle de Mezo and was making his

way back towards the Dorsoduro district where he had left his vessel, when he abruptly came face to face with a woman who had rounded a corner ahead of him. A pair of determined eyes widened as they recognised him.

That woman, not Italian law enforcement, but some other sort of police officer, had burst into the room as he was interrogating Lightstone. Spotting him, her hand went to the weapon at her hip.

Necro could not risk trying to apply The Kiss with a firearm in play. And there was no water to jump into in the alley.

He turned and fled.

෩

Umiko did not pull her gun—the narrow, twisting streets of Venice made it impossible to get sufficient line of sight on a fast-moving target, especially at night. She could not risk hitting an innocent person or drawing anyone into the street in response to the sound of gunfire.

She took off after Necro, hoping he would run into a dead end, or at least somewhere she could safely take a shot. At this time of night and this time of year, the streets were deserted. Most of Venice's population were at one of the many Carnevale soirees or snug inside their homes.

Pounding footsteps echoed around the narrow streets of the city as Umiko and her target raced along them, the pace slowing as they pivoted around corners, then accelerated, the vapour of their exertions puncturing the foggy night air.

Although he had had a path mapped out in his head to find his way back to the aquapod, Necro realised he was now lost. He was completely disoriented after so many twists and turns—down this *calle*, across that bridge, through a square and along a *sotoportego*, the passageways underneath buildings.

He skidded to a halt and recognised the Rialto Bridge—scene of his recent crime—to his right. He ran up the bridge and down the other side, striving to put distance between himself and his pursuer, trying to keep close to the edge of the streets in case the woman was tempted to draw her weapon.

The almost-full moon emerged from behind the clouds. Necro flinched in pain at the moon-burn, his pace slowing. It hurt him to even move, but though every muscle was stinging he pushed himself to keep going.

A light snow began to fall, dusting the ground white. The fog that had been creeping into the city intensified.

Necro was following the signs *Per S. Marco,* where he imagined St Mark's Square would be full of people in Carnevale masks, enabling him to disappear into the crowd.

The moon was shrouded by cloud once more. He turned right from Calle dei Fabbri and then left onto Sotoportego del Cavalletto, which led straight to the piazza, where he could lose the woman chasing him.

But even as he ran toward the famous square, he knew

he had misjudged the cover he thought it could offer. There was no colour, no noise.

Breathing heavily, he emerged into the dimly lit square to find there was no one in it. The *campanile,* St Marks's famous bell tower, watched over the square, seeming to anticipate his next move.

Necro cursed under his breath. He knew he had to get across the square, past the *campanile* to the water, so he could make his way back across the Grand Canal to Santa Maria della Salute, and then to the outer edge of Dosorduro. It would be bitingly cold, but then the woman would not be able to follow him, and he could quickly make his way to where his aquapod was docked.

In the seconds he had to contemplate his path forward, Necro's mind flipped through multiple scenarios at once.

If he ran across the square, he would leave himself open to being shot. If he stuck to the side of the square, it would slow him down and allow the woman to catch up. He was not familiar enough with Venice to chance slipping out of the square and trying to find another way around.

As he contemplated what to do, the creeping fog thickened. Within seconds, the square was shrouded in white. Visibility was reduced to a few metres.

Necro realised he could move straight across the square, if he moved carefully and quietly.

He zipped up the collar of his jacket over his mouth to conceal his breathing and began to tiptoe into the fog.

Behind him, he heard the woman's footsteps grow

louder and stop, as she also was confronted with what to do next.

Like a tightrope walker, hardly daring to breathe, he inched closer to the bell tower, navigating towards the spire, the tower's base now hidden in the fog.

❧

To slow her breathing, Umiko inhaled several lungfuls of cold air through her nose and out of her mouth, before tentatively stepping into the fog, like a swimmer testing the water with her toes.

She could not hear a sound. It was completely silent, except for the distant lapping of the canal waters. She assumed that Necro would head for the water, but instead followed the edge of the square so she would be less likely to become lost, or worse—for Necro to sight her before she did him.

Umiko winced as she risked some faster, audible steps. Her hand went to her holster, and she drew her weapon.

A sudden movement at her feet startled her—a cat running across her path.

She held her breath as she crept forward, hoping to pick up on any sound that would reveal Necro's location.

Nothing.

Umiko realised she had reached the edge of the square, which opened out on to the water. If she could get there ahead of Necro, she could cut him off. Holding her gun aloft, she quickened towards the water's edge.

Suddenly, she heard soft footsteps behind her. She swung around and emitted a sharp intake of breath.

A tall man dressed in the startling Carnevale attire of the plague doctor loomed over her. He cut a terrifying figure with his face concealed behind the long-nosed mask. He held out his arms and grasped her shoulders.

'*Sta bene?*' he asked. '*Dov'e sta andando?*'

'Let me go!' hissed Umiko, as she broke the man's grasp.

But the incident had disclosed her location to anyone within earshot, and she was barely twenty metres from the water's edge.

The sudden sound of running feet jolted her into action, and she raced towards the canal.

Umiko could only discern the size and shape of the figure who half emerged from the fog, but she knew it was him.

'NECRO!' she shouted, but she was too late.

Without reacting to Umiko's shout, Necro dove into the icy waters of the lagoon once again.

Umiko levelled her weapon and fired several shots into and ahead of where Necro had vanished into the water. She knew she had little time before someone would arrive to investigate the sound of gunshots, but she waited and watched.

A minute later, she saw a dark head break the water's surface further across the Grand Canal, in front of Santa Maria della Salute.

In desperation, she fired two shots at the black form as it slunk from the water and back into the urban maze, but neither hit their mark.

Gone.

Umiko roared a white cloud of anger into the chilly Venetian air.

As she caught her breath, she noticed something on the ground, gently wafting towards the water. She raced to grab it before it was lost to the canal. It was a half-folded piece of paper. Had the Plague Doctor dropped it?

She opened it to reveal unfamiliar written characters and a strange diagram—a long row of markers, a sketch of some sort of metal fixture, and a cross section that showed how deep the markers were, but not exactly where they were.

Deep?

Then she noticed the diagram's label in the corner of the sheet, in English. It was a word she knew all too well, a word that verified the owner of the diagram: NADIR.

Her heart froze.

ATLANTUM

Princess Lumina of Onda was well-named—she *was* luminous.

All eyes were on her as she seemed to float into the Grand Ballroom of Atlantum. Her short, wavy blonde hair and translucent skin were complemented by her green eyes and her sea-green, halter-neck silk dress, with a long skirt into which hundreds of miniature crystals had been hand-sewn. She wore no jewellery except for sparkling diamond studs in her ears, and a single pearl ring that gleamed on her right hand.

Ambra admired the princess as she waved at the crowd before being seated.

The princess's mother, Queen Cresence of Onda, wore a floor-length ivory jacket with a high collar over a silver dress. Her white-blonde hair was cropped short, and around her neck was a heavy silver necklace.

Both wore silver tiaras decorated with mother of pearl, which glowed in the evening light.

After the Queen was seated, Chancellor Aroz gave a

short speech welcoming the Queen, the princess, and the guests.

The Queen's blue eyes smiled as she surveyed the gathering.

Aroz led the crowd in a joyful rendition of 'Happy Birthday' for the princess, and then a thousand people sat down to enjoy a marvellous feast.

As vast as the Grand Ballroom was, it began to fill with the scent of delicious food.

There was every type of fresh seafood imaginable served on platters of ice, along with a variety of dishes from both Ondan and Terran cuisines served by elegant, fleet-footed waiters in black ties and coat-tails.

'This food is incredible,' said Jevon through mouthfuls, though Ambra was barely aware he'd spoken to her—she was lost in savouring the range of familiar and new flavours and textures.

Dessert consisted of a selection of sorbets and the princess's champagne-flavoured birthday cake, decorated with sea-green mousse frosting and edible silver sugar shells.

The sun had set, and as its light diminished, the Grand Ballroom was lit with thousands of red-and-gold fairy lights, the perfect contrast to the blues and greens of Atlantum.

As Ambra and Jevon finished their dessert, they caught sight of a tall, gangly man urgently weaving his way through the hall towards their table, his gaze fixed on Quill. His bushy grey eyebrows were knitted together.

Quill rose as the man approached the table, and his face creased into a smile.

'Mabul, how lovely to see you!' greeted Quill, spreading his arms wide.

'Greetings, sire,' said Mabul, his face serious.

'Oh, come now! Such concern? It's the princess's special birthday. Won't you have a glass of iced coral tea?'

'Perhaps later, sire. May I have a word?'

'Of course,' Quill said, rising from the table and leaving his napkin on his seat.

The two made their way to a quieter alcove at the side of the ballroom, where Ambra observed them in deep conversation for about fifteen minutes, Mabul gesturing animatedly, Quill's brow furrowed. Eventually, Mabul slipped away and Quill made his way back to the table.

'Everything okay?' Ambra asked, looking for clues on Quill's face.

'Yes and no,' replied Quill.

'What does that mean?'

'That man, Mabul, is the head of Ondan intelligence. He has received reports that the night before last, a colleague of your mother's was violently murdered in Venice.'

'*What?* Oh no!' gasped Ambra.

Quill pulled the front page of that day's *Raw Prawn* from a pocket inside his vest. He unfolded it and placed it on the table for the siblings to see. Along with the main image of the ornate bridge, there was also a photograph of a young woman.

'Oh—I recognise her name, but I don't recognise her face from that picture,' said Ambra. 'That's just horrible. Do the police have any idea who killed her?'

'We know who killed her—because the way this young woman died is the method of someone with a most unusual ability,' said Quill, tapping the pictures of the bridge and the photograph of the dead woman with his forefinger.

'What do you mean?' asked Jevon.

'The victim was drowned—and found on top of the Rialto Bridge.'

'So, whoever did it drowned her and then took her to the top of the bridge? That doesn't make sense,' said Jevon.

'Not quite.' Quill pointed to the article, which was written in the Ondan script. 'She was killed by someone who applied the Nerean Kiss. Only two living souls have mastered the technique. Queen Nefaria of Nautila—who has never visited Terra and is unlikely to—and her eldest son, the heir to the Nautilan throne, Necro.'

'Nerean Kiss? What's that?' asked Ambra, looking apprehensively at Quill.

Quill's steady blue eyes met hers.

'The Nerean Kiss is the rapid summoning of large volumes of seawater from within the lungs of those who know the technique. It is applied literally as a kiss, such that the victim ingests and inhales so much water that they drown.'

Ambra put her hand to her mouth. Jevon placed his hand in the middle of her back.

'The other part of Mabul's report that is not yet in the papers is that last night, your mother was the victim of a theft,' Quill continued. 'The materials her team planned to use in their media announcement have been stolen, almost certainly by the same person who murdered the young scientist—Necro.'

'Oh God! Is Mum okay?' cried Ambra.

'Yes, she's okay, but because of the theft, the press conference has had to be delayed until I can deliver her the backup copy she entrusted me with. To minimise the possibility of it being stolen and misused, none of the rest of her team has a copy, and it is nowhere online or in the Terran clouds,' said Quill.

Ambra turned to look at her brother. 'I'm not staying here. We have to go there, to Venice,' she said.

'How? We're in this massive structure in the middle of the ocean. We don't have the money to buy two international airfares. We don't have our passports,' said Jevon. 'And don't forget, we're here because Mum is concerned for our safety. She clearly didn't think flying us to her was safe. And it's certainly not, with a lunatic like that on the loose!'

'And what's to say his next target isn't Mum?' countered Ambra.

'The police are involved now. You don't need to put yourself in the middle of it!' shouted Jevon, his raised voice causing pauses in the dining of nearby guests.

Quill put his hand on Jevon's shoulder.

'Given what we feared has unfortunately transpired, you can both safely come to Venice with me. Now that Necro has stolen that research, he will be long gone. And never mind planes! You will travel the Ondan way—but I need to get permission from Aroz to take you. Just wait here for a minute.'

Quill made his way to the next table where Aroz was loudly debating Ondan–Terran politics with another guest.

'Ambra, we really should stay here. If Mum had wanted us to be in Venice, that's where we would be,' said Jevon. 'Let Quill take the backup to her.'

'I'm going there, and I will be another form of back-up—I want to be gene-edited live during the media event,' declared Ambra.

'The hell you are!'

Ambra rolled her eyes. 'Well, unfortunately, Jevon, the only member of the team who was edited a year or so ago to be monitored and studied is the one who is now dead, which makes her a bit awkward to have as an exhibit. Anyway, Mum was going to be edited live during the press conference to maximise the impact of the announcement. But it will have *more* of an impact if she edits her own daughter, not herself, especially if her work is about to be hijacked—she'll need a big attention grab to counter it. And protect her professional reputation.'

'You're bloody well right it will have more impact, because you'll pass it on to any kids you might have! How do you know it's not going to be a problem for them down the track?'

'They know it works in the same way they know this process works for editing for disease prevention, in the absence of someone actually getting sick—they can *show* the edit in the gene. Anyway, it's my choice, Jevon, whether you like it or not!'

'Mum is NOT going to agree to this!'

'I'll convince her. I reckon she'll go for it, especially if this Necro character is out there somewhere about to ensure a different version of what it all means is announced first.'

Quill returned.

'Listen, Aroz has said we can use one of our rapid transit submersibles. It could get us to Venice in about nine hours.'

'From here? That's almost twice as quick as a plane!' calculated Jevon. 'Whoa, it must go at a cracking speed!'

'Oh, it does,' said Quill, grinning. 'I wish we'd had them in my own boy racer days. They've been engineered by the Ondans to move small groups much faster than these gargantuan pods that contain our cities. The Terrans don't know about our technology. They'd be so envious, but we don't trust certain groups of Terrans with such a gift, not just yet.'

Quill looked at Ambra. 'Don't worry, you will be perfectly safe. Come on, I'll show you.'

They left the Grand Ballroom and followed Quill to one of the many transportation docks that connected

Atlantum to the wider world. Eventually, they arrived at a set of sturdy double doors made of metal, with a security keypad that blinked red and yellow. Quill's fingers played the keys and the lights changed to blue. There was a bronze plate on the door that was etched in both Ondan and English: 'HIGH SPEED SUBMERSIBLE USE WITHOUT PERMISSION IS AN OFFENCE PUNISHABLE BY IMPRISONMENT.'

The doors groaned as they swung open. The sound echoed in Ambra's mind. She closed her eyes.

TOKYO

THE DIRECTOR-GENERAL OF the Japan Meteorological Agency sat in Kaito's office in the TIA's headquarters. He had once worked for the TIA and remained a useful source of information for its operations.

Particularly today.

'My colleagues in California have contacted me about some concerning tectonic activity in our area,' said the Director-General. 'It mirrors similar activity we have been monitoring. Based on our knowledge of the behaviour of our plates, we do not believe it is originating from them.'

'Then what do you think might be causing it?' asked Kaito.

The Director-General gazed steadily at Kaito. 'We were hoping you might know something about it,' he said. 'Our American friends are no wiser. Nor are the Russians or Chinese. They are conducting their own investigations as we speak and will share any findings they make.'

Kaito tapped his fingers slowly on the table. 'This is a crucial issue for all of our countries,' he ventured. 'I can assure you, it's nothing we are up to. I do have an operative who is undertaking some sea-floor reconnaissance for us, which should provide some insight, but he's still in the field and it's too soon to be able to tell you anything.'

'Please let me know as soon as you hear.'

'Of course,' said Kaito.

THE DEPTH CHARGER

AMBRA AND JEVON followed Quill down a dimly lit spiral stairway to the docks underneath Atlantum.

Ambra surveyed the vessels moored. There must have been a hundred of them, all shapes and sizes, clearly designed for different purposes—research, travel, supply ships, and a fleet of two-passenger aquapods.

'Not like a Terran dock, is it?' said Quill. 'You'd expect to find yachts, trawlers or cruise ships, with their decks open to the fresh air. Of course, we Ondans travel underneath the sea to avoid detection, and thus all vehicles in our fleet are designed for submarine travel.'

Quill made his way along a gangplank to a series of gleaming vessels, the sea lapping at their hulls.

'Here we are,' he said, pointing proudly, as if introducing his Terran guests to an old friend, 'The *Depth Charger*.'

'Oh yeah,' said Jevon, nodding his approval.

'I'm not getting into THAT,' exclaimed Ambra. 'It

looks like it will sink at any second! Don't you have anything more … modern?'

From the outside, the vessel looked like something NASA would have built if they had a Marine Steampunk Division. More like a work of art than a transportation vehicle, it was streamlined, yet exquisite in the intricacy and craftsmanship of its design.

'It's perfectly seaworthy,' Quill reassured her.

Ambra could see her reflection in the burnished bronze sheen of the *Depth Charger*'s exterior. Quill opened the entry porthole to the ship, and the three of them clambered on board.

'So, this thing can travel anywhere in the world, super-fast,' mused Ambra, while opening doors and exploring the layout of the vehicle.

It was big enough to accommodate six people in three different rooms, along with a common area and small galley, as well as the navigation room. There looked to be enough supplies in the galley to last a week.

'We can get to the coast of anywhere on the globe inside fifteen hours—we took the best of Terran hydro engineering and developed it further for use in our fleet. Once up to speed, these things require no fuel. They simply run on churning seawater through a hyper-efficient turbine,' said Quill.

'Can I drive it?' asked Jevon, running his hands lovingly over the banks of lights, controls, dials, and switches.

'You don't need to—well, not once we are in the open water—they are autonomous vehicles,' explained Quill.

Ambra disguised a grin as Jevon's face fell.

'Shall we get underway?' suggested Quill, as he began the *Depth Charger*'s ignition sequence, and entered the coordinates for Venice, Italy. 'We have to get these materials to your mother ASAP so she can make the announcement before Necro is able to misrepresent it for his own purposes. And we cannot delay.' Pointing to two seats, he added, 'I must insist you strap yourselves in for now, at least until we get going in the open ocean.'

Ambra and Jevon obeyed, settling into their seats and securing themselves. A powerful engine began to shake the ship, as Quill deftly manoeuvred the craft away from the dock.

Throat constricted, Ambra's eyes followed the waterline as it rose up the outside of the ship until the vessel was completely immersed. The lights in the cabin glowed brighter as darkness enveloped them.

Quill clicked a series of lit buttons on the navigation panel, which opened the dock gates directly beneath them.

As she watched the blinking red and yellow lights on the gates rising past the ship as it descended into the deep, Ambra placed her hand on her stomach and commenced a breathing technique she had learned in therapy.

Then the *Depth Charger* was clear of Atlantum.

Quill pushed a lever to increase the power and another to thrust the vessel forward.

As he did so, a G-force greater than a Boeing about to take off kicked in, triggering an acute adrenalin rush.

'Whoooooooo-hooooo!' yelled Jevon.

Ambra laughed with glee, momentarily forgetting her fear of being submerged.

Quill chuckled at their reaction, twisted the navigation lever to bank left and upward slightly, then switched to autopilot. They were off.

NAUTILA

'**YOU CAN'T GO.** It's far too risky.'

In her chambers, Princess Nemeia, daughter of Nefaria, pulled a face at her brother Neven's cautionary words.

'If you don't tell her, she won't know—I'll be there and back before she even notices I've gone.'

'She expressly forbade you to have any more contact. You know what she's like,' warned Neven, leaning on the door of his sister's room as she readied herself to leave.

'It's been two years since I've seen Lumina, and today is her twenty-first birthday. I'm going to her banquet. If she asks, will you please tell Mother I'm out?'

'And where do I tell her you've gone?'

Nemeia was already dressed in her party attire, a floor-length sleeveless midnight-blue gown and sparkly silver kitten heels. Her long dark hair was gathered up, loose waves framing her face.

'Just out! On a research expedition. Whatever!'

Neven tried to conceal his amusement. His sister was hardly one for documenting the denizens of the deep.

'Alright, but I'll have to think up a more plausible excuse than that. Hope you're ready for the consequences if she catches you out.'

Nemeia's shoulders dropped as she turned away from checking her appearance in a full-length mirror and faced her brother.

'Don't care anymore, Neven. It was Necro who caused Lumina's father's death, but it was Lumina and I who were punished for it when Mother forbade contact with the Ondans. We've been friends since we were little.'

'I was punished too. Ramir had agreed to Lumina's engagement to me, and because of the way he died, that's never going to happen.'

'Neven—I'm sorry. I know it hurt you, too.'

'Will you be welcome in Atlantum? After what happened?'

'Of course. Both Queen Cresence and Lumina have always known it was Mother and Necro who were responsible, not me, or you,' Nemeia said.

'Are you sure? I thought they'd blame our family.'

'I'm sure. We've stayed in contact,' said Nemeia.

'How?'

'The Sea Nags.'

Clever, thought Neven.

A specially bred species of seahorse, designed to swim

long distances and to great depths, the Sea Nags were essentially submarine carrier pigeons—messengers of the ocean.

Neven ran his hands through his short black hair. Though he was the image of his twin brother, it was easy to tell them apart. Necro's ruthless nature was apparent in his eyes, his demeanour.

There was no persuading his sister not to go.

'Try to stay out of trouble. And don't be too long. There's a limit to how much I can cover for you before she gets suspicious.'

'I have to wait until after the sun has set to arrive at Atlantum, so I'll only be gone a few hours,' soothed Nemeia.

She picked up her clutch bag, kissed her brother on the cheek, and slipped out of her chambers toward the dock.

'Tell her I said hi,' called Neven, as his sister left.

Perhaps, if Lumina was still talking to Nemeia, there was hope.

'I will,' sang Nemeia's voice.

Neven sank onto the chair in his sister's room. He wished he was going too but wasn't sure he could face Lumina.

Damn his brother.

LORD ABZU

HALFWAY INTO THEIR journey to Venice, the *Depth Charger*'s engines cut out.

'What's happening?' Ambra grabbed onto the back of Quill's chair and the navigation desk as if to steady herself, though the vessel had lost forward momentum quickly, and was barely moving.

With the *Depth Charger*'s engines shutdown, the sudden silence was loud.

Quill was rapidly flicking through the screens on the navigation dashboard, which offered a 360-degree view of what was in range of the vessel.

He stopped at one of the images, which showed a presence four times as large as the *Depth Charger* moving slowly and carefully towards them. It was a dark-grey hulk of a ship, which had neither the beauty nor grace of the *Depth Charger*.

Along the side of the ship was painted a large silver trident and the name *Neptune's Revenge* in silver script.

'Oh no,' groaned Quill, closing his eyes.

He craned his neck out of the navigation room window.

'What? Are we about to be attacked?' asked Jevon, his gaze following Quill's.

'No. It's Lord Abzu—he's remotely disabled our vessel. Abzu is a sort of Nautilan equivalent of a Terran sheriff, but he's very much a law unto himself. And he is what you could best call a little bit mad. He was banished from Nautila by Nefaria because of his unpredictable behaviour, largely as a result of some unorthodox experiments he was conducting on his own mind, and he's now a mercenary for whoever hires his services.'

There was a painful grating noise, metal on metal, followed by the sound of an airlock opening.

Quill's shoulders drooped.

'Ah. He has rendezvoused with our vessel, docked, and is about to board. Whatever he says or does, just play along with it as much as you can. And let me do the talking. We don't want to …'

'QUILL!' bellowed a nerve-shredding voice.

Quill flinched as the larger-than-life figure of Lord Abzu strode into the cabin. At seven feet tall, with long curly black hair, covered in body armour of blue and green scales, and clanking with various kinds of weapons, he was a formidable presence.

To Ambra's mind, he looked much like the god of the sea his vessel was named after.

The giant submariner swept up a reluctant Quill in a bear hug.

'Hello, Lord Abzu,' said Quill mildly, looking like a doll in the Nautilan's arms. 'What are you doing in this part of the deep?'

'The Terran TIA have got me doing some sea-floor reconnaissance. Lot easier for me than them,' boomed Abzu, setting Quill down.

'Reconnaissance? What are they looking for?' asked Quill.

'Oooo, any unusual activity. The brief was vague to say the least. Seems there's some funny stuff going on with plate activity, and the Japanese, as you can imagine, are a bit toey.'

'Plate activity?' queried Ambra.

'As in tectonic plates,' explained Quill.

Ambra pressed her lips together and decided not to ask any more questions.

Abzu's gaze turned to Ambra and Jevon. 'Who do we have here?'

'Two of our Terran friends,' said Quill.

'Aha! Exactly what I need!'

Ambra and Jevon exchanged glances.

'No, you don't,' said Quill firmly, without even bothering to enquire into Abzu's need. 'We are on our way to Venice for urgent reasons.'

Abzu either didn't hear Quill or ignored him.

'Another client of mine's running experiments on Terrans, and I told 'em I'd design one. I gotta test it before I go to 'em with it, and, by Neptune, down here it's hard for me to source Terrans for such purposes.'

'What do you mean *experiments*?' Quill asked.

'The ones to save Terrans from themselves. To break and rewire their neurological patterns.'

Whatever that meant, Ambra didn't like the sound of it.

'Lord Abzu, I must insist that you allow us to continue on our journey,' said Quill.

Abzu was prowling around the cabin, closely examining the Lightstone siblings.

'This one'll do nicely,' he said, as he gripped Jevon's shoulders.

'Jevon!' cried Ambra.

'Lord Abzu, you will need to find another Terran for your experiment,' said Quill.

'Yes, you will,' said Jevon, struggling to break free of Abzu's grasp, and failing.

'I'll do yer a deal,' said Abzu, a glint in his eye. 'If he can beat the game I've designed, then I can tell the Terrans it works, and you'll get him back. If not, well—he'll have to stay with me for a while, and I'll let both of you go on your way. Win-win.'

'What win-win? For whom? If he succeeds, presumably your client will pay you handsomely. If he doesn't, you get to keep him as one of your lab rats and refine your experiment. What sort of a deal is that?' said Quill.

'What game?' said Jevon, whose eyes had lit up.

'It's an immersion simulation. The game occurs in your mind,' said Abzu.

'What type of simulation?' pressed Jevon.

'Ahrrr, well, I can't tell you that! It would pre-empt how you play it—and mess up the experiment.'

Quill sighed. Ambra felt the pit of her stomach sinking at Quill's resignation.

This was going to have to play out according to the rules of Lord Abzu.

NAUTILA

QUEEN NEFARIA TURNED Lillian Lightstone's memory stick over and over between her thumb and forefinger.

Her stare was fixed on the diminutive man kneeling before her, his eyes downturned, his midnight-blue robe pulled around him. Navy light cast from the lamps behind Nefaria's black-rock throne flickered over his face and smooth scalp. The room was completely silent.

'Saphiro, you are my best intelligence agent. You say you have tracked down a source for a superconductor.'

Nefaria's voice, though soft, seemed to fill the cavernous room. Without raising his eyes, the man nodded.

'Tell me what you have learned over the last year of your mission,' the Queen ordered.

Saphiro looked up at Nefaria with his almond eyes.

'The Terrans had a theory that the unique chemical composition of the planet Saturn was producing diamonds—the lightning storms that rage there turn methane into carbon, which hardens into chunks of graphite and then diamond. These Saturnian diamonds are extremely powerful superconductors.'

'What use is this? Saturn is a long, long way away, and you speak only of a theory.'

'The Terrans undertook a classified mission to Saturn some years ago called *Chronos 6*. Mission *Chronos* was designed to navigate a special probe through Saturn's rings, something never before possible without contemporary technology. The specimens collected included a Saturnian diamond. This diamond is the most powerful superconductor humanity has ever had in its possession.'

'You are a liar. Saturn is a gas giant, and probes cannot land on gas planets. And probes never return—they stay on their trajectory until they are damaged or out of range.'

'Your Majesty, the probes were designed to. be able to gather samples while in motion during their orbit around Saturn, and to return to their launch site. On this secret mission, one of the probes was destroyed on its way back to Terra. But the other did return—with a Saturnian diamond.'

Nefaria did not shift her gaze from Saphiro.

'Where is this diamond now?'

'When it first arrived on Terra, it was in the possession of the National Aeronautics and Space Administration in Washington, DC. It was the subject of intense research, until stolen from a high-security laboratory about 18 months ago.'

'Who took it?'

'It is not known to me who took it. The whereabouts of the diamond is known by an international dealer in such items, known as The Jeweller. If you want your superconductor, you must find The Jeweller.'

'What is his name?' demanded Nefaria.

'The Jeweller has no name besides The Jeweller.'

'Where can we find him?'

'The most recent intelligence I have is that The Jeweller is in Mumbai, India.'

'And what might The Jeweller want in return for the Saturnian diamond?'

'That depends. The Jeweller would need something of equal or greater value, something scarce, something that can be sold to a buyer who urgently wants it but cannot get it elsewhere.'

Nefaria turned Lillian Lightstone's memory stick over and over between her thumb and forefinger.

THE GAME

LORD **A**BZU MARCHED Jevon onto his vessel, *Neptune's Revenge*, with Quill and Ambra following.

They entered a room that was a hybrid of laboratory and data centre, and strangely ordered given that the rest of Abzu's ship appeared to be in a state of chaos.

Jevon winked at his sister.

'Don't worry. You know how much time I've spent playing and beating computer games.'

'Yeah, Jevon, but I don't think this is going to be anything like that.'

'Right, first you'll need these,' said Abzu, tossing an armful of equipment at Jevon.

Ambra watched as Jevon donned the simulator gear, including a headset and sensors on his wrists and ankles.

'Now into the VR room,' Abzu pointed at a smaller room that led from the main room, separated by a glass partition. A row of red-leather recliners stretched across the width of the room.

Jevon settled back into one of the oversized chairs, which was hooked up to a vast network of cables, lights, displays, and screens.

Abzu jabbed at a bank of buttons and the big screen atop the chair flickered on, but showed only a grey test pattern.

Ambra watched her brother's jaw and limbs go limp. Then his face began to twitch in response to a stimulus that he could see, but she could only imagine.

Abzu flipped a switch and the screen above Jevon's head came to life.

Ambra could see both the broader scene, and a point-of-view shot of everything Jevon was seeing, but unlike him, she was not feeling it, and was aware it was not real.

❦

Jevon was in a vast, palatial open-air pavilion, kneeling in front of a richly dressed man wearing a headdress of purple silk who presided over the room from his throne.

At the side of the throne sat a tiny, adorable-looking creature, gently panting. Its fur caught the late afternoon sunlight that came streaming in through the side of the pavilion, giving it a golden halo.

The grand man spoke to Jevon in a tongue that was completely unfamiliar, but that he was somehow able to understand.

'This creature represents the rulership and ancestral lineage of my family. You will feed it, and it will grow and flourish. On pain of death, you will feed the creature whatever it needs.'

Jevon understood that at all costs, the creature could not die, as it was symbolic of the strength and right to rule of the royal family.

He led the sweet creature away to his modest quarters and took on the responsibility of caring for it.

It was so innocent and cute, and on the first day, it only ate one grain of rice.

The next day, the creature was happy with only two grains of rice. As it grew, it needed more food.

The following day, it wanted four grains, and the day after that, eight. All was well, and manageable.

But the more it ate, the bigger it grew. And the bigger it grew, the uglier it grew, demanding ever more rice.

Jevon quickly identified a pattern and realised the creature required double the amount of food it had eaten the day before, every day.

Trying to anticipate the creature's needs, he did some basic sums to determine the amount of food the creature would need. As the calculations became bigger, his ability to do the maths slowed.

At two weeks, he became alarmed.

At four weeks, the horror of his predicament dawned on him.

He tried to warn the royal ruler, but he wouldn't listen.

What was wrong with him that he couldn't see where

things were heading? He was imperilling his empire, his subjects and himself, though the evidence was right in front of him.

Jevon's calculations could only extend so far using ink, paper, and his brain, but he knew he was in a no-win situation.

What he couldn't know was that by the ninth week, the creature would need over 18,000,000,000,000,000,000 grains of rice, weighing over 461,000,000,000 tons—a heap of rice larger than Mount Everest, and a thousand times the world's total production of rice.

There was not enough rice in the world to feed the creature's insatiable, exponentially growing appetite.

But it was Jevon's task, and the only way to ensure his own survival, to keep feeding the beast.

⧖

As she looked at the numbers her brother was scribbling down, which were getting larger and larger, the truth slowly dawned on Ambra.

'That creature's food requirement is doubling *every* day!' gasped Ambra, as she spun around to face Quill.

Quill's forehead was creased, and he was silent.

'If he stops feeding that horrible creature, it will die, and Jevon will be killed! But if he keeps feeding it, the food staple for that country will be gone within weeks, and they will all starve!' said Ambra.

'That's precisely the challenge of this experiment,'

beamed Abzu, wagging his finger at Ambra. 'Will he find a way to break out of this catch-22 he finds himself in?'

Ambra turned on Abzu, no longer in awe of the giant Nautilan. 'If he is killed or dies in the game, does he actually die?' she demanded.

Abzu did not respond.

'You let him go, right now!' hissed Ambra.

'He will stay with me while I refine this simulation,' declared Abzu.

'I'm not leaving him here!'

Ambra made a charge for Jevon but found herself caught in Abzu's iron grip. Abzu lifted her up by the arms, so her face was level with his. His eyes locked onto hers.

'Now that he's been in longer than a few minutes, he believes this is his reality. Any touch, any loud sound will send him into shock, as he will feel he's in two realities at once. I don't know what the consequences will be for him.'

Abzu put Ambra down and released his grip. Ambra shook herself free, glaring at Abzu, but did not attempt to approach her brother.

'When I say he can go, I'll release him. He will be returned to you,' promised Abzu.

'What is this experiment?' asked Quill, face worried as he looked at Jevon, stuck in a double bind.

'Oh yes, I should name it! The Terrans love names for such things. What'll I call it?'

Abzu thought for a moment and then turned to Quill, with a satisfied look on his face.

'Jevon's Paradox.'

THE DEPTH CHARGER

AMBRA WAS SILENT as Quill manoeuvred the *Depth Charger* away from *Neptune's Revenge*.

Lord Abzu's ship faded from view, and the *Depth Charger* began to pick up speed.

Quill looked at Ambra as he checked the navigation settings.

'Don't worry. Abzu is an odd character to say the least, but he will not hurt Jevon. And he has a background in law enforcement.'

'He *used* to. And for the Nautilans!' huffed Ambra. 'Even they think he is too unpredictable, as you said yourself.'

'I've known Abzu a long time. Once he fixes his mind on something, there's no use arguing with him. He has to arrive at conclusions of his own accord,' reassured Quill.

'And when will that be?'

'When he is good and ready, I'm afraid. He will likely deliver Jevon back to Atlantum. In the meantime, we need to focus on the task at hand. Your mother needs this copy of her team's work, as fast as we can get it to her.'

Ambra slumped back in her seat, resigned.

Hour after hour, the vessel sped along through the ocean depths, its powerful headlights showing a clear path ahead for the speed at which they were travelling, yet they were a pinpoint of light in a vast blackness.

The ship's bow lights illuminated a parade of unusual deep-sea creatures Ambra had never heard of. In and out of the beams they came and went, each with a moment in the spotlight, as the *Depth Charger* wove its way around them, threading a path through various valleys and rock formations jutting up hundreds of metres from the sea floor.

The hum of the vessel's engine, and Quill's gentle low whistle as he busied himself with various tasks, lulled Ambra into a sleepy state.

She was halfway between being asleep and awake when Quill jumped up and cut the power to the engine and killed the lights.

'What? What's wrong?' cried Ambra, startled.

'Lucky I was watching! The navigation instruments somehow missed alerting me to that!' Quill exhaled loudly as he peered at the navigation screen.

'Miss *what*?'

'Nautila,' said Quill, pointing at a barely discernible, but colossal circular shape looming on the screen, about two nautical miles ahead of them.

Ambra peered out of the cockpit window.

'You won't see it. It's too far away—not to mention too dark—but it's there. We must stay undetected, or we will be captured and searched, and then …' his voice trailed off. 'Let's just say, at best, we'd make for a good ransom, especially a Terran captive. And there are rumours of nasty experiments on prisoners. But what are they doing north of the Equator? And how on Terra did their presence not trigger a warning from our radar?' he muttered, poking at buttons and flipping levers on the navigation panel.

'What do we do now?' asked Ambra, trying to read Quill's anxious face in the dim light reflected from the navigation instruments.

'Stay very low, very quiet, very dark, and very slowly back away until we are clear of them,' said Quill.

'You know where you are going, though, right? I mean, you don't have lights, but you have radar, don't you?'

'I can't use the radar right now either,' admitted Quill. 'That's what will alert them to us, and I am surprised it didn't beforehand. What I don't understand is how we didn't pick them up well before we were in range.'

The *Depth Charger* was slowly sinking, Quill guiding the craft inch by inch, waiting for any grating sensation and ready to course-correct.

Suddenly, all was illuminated with a flood of light. Nautila had lit the bottom of the ocean up like a Terran day, as high-powered beams scanned the surrounding area.

'Oh boy,' breathed Quill.

'Have they seen us?' whispered Ambra.

The light wasn't hitting the *Depth Charger* directly, because Quill had managed to navigate the craft behind a section of jagged rock, where it was out of the direct line of sight.

'They rarely use those lights, because they don't need to, and because they prefer to stay hidden. They've picked up on something,' said Quill.

'What if they discover us? They're big and slow, we're small and fast—surely we can outrun them?'

'We can outrun Nautila, but not the smaller vessels they will send out after us,' said Quill.

The beams scoured the ocean for a few minutes, Ambra holding her breath and Quill ready to spring into action.

The lights went out. Ambra exhaled.

'We're not safe yet,' cautioned Quill, guessing Ambra's next question.

It was another agonising half an hour before Quill managed to steer the craft to a position that he deemed far enough away for it to be safe to turn the lights and engine back on.

One eye carefully on the navigation screen, he opened the throttle and the *Depth Charger* surged forward.

They were clear of Nautila.

Ambra sat back in her seat, her eyes closed. She opened them and looked at Quill.

'Why is this research my mother has been working on causing all this drama?' she asked. 'I know it's about editing out a destructive gene that humans have, but that's a good thing, right?'

Quill turned to face her.

'There is a concern that human beings are wired, *genetically*, to expand and fill every available space on Terra with their presence and their demands for resources—though some Terrans have much less than others, and, of course, Terrans are only one species among billions who live on this planet. There are genuine and well-documented fears that humanity is headed for a full-scale ecosystem collapse, which would end civilisation as we know it. Altering this gene, en masse, will help divert us from our current dangerous trajectory.'

'I get that. So why would anyone want to stop this technology?'

'There are vested interests who want to see humanity continue on its current course, and those who either don't see the situation as a problem that will affect them, or who don't care about what it will mean for their descendants.'

'Jevon understands why she does it, but he doesn't like Mum's gene tech work as a way to address the issue,' confided Ambra. 'My Dad too—he's had huge fights with Mum over it. He thinks it's risky and could be used for unethical purposes, but Mum says we're out of time, we're not going to change quickly enough, and that it's far more dangerous to *not* try the gene editing. Dad reckons its our culture that needs to change, that we could just choose to be different— before we end up at a point of no return,' said Ambra.

'But will you?' said Quill. 'This is the question at the

core of your mother's research—given you've known for decades the implications of continuing this pattern, why haven't you changed already?'

'Lots of reasons, I guess,' said Ambra.

'Are any of them stronger reasons than preventing the demise of your species?'

'They shouldn't be.'

'We are in a race against time and misinformation, Ambra,' said Quill. 'Necro has undoubtedly sold or traded that research documentation to a Terran buyer who plans to misuse it or misrepresent it. It will be difficult to convey the true meaning once mainstream and social media networks are alight with the incorrect or incomplete version.'

'And you have the only copy?'

'Yes. There are Terran and Nautilan spies, double agents, and hackers everywhere, and although it is not entirely free of espionage, Atlantum was the safest place to store your mother's research backup. The more copies that exist, the greater the risk of one being stolen and falling into the wrong hands—and as we've now learned, even with all our precautionary action to minimise that risk, it still happened.'

A lapse into silence.

'How far out are we?' asked Ambra.

'Another two hours to Venice, assuming no other close encounters,' said Quill.

Ambra nodded, reclined back in her seat, and closed her eyes as the *Depth Charger* carried them swiftly on to their destination—the iconic city built on a lagoon.

ATLANTUM

The double doors to the royal bedchamber were flung open, and two young ladies in formal gowns swirled in.

Shoes were kicked off, tiaras and handbags tossed onto a chair.

Lumina fell back onto her bed, limbs sprawling in an unprincess-like manner.

'That was the best birthday!'

Nemeia smiled at her friend.

'I am so stuffed with gorgeous food, and champagne cake and featherlight sweets, and my feet hurt from dancing with Lord Aroz!' cried Lumina, flexing her toes.

'It was a lovely celebration,' agreed Nemeia, as she sat down next to Lumina.

Lumina sat up, propped on her elbows. She eyed Nemeia.

'How is Neven?'

Nemeia's smile faded.

'He's okay,' she said.

Lumina waited with expectant eyes.

'He said to say hello.'

Lumina let out a long sigh and fell back on the bed.

'Is that all? It's been two years since we've seen each other.'

'I know, and that might have been all he *said* to say, but he talks about you a lot.'

'He didn't want to come and see me for this special birthday?'

'If we had both come, Mother would have noticed, and there would have been hell to pay,' soothed Nemeia.

'Will anyone ever stand up to her? I'm sorry, Nems, I know she's your mother … and a queen …'

'It's difficult for us. Even if we decided to leave, where else can we live? Nautila is the last place for our kind.'

Lumina put her hand on her friend's arm. 'You are always welcome in Atlantum.'

'I worry about what Mother would do if I—if we—left,' said Nemeia.

'We?'

'Neven would have to come too. If only one of us goes, life would be deeply unpleasant for the other left behind.'

'Why don't you both plan to leave? Come here. Live with us,' pleaded Lumina.

'We've thought about it,' admitted Nemeia. 'But we can't—not just yet.'

'What's stopping you?'

'Mother and Necro are up to something. We need to stay until we can find out what it is.'

'Up to what?'

'They are planning—well, we don't know what they're planning. But it is about reclaiming the supremacy of the Nautilans ... something that will hurt the Terrans.'

'The Terrans are our friends!' cried Lumina, sitting upright.

'Some of the Terrans are friends of the Onda. But some of them are working with Mother and Necro—their interests are aligned with Nautilan interests.'

'And you don't know what they are planning? Your mother and brother, I mean,' pressed Lumina.

'All I know is it requires a huge source of energy, and Necro has been tracking this down for the last ten years. They need it to power some sort of device ... but I don't know what its purpose is. Mother and Necro are careful never to discuss it in front of us.'

'I don't like the sound of this. We need to find out what it is. And we need Neven's help.'

Nemeia looked anxiously at her friend. 'If we're caught ... Mother will not forgive us.'

A long moment of silence, as both young women considered the consequences.

'I am seriously worried about it, Lumina.'

'I know,' said Lumina, clasping Nemeia's hands in hers. 'I can only imagine what this means for you—to leave your home, and your surviving parent.'

'No—I mean I am seriously worried about what Mother and Necro are planning.'

Lumina rose from her bed and went to ring a small silver bell that hung in the corner of the room. 'Let's work out what to do over a cup of tea,' she said.

Nemeia smiled, but it fell away as quickly as she could summon it.

In what seemed like moments, there was a soft knock at the door, and a servant delivered a silver tray with a pot of steaming pearl tea, along with two delicate cups.

The young royals settled in at the small round table in Lumina's chambers and, sipping on the pearly tea, began to form a plan.

VENICE

THE *DEPTH CHARGER* slipped silently into the Venetian lagoon under an almost-full moon that glowed through the foggy night sky.

Quill manoeuvred the vessel towards a more isolated area in the north-east of the island to dock.

'We can hardly park this thing at St Mark's Square,' he said with a grin. 'From here, we'll have to make our way on foot to San Polo, where your mother is staying,' he added, offering Ambra a hand as she clambered out of the hatch onto the roof.

The cold burned Ambra's lips as she stepped onto the dock, her breath hanging in the icy air. She was grateful for the ship-issue black jacket, navy pants, thermals, socks, and boots that Quill had supplied her with, which kept the northern winter night at bay.

Quill led Ambra as the two wove their way through the cobbled streets, bridges, and archways of Venice. It was late at night, and the streets and squares had long since emptied of Carnevale revellers.

The city ached with cold.

There was not a soul about, only a rat scampering along near Teatro le Fenice, and even he dove into a hole in the side of the building as fast as he could.

'He must be late for a show,' quipped Quill, causing Ambra to giggle at the idea of a rat at the theatre.

It took them a good twenty minutes on foot at a decent pace to make their way from Castello towards San Marco, then follow the signs *Per Rialto*.

Ambra kept thinking of the front page of *The Raw Prawn* and the story Quill had told her about the murder of her mother's colleague on top of the Rialto Bridge. Though she had warmed up from the brisk walk, she shivered as she reached the top of the arch and hurried quickly down the steps into the San Polo district.

Quill led Ambra on a route she was certain she could never find again—left from the square with a church and well in the middle, left on another small calle with a quaint bookshop on the corner, into another small piazza, a left turn into Calle del Forno, then turn right, another left turn ... she was dizzy.

Finally, they arrived at a small, four-storey building. There were two windows with wrought-iron grilles on either side of the sturdy wooden door that was the main entrance to the building. Warm yellow light shone into the courtyard through the glass.

Ambra noticed there were black shadows moving around inside the lobby. Armed security? Police?

'Oh,' muttered Quill, standing a few feet back from the door as he pondered what to do next.

'I wasn't expecting having to deal with—'

'Fermati!' came a shout from inside the lobby.

The door was flung open.

Quill and Ambra froze as several black-clad figures emerged from the building, levelling assault weapons at them. Instinctively, they both held their hands up, palms facing the security guards.

'Chi siete?' demanded one of the armed men suspiciously.

'We are here to see Lillian Lightstone. This is her daughter,' said Quill, nodding sideways at Ambra.

No response.

'Siamo qui per incontrare il professore in questa casa—questa è sua figlia,' offered Quill.

The guns were lowered, but before Ambra or Quill could try to explain their presence further, Lillian Lightstone appeared on the staircase leading down to the lobby.

'Mum!' cried Ambra.

'Stay put!' she ordered her daughter, before gesturing to the guards that the visitors were welcome.

The guards stood aside, then moved beyond Quill and Ambra, to ensure the area behind the newcomers was secure.

Lillian Lightstone's weary face wore an expression of surprise mixed with relief as her daughter rushed to embrace her.

Ambra pulled back and looked more closely at her mother in the low light, scanning her for any signs of injury.

'Are you alright? What happened?'

'I'm alright,' said Lightstone, stroking her daughter's forehead.

'I'm glad the Sand Poet got you safely away. But where's Jevon?'

Ambra didn't know where to begin.

'Let's go upstairs and talk,' suggested Quill, and the three went up to Lightstone's third-storey apartment.

Over coffee, to keep them both warm and awake, they filled each other in on the news of Jevon's capture by Lord Abzu and Necro's theft of Lightstone's work.

There was a quiet knock at the door.

'Professor Lightstone?' came a woman's voice.

Lightstone got up to open the door to Umiko. After her fruitless pursuit of Necro the night before, an exhausted Umiko had slept late, then accompanied the professor on her second trip in as many days to meet the Italian authorities, where they had both given a statement.

'Umiko, this is my daughter, Ambra, and this is Quill, our Ondan ally,' said Lightstone.

Umiko introduced herself to the newcomers.

Lightstone turned to Quill. 'Quill, do you have the backup copy with you?'

Quill produced a memory stick from inside his vest and handed it to her.

Lightstone exhaled.

'Now what?' said Umiko.

'Necro knows our announcement is imminent, and will quickly have what he stole in the hands of those who will use it to misinform people about what the findings mean. It will be difficult to counter that once it is in the public domain,' answered Lightstone.

'Then why don't you make your announcement first?' asked Umiko.

'Well, there's the complex logistics of having to rearrange an international press conference, especially with the theft throwing things into further disarray. And my team are still in shock. It will hopefully take place late tomorrow. I can only hope an extra forty-eight hours won't matter, that he won't be able to move that stick quickly,' fretted Lightstone.

'Where might Necro be headed with that stick, and how much of a head start could he have?' wondered Umiko.

Lightstone shrugged and shook her head.

Ambra glanced at Quill, whose face looked as apprehensive as she felt.

NAUTILA

NEMEIA AND LUMINA had slipped away while the city was asleep after the celebratory banquet, finding their way to the royal dock of Atlantum where Nemeia's aquapod was waiting.

They arrived back at Nautila without being discovered and crept through the corridors to Neven's quarters, which were near Nemeia's rooms.

The door was open.

'Neven?' whispered Nemeia into the darkness. She touched a button near the door frame and a low light filled the room. It was empty, and the bed had not been slept in.

'Has he left?' whispered Lumina.

'I don't think so—he was concerned about Mother noticing my absence, so I don't think he would have chosen now to go anywhere. But I know where he might be.'

Nemeia dimmed the room light and motioned for her friend to follow her.

Taking every precaution to ensure they were not

detected, Nemeia and Lumina tiptoed their way to the Nautilan library, a good five-minute walk from the royal quarters.

Nemeia pushed the door open, and after checking the entrance, ushered Lumina into the darkened library.

One half of the main room comprised shelves stacked with thousands of texts, from bound books to paperbacks sourced from Terra. There was a pod of computers near the far wall, and a series of reading desks with lamps in the centre of the room.

In a far corner of the library, there was a faint glow from under a door.

'That's where Neven is—that's a private royal reading room where restricted texts are stored,' whispered Nemeia, pointing to the thin yellow bar of light.

The girls hurried to the other side of the library, and Nemeia pressed her palm to an electronic reader adjacent to the door.

The steel door to the vault slid open.

Neven looked up from his reading, looking startled at the unexpected entrance. His eyes widened.

'Lumina?'

The light colouring of the Ondan princess was a vivid contrast to the dark surroundings of Nautila.

Lumina's face broke into a glorious smile as she ran towards him. Neven rose to meet her with an embrace.

He pulled back, cupping her cheek in his hand.

'I can't believe it! What are you doing here? It's so dangerous.'

'We don't have much time,' Nemeia said, touching her brother's arm. 'How are you going with the research?'

Neven ran his hands up his forehead and through his hair. 'Whatever it is, it's nothing that our archives are offering any clue to,' he said.

Nemeia began rummaging through the texts Neven had piled across the desk. There were heavy, bound volumes of handwritten Nautilan history, centuries old. There were recent copies of Terran novels related to the ocean, and Terran texts on marine biology and naval warfare. Technical volumes on the construction and maintenance of deep-sea structures and submersibles.

'Neven, this is a mess!' she admonished her brother.

'What are you looking for?' asked Lumina, as Nemeia began investigating the contents of an open safe, taking out what looked like a journal and flipping through it, her eyebrows knitting together.

'Any evidence that Nautila once waged war on Terra, and if so, how,' said Neven. 'We're trying to find anything that might help us discover what Mother and Necro are planning.'

'According to Quill's Ondan chronicles, I don't think Nautila has ever waged war against the Terrans,' said Lumina. 'Certainly not while your father was alive. Nazer was always working to maintain peace,' she said, placing her hand on Neven's arm.

'Maybe, but some of his decisions had the opposite effect,' lamented Neven. 'Necro was incredibly jealous when Father arranged your engagement to me.'

'But he *knew* that as Crown Prince he would have to marry a Nautilan, and that our engagement was part of Nazer's peacekeeping efforts,' said Lumina.

'That didn't matter to Necro, and I am certain it was a factor in his decision to let Ramir die when he could have saved him during …' Neven's voice faded as he saw Lumina's face fall at the mention of her father's name.

'I'm sorry.'

He put his arm around her shoulders and gave her a gentle squeeze.

'We can't do this from here,' declared Nemeia, tucking the journal she'd been looking through down the front of her dress.

'We need to go back to Atlantum and find out what's going on—the Ondans have much closer ties with the Terrans and will have more intelligence that will help us find out what Mother and Necro are up to.'

'Is that so?' came a cold voice from behind them.

The three young royals spun around, faces struck with horror.

'You treacherous young fools. Do you think anything happens in Nautila that I don't know about?' said Nefaria, emerging from the shadows.

'Mother … listen to me,' began Neven.

'I understand everything!' spat Nefaria. 'You wish to betray your own kind. Since you have shown no loyalty to your people, or your Queen, you are both hereby banished from Nautila. Do not return.'

'Mother!' cried Neven, his face contorted with anguish.

'You are no longer my children!'

Nemeia's face reflected no emotion.

'Give me that journal,' demanded Nefaria, holding her hand out to Nemeia.

'What journal?'

'The one you put down the front of your dress.'

Eyes flashing, Nemeia pulled the journal from inside her dress and slammed it onto the reading table.

'And you …' Nefaria's lip curled as she turned to Lumina. 'The only reason you will leave alive is because it will cause more trouble for me to give you the Nerean Kiss than it will to let you leave.'

Lumina set her jaw and fixed the Nautilan Queen with a defiant look.

'We will all leave,' said Lumina, in a quiet voice. 'We will find out what you are planning. And we will end you.'

Nefaria laughed, a reaction Nemeia and Neven had rarely seen from her.

The smile faded from Nefaria's face as abruptly as it had appeared. 'You have thirty minutes to gather whatever you can take with you and go,' she said.

Lumina grabbed Nemeia's hand, turned on her heel, and marched out of the library.

Neven faced his mother. 'You've strayed so far from what Father wanted for our people …' he began.

Before he could say any more, his mother slapped him hard across the face.

'Do not speak to me of him!'

Neven's face had changed from one of shock to one of fury. For a moment, Nefaria shrank away from her son. Neven's furious face faded to one of contempt, then pity.

'This lust for power … you've already lost your husband, your king. Now you've lost two of your three children. Whatever it is you are seeking, it won't be worth what you've sacrificed,' whispered Neven.

For a moment, things were silent, as mother and son locked eyes. Neven broke the stare and turned his back on his mother. Then he was gone.

THE JEWELLER

THE CACOPHONY OF noise hit Necro with physical force as he picked his way along the streets of Mumbai.

Even at night, this city was hard for him, used as he was to cool, quiet, and dark places. The humid heat, along with the incessant torrent of people, traffic, and blaring horns, was jangling his psyche.

He decided he was going to get this mission over and done with as fast as possible.

Through his networks, Saphiro had managed to find and arrange a meeting with The Jeweller.

Necro set about making his way to the meeting point, an open-air rooftop bar, which few people seemed to know about when he asked for directions.

The building at the address he had been given was down a side alley and was shabby to the point of looking as if it should have been condemned. He got into a worryingly rickety-looking antique lift, clanged the cage door shut, and rode slowly up to the eighth floor.

As he emerged onto the roof, the sound and smells of the city below faded away. He knew there was a full moon, though it was too well cloaked by cloud to cause him a problem.

The place belied its decrepit façade—his eyes took in old-world glamour, heavy wooden fixtures, and luxurious furnishings. Ornate brass lanterns glowed softly. He inhaled the scent of sandalwood incense, carried on the warm night air.

A number of patrons were gathered at the bar, and around tables, with many engaged in low conversation over semi-private tables screened with sheer, bronze-coloured drapes that shifted in the gentle breeze. The bar was a pleasant murmur, not the raucous hubbub he had expected.

This meeting was a gamble, and he did not know if it would pay off.

He made his way to the appointed table and pulled aside the gossamer curtain.

Across the table sat the most striking-looking woman Necro had ever seen. She was a few years older than him. Her espresso-coloured hair fell in loose waves around her face, and her tawny eyes reflected flickering light from the lantern at the side of the table. Her burnt-orange sari complemented her brown skin. She wore a gold stud in her nose. A delicate jewelled necklace sat at her throat.

'I'm looking for The Jeweller,' he said.

The woman greeted him with a charming, almost flirtatious, look.

'And here she is.'

'She? You?'

The woman motioned for him to sit down. As he did so, Necro made a mental note to stay focused on the task at hand, and not the distracting creature in front of him. The two looked at each other in silence for a few moments.

'I'm here to make a deal with you—something of value you can trade, for something I've been told you can help me with,' said Necro.

'Now what have you got that I might want?' The Jeweller asked, the hint of a tease in her voice.

'The only copy of years' worth of research by an international team of leading scientists—research that is about to make global headlines, one way or another.'

'And?'

Necro leaned forward over the table and kept his voice low.

'The research is called the Rapa Nui Gene Project. Rapa Nui is the Polynesian name for Easter Island, a Pacific civilisation believed to have collapsed around the seventeenth century. The island population became obsessed with building large *moai,* or statues, apparently having no regard to the environmental destruction they were inflicting on their own life-support systems, and despite being completely dependent on the resources in their immediate surroundings. It has become a Terran metaphor for concern about the collapse of civilisation on a global scale.'

'I am aware of it. Though the reason for the collapse

of that civilisation in the Pacific is contested, yes?' said The Jeweller, as she poured a gold-coloured liquid into a small crystal glass. 'Drink?'

Necro ignored her offer.

'The Rapa Nui Gene Project research proves that Terrans are biologically hardwired to bring about their own destruction,' he said. 'This is of interest to Terran climate deniers.'

The Jeweller paused mid-pour and looked sideways at Necro, her interest at last kindled.

'The research also shows that it is possible for the Terrans to override their genetic programming with gene-editing nanotechnology. This is of interest to Terrans who are seeking to avert catastrophic climate change. What elements of this research are released, and by whom, will have critical political, economic, and social implications.'

'I see. Now we have a basis for some negotiation,' The Jeweller said.

She finished pouring her drink and took a sip, her cat-like eyes on Necro all the while. 'Where is this material?'

Necro placed the memory stick with Lightstone's research and the capsule containing the gene-editing nanotech on the table between them. He kept his fingers on the stick.

The Jeweller's eyes slid slowly from the stick back to Necro's face. 'There are people I can offer this to who would be anxious to have it, and to influence what is released, and how,' she said. 'But why did you not offer it to your Terran allies?'

'They have not been able to provide me with a super-conductor, though many promises have been made over the years. According to one of our intelligence agents, it is you who can deliver a superconductor. And I know which Terrans will pay you the larger sum for the information, so that it will be released to serve Nautilan interests. Now, show me the Saturnian diamond.'

'I don't have it.' The Jeweller's mouth smiled at Necro, but her eyes did not.

Though he was looking at the same person, he realised her warmth and beauty had gone. Without the mask of charm, her true nature was evident—her visage was that of a calculating mercenary, not of an exotic dealer in rare gems.

'What do you mean you don't have it?' growled Necro.

'I can tell you where you will find it. The deal was to assist you in sourcing a superconductor. I know exactly where it will be heading.'

'Where it *will* be heading? The deal was the memory stick for the diamond!' Necro hissed.

It was all he could do to not launch himself across the table and submit her to the Kiss.

The Jeweller's eyes were cold. 'The deal was to source a superconductor.'

'Where is it?'

'You will find it in the Doomsday Vault in Svalbard, Norway.'

'The *what*? Where?'

'The Global Seed Bank. Established on the Norwegian island of Svalbard several years ago. It is a state-of-the-art seed-storage facility that stores copies of seeds to protect against their loss through sabotage, war, climate change, accident, natural disaster, you name it. It will enable key crops to be re-established if needed. Hence its nickname, the Doomsday Vault.'

Necro tilted his head sideways.

'Why would a seed bank need a superconductor?'

The Jeweller shrugged.

Necro's eyes narrowed—she knew more than she was telling him.

His mother's spy had advised that the Saturnian diamond had vanished from NASA's research facility eighteen months ago. How could it be possible that there were experiments with seeds that required a superconductor?

Necro rose. He left the memory stick on the table. The Jeweller would ensure it was bought by those whose interests aligned with his. At least now he had a solid lead on a superconductor that was powerful enough for his purposes—if this woman was telling the truth.

He paused on the other side of the sheer curtain, without looking back at her.

'You'll be seeing me again, if what I seek is not where you say it is.'

He did not see the Jeweller gazing steadily at him, her face devoid of expression.

TOKYO

Kaito and his team were gathered around the TIA's board-room table in Tokyo.

The flat screen at the far end of the table flickered to life. Sounds of a press conference.

Accents—American?

Kaito's brow creased.

He had not heard from Umiko since she had left for Venice and had received no reply to his message requesting a meeting on her return.

An image took shape. The press corps briefing room in the White House.

'What happened to the news briefing from Venice?' he enquired, scanning the faces of his team.

Blank looks, shrugs.

All eyes turned to the screen as an official approached the podium to address the assembled media.

'Ladies and gentlemen, thank you for your attendance today,' intoned the official, sounding as enthusiastic as if he was reciting the phone book. 'I know you're all excited to be part of this announcement about the Rapa Nui Project findings, one of the most ground-breaking scientific discoveries of our time. This press conference is the subject of intense media and public interest. As usual, it is being livestreamed via the web, and is currently the number one trending topic on social media— including on Easter Island.'

Polite laughter rippled around the press corps room.

'In a moment, we'll learn about the results of the Rapa Nui Project, a six-year, collaborative study undertaken by some of the world's most pre-eminent scientists, led by Professor Lillian Lightstone. We are about to discover what their findings revealed. And now, please welcome the Director of the Office of Science and Technology Policy, Tony Denari,' announced the official, gesturing to his right, as Denari bounded onto the podium, all sharp suit and winning smile. There was a collective sigh of dismay around the TIA table.

'Agh—Denari! He's well and truly compromised. He's worked for fossil fuel companies and major banks funding oil, coal, and gas projects,' groaned Kaito's communications director, running his hands down his face.

'What is going on? Why are policy people from the White House making this announcement and not the scientists themselves?' asked the TIA's director of strategy.

A good question, thought Kaito.

The press conference began with a lengthy description of the project—the funding partners, the biographies of participating scientists, the existing academic literature around the research question.

Finally, Denari turned to the research findings, his face solemn.

'The Rapa Nui Project offers insight into an age-old and long-contested question: are human beings controlled by our genetic makeup? And if so, are we destined—and this is the critical part. The critical part …'

Denari paused for dramatic effect.

'… is: are we *biologically programmed* to bring about our own downfall as a species? The answer according to this research is: yes, we are.'

'Even more disturbing,' Denari said once the ruckus had died down somewhat, 'is that a group of scientists who identified this gene want to *edit* it. They plan to collude with governments to enforce this on us all of us, billions of people. They want to inject you with nanotechnology containing a virus so they can change *your* DNA and alter the very core of who you are. But I can tell you now …' he pounded the podium with his fist, '… *this* government is *not* going to allow it!'

The briefing room erupted—hands raised, messages sent, questions shouted.

Denari held his hands up, facing the audience. 'I know you will all have many questions, and we've got some time for those following this short explanation of the findings, so please bear with me …'

Kaito's phone jangled, jolting his attention back to the TIA boardroom.

He looked at the screen. Umiko. His finger slid across the screen as he walked out of the boardroom into his office.

'Are you watching the press conference from the White House?' asked Umiko.

'They have just announced the findings of a research project, presumably the one you mentioned. How is it happening in Washington and not in Venice?'

'It is a fake report. I mean, *some* of what they are saying is true, but it's not the *whole* truth, because the people presenting the findings are misrepresenting what is *actually* the case according to the real research findings, and …'

'Wait—stop. What do you mean, a false report?'

'I told you he was after this research, due to be launched by that group of scientists!'

'By "he", I assume you mean Necro?'

'Yes! He stole the research from Professor Lillian Lightstone, the lead researcher, in Venice. I caught him in the act, but couldn't take the shot, and he got away. Now he's traded off that research for something—I don't know what yet, but it has to be related to—'

'One thing at a time!' snapped Kaito.

Umiko took a breath.

'What did this Professor Lightstone say the findings of the research were?' Kaito asked.

'Lightstone's team have been researching whether

humanity is biologically— genetically—wired to engineer our own extinction, and if so, whether we can overcome our "programming".'

'So the announcement revealed—but what were the real results of this research?' pressed Kaito.

'Lightstone's team have discovered that we are, indeed, genetically programmed to bring about our own demise, but what was omitted from the press conference was that it is possible to break that "programming". Lightstone's team have developed a way to edit the gene with nanotechnology.'

'So—this press conference in Washington is revealing the first part of the findings—but not the second?'

'Correct.'

'I see,' Kaito exclaimed softly, the implications dawning on him. 'Necro has channelled this material into the hands of Terran climate deniers who have been selective in what they reveal.'

'Yes. He doesn't have the ability to influence the Terran media on his own, but he would have realised that if he found a buyer whose motivations were aligned, they would serve his interests.'

'Now people will be more likely to believe that whatever they do, whatever we do—it won't matter. That our genetic fate is sealed,' mused Kaito.

'And they will believe that because they haven't been presented with the *other* significant part of the finding— that by editing the gene responsible, we can override our tendency to colonise every part of the planet, consuming our way through our resources and altering the climate,' said Umiko.

'Can't Lightstone and her team simply set the record straight? Weren't they due to hold their press conference in Venice soon after the death of that unfortunate young woman?' said Kaito.

'It won't matter what they do, not now. A retraction, a follow-up clarification, an apology—it never gets the same amount of oxygen as the initial sensation, especially when such a story comes from the White House,' said Umiko. 'You can bet that any tick of the clock now, the internet will be alight with an explosion of gene memes, most of them feeding on the frenzy of misinformation just announced.'

Kaito was silent, thinking.

'If people believe we are genetically fated to bring about our own extinction,' he said finally, 'it will sow despair, hopelessness, undermine many efforts, at many levels, especially in political response—and that's been an uphill battle as it is. And if they believe that the technology to address this is some kind of conspiracy…our demise will become a self-fulfilling prophecy.'

'Exactly.'

'There is nothing we can do about this Rapa Nui issue right now—let Lightstone handle it. Our main concern is Necro. He would not have given that valuable material away. Find him. More importantly, find out who he did a deal with, and whatever it was he got in exchange for it.'

'I'm on it!' said Umiko, upbeat as usual, though Kaito thought she sounded depleted.

Kaito's phone screen went dark. Umiko was not the most orthodox of his agents, but she was one of the best in getting results. Now it was up to her—he could only hope her dogged pursuit of Necro would bring a successful outcome.

He gazed across Tokyo from the eighteenth floor, the snow whipped into patterns by the wind, the city wrapped in a smooth blanket of white.

It was snug and warm in his office. The last thing he wanted to do was go on a journey, but he had a meeting to attend—one no one else in the TIA knew he had scheduled. The following day was a national holiday, and he had arranged for his personal assistant to manage his calls, so that he was less likely to be missed.

Collecting his thick grey overcoat, scarf, and gloves, he descended into the metropolis and ventured out into the blizzard.

SERIOUS GAMES

DEEP IN THE Iya Valley, on Japan's smallest island of Shikoku, the snow was swirling furiously.

A silver four-wheel drive, barely visible as it manoeuvred gingerly through the snow, approached a remote farmhouse surrounded by forest.

Onmitsu Kaito had driven himself to this meeting from Tokyo in order to be as far from being overheard, traced, or followed as was possible for him to be. He had no phone and had purchased no flights or train tickets. He had hired the vehicle using a false ID.

Kaito stopped directly in front of the farmhouse, noting a black four-wheel drive vehicle was already parked at the side of the house. There was barely an hour or two of light left, and he wanted to get this meeting done quickly so he wouldn't have to navigate back in the pitch dark.

Kaito trudged through the already thick snow and biting wind to the stone steps leading up to the house. As per instructions he'd been provided with, he found the hiding place for the key, and entered the *minka*, removing his shoes, and brushing the white flakes from his hair and heavy grey coat.

The sound of the blizzard faded as he entered and made his way to the *zashiki*, the main room at centre of the structure, inhaling the scent of cedar wood.

The 'House of the Flute' had been lovingly restored over decades. It had become an attraction for travellers and volunteers who participated in the restorations, but with essential safety renovations planned toward the end of winter, the entire site had been closed to visitors for months.

The hearth in the central room cast a warm, golden glow over the polished wooden beams, the thatched roof ceiling, the *shoji* screens at one end of the room, a samurai banner that hung across the width of the room at the other end, and the two men already seated around the *irori* hearth.

'I am Onmitsu Kaito, Director of the TIA,' said Kaito, bowing to the men, who were sipping tea from a cast-iron pot that hung over the orange embers of the hearth. They did not rise to greet him. Kaito grimaced, as he noted that neither of them had removed their footwear.

'Kerr, MI6,' offered the sandy-haired man in a northern English accent.

Kaito tilted his head slightly—what interest did MI6 have in this?

'David Adams, Malvern Media,' said the dark-haired

man with a closely cropped beard, as he motioned for him to sit down. He spoke in an American accent.

Settling cross-legged on the flat cushions around the fireplace, Kaito accepted a cup of steaming green tea.

'We are an offshoot of the Serious Games Institute, which was established in Coventry University, Britain,' began Adams.

That might explain the MI6 presence, thought Kaito. 'Serious games? Sounds quite a contradiction in terms,' he said to Adams.

He sipped the tea, feeling its warmth thaw the chill that had permeated his bones.

Adams's grey-blue eyes smiled.

'It seems that way. Serious games are those that seek to help people learn, or shift human behaviour, by harnessing game dynamics. My organisation develops what we call "mission critical" games—those that can help humanity address complex problems, or overcome barriers, that are vital to civilisation continuing.'

Kaito nodded slowly. 'How may I help you?' he asked.

Adams gave Kerr a look. Kerr got up and produced a packet of cigarettes from underneath his thick wool jacket, then went out into the freezing air.

The American is calling the shots here, observed Kaito.

'Your organisation seeks to create shifts in perception, yes?' asked Adams.

'We do many things. However, the nature of our work

is such that if it is to succeed, it must remain concealed,' replied Kaito.

The hearth embers crackled and popped.

Adams looked intently at Kaito, turning his teacup around and around in his hands.

'What use might the TIA have for a game that helped people experience ecosystem collapse?'

Kaito leaned forward. 'It would be of interest. As you know, my agency creates the appearance of crises before they happen, but our work is restricted in that we cannot cause actual harm to people or ecosystems, especially not irreversible harm. Also, we are unable to execute events that are complex or large scale, so they are typically single-issue exercises.'

'Ah yes.' Adams grinned. 'I believe the TIA was responsible for turning Los Angeles's air pink some years ago?'

The corners of Kaito's mouth turned upwards. 'A simple additive to the city's fuel supplies—harmless, but effective in raising awareness of otherwise invisible pollution.'

That TIA mission had been a success—the pink haze that lingered over the City of Angels for days was followed by public outcry, and a shift in policy and investment to cleaner energy sources and high-quality, comprehensive transit networks.

'For the last two years, we have been working on a prototype, and it is almost ready for testing,' said Adams.

'What exactly is this project?'

'A deep immersion simulator of future scenarios for

humanity's existence on Earth, developed through harnessing various scientific and military capabilities.'

'So, it is like a virtual reality experience.'

Adams nodded. 'In the same way that pilots train in simulators to prepare them for real-world emergencies, this simulator can prepare people to respond now to the "long emergency" of a future yet to arrive. But it is much more sophisticated. Participants will believe that they are truly there and experiencing it, and oblivious to the fact that they are actually having a VR experience.'

Adams reached for the pot hanging over the fire and poured himself and Kaito another cup of tea.

'How does it work?' asked Kaito.

'On entering the virtual simulation world, participants can experience *through their senses* what it would be like to live in a world drastically altered by climate change and ecosystem collapse. It connects the cognitive—or what we understand as the intellect—with our emotional response to what we sense and feel.'

The possibilities began to dawn on Kaito as he listened to Adams.

'In effect, it is a time machine that allows people to *experience* the future.'

Kaito pondered this information.

'This is a game, a simulator,' observed Kaito. 'Why is it necessary to meet so remotely, so secretly … with …' he jerked his head in the direction Kerr had gone.

'Because this is far more than a game. Once we get a

working prototype, it will have profound consequences, and certain interests who do not want it to become operational will take any action necessary to stop it.'

Aha, Kaito thought. He now suspected the American might have links to the intelligence community.

'Where is this prototype?' enquired Kaito.

'It is in the northern hemisphere, in the Arctic,' said Adams evasively, apparently waiting for Kaito's reaction before revealing more.

Kaito nodded. 'I will, of course, need more details, but I think we can do business, Mr Adams.'

The American extended his hand, but before Kaito could shake it, there was a loud crack outside.

A flowering red stain appeared on the window of the farmhouse.

Through the frost-crusted glass, they saw Kerr's body drop to the ground. Both men sprang to their feet.

Adams held a finger to his lips and motioned for Kaito to move to the far side of the room, closest to where the black four-wheel drive was parked. Though he was wearing boots, Adams somehow managed not to make a sound while crossing the wooden floor. The men crept towards the car, Kaito silently gathering his shoes on the way.

Adams produced a revolver from under his coat, cocked it, and held it aloft. He turned the door handle cautiously, and the two men bolted from the farmhouse. A white-clad figure emerged from the snow swirl, and levelled a gun at Kaito, but before the figure could pull the trigger, Adams had already fired with deadly accuracy. The body slumped to the ground, leaving a crimson streak as it sank into the soft snow.

Kaito stared in shock—he was a strategist and an analyst who spent most of his time directing operations from an office. He had never been close to the sharp end of fieldwork like this.

'Quick. In case there are others,' Adams urged, motioning to the car.

Leaping into the vehicle, they slammed the doors shut as Adams gunned the engine and they began moving. The black four-wheel drive sped along the valley road, faster than it was safe to drive on the snow and ice.

Kaito eyed Adams sideways as the American negotiated the terrain, his eyes darting to the rear-vision mirror, to the road ahead, and back again.

'Which agency?'

Adams seemed to not want to answer, but eventually he said: 'US State Department. Counter-terrorism'.

'And there is something more you want from me than a partnership to develop a simulator, is there not?'

Adams glanced at Kaito. 'The Saturnian diamond you have in your possession.'

Kaito's eyes closed. 'How do you know about that?'

'I was working at NASA as part of the *Chronos 6* mission ground crew at the time when the diamonds were stolen. One of your agents, on your instruction, carried out that theft. I have been tracking those diamonds ever since.

There's a chance the missing ones are doing the rounds of the international black market for rare gems, and while they are considered merely precious stones the situation is safe, but they are still on the loose. We cannot risk their true nature and power being discovered.'

'I agree. That's why I ordered the diamonds stolen and decided to lock them away until I could find out how to destroy them. As far as I am aware, there is no material or energy source on planet Earth strong enough to do so. However, I only have one of the diamonds. The others went missing, and I am not sure if they did before or after the mission I ordered. I strongly suspect my agent lied to me and sold them,' said Kaito.

'I'll continue to track the missing gems, but for the simulator, one is all we need. Where is it?'

Kaito was silent.

'How do I know I can trust you, to just give you a valuable artefact I have sought to protect the world from? Because our mission is aligned?'

'Because I have not yet turned you in to the US authorities, and I have evidence to do so,' said Adams pointedly.

'So—blackmail?'

'Think of it more as a mutual favour.'

Kaito realised if he wanted to avoid jail and keep his job—indeed, his life's purpose—he didn't have much of a choice other than to comply. And the intended use of the diamond was aligned with his own work.

'It is in a Swiss bank deposit box. If I go to retrieve

it and take it to Norway, my absence will be noticed. I will give you the instructions and authority to do so,' said Kaito.

'Good. I'm leaving on a flight out of Osaka in a few hours.'

The black four-wheel drive sped deeper into the blizzard, and on through the night.

RARE JEWEL

I**T WAS 3** am, and all was quiet in the San Polo apartments where Ambra and Lillian Lightstone had retreated to the bedrooms and succumbed to exhaustion. Quill was softly snoring in a recliner chair.

Umiko was half asleep on a couch when her phone buzzed.

'Kaito-san,' she answered groggily.

'Umiko, are you still in Venice?'

'Mmm. I need to rest for a couple of hours and find out where Necro might be headed next. Where are you?'

'There's been an incident …' began Kaito.

Umiko shook herself awake.

'What? What incident? Where are you?'

Kaito filled his agent in on the events at the farmhouse, mentioning both the simulator and the interest in acquiring a Saturnian diamond, but omitting his prior knowledge of its whereabouts and his exchange with Adams.

'The TIA has been aware of the development of this

simulator for some time, though not its exact nature, location, or the extent of its potential influence. Our agency is now a partner.'

'And Adams's organisation is … a *media* company?'

'Yes. However, Adams is US intelligence, and the organisation is a front for more significant work, such as the simulator.'

'And where is this Adams now?' enquired Umiko.

'On a flight out from Osaka.'

'Do you know where he has gone?'

'No. He said he'd be in touch.'

It was only a little white lie, Kaito told himself. He could not reveal to Umiko that he had already provided the diamond to Adams for the simulator project without giving away his role in the theft of the diamonds from NASA.

'This guy's made us a target! An MI6 field operative was killed, but it could easily have been you!'

'Our work means we are always at risk of being a target, Umiko. The project his organisation is working on is important to our mission.'

'A goddamn video game!' exclaimed Umiko.

Kaito chuckled.

'He described it to me in greater detail on the drive back from Shikoku. There is more to it than it seems.'

'How so?'

'I'll explain it later. For now, it is enough to say that an ultra-classified project they have been working on requires an immense power source to work, one they have not been able to acquire so far.'

The realisation dawned on Umiko. Her mouth went dry.

'A superconductor—he's after that Saturnian diamond you mentioned,' she said, her voice hoarse.

'Adams?'

'Yes! No - well, yes him too - but I mean Necro! If that diamond is out there, if this Malvern organisation's project is working to source the diamond because they have built a device that needs one, then that's exactly the place Necro will head if he finds out about it!' exclaimed Umiko, rousing Quill from his slumber.

'We've been over this before. Nadir is not possible—it's a myth,' said Kaito.

'Oh, I think it is more than a myth. And if he's planning to do it, and he knows the whereabouts of the diamond, he could well have the means to make it work,' argued Umiko. 'Take a look at what I just sent you,' she said, pinging Kaito a picture of the diagram labelled "NADIR". 'Necro dropped that in St Mark's Square.'

Kaito was beginning to agree with his agent's assessment. If Necro had any clue that the Svalbard simulator team was sourcing an extraterrestrial jewel, that is where he would head.

And if Umiko was right, if there was even a remote chance that Nadir *was* more than a handful of intelligence yielded in the last decade, if Necro got wind that there was someone else looking for the Saturnian diamond and then discovered the location of the project … it was critical to intercept Necro before he made his way to the far north. But he could not let Umiko follow that lead by disclosing that there was a diamond, which he had provided, en route to the simulator with Adams. It would either jeopardise his position, as she would be legally required to report his actions, or if she chose not to, it would implicate her in a theft from a US Federal agency.

'Umiko, listen to me and do as I say: the project that Adams's organisation is developing is on Svalbard, an island close to the North Pole, which is part of Norway. My sources have confirmed that Necro is currently nowhere near Svalbard.'

'For now, but we know how fast he can move,' said Umiko.

'True, but even if he did head there—and right now he has no reason to—he will not find access to the Terran project as straightforward as he expects.'

'What does that mean?'

'Umiko, I need you to focus on Necro and his activities, not an elusive diamond, the whereabouts of which is unknown. Lord Abzu can help—I have him doing some work at the moment concerning unusual activity on the seabed in several locations.'

'*What?* That can only mean tectonic activity. I told you! All this time I've been saying …' cried Umiko.

'We don't *know*,' Kaito said, cutting her off. 'It could be military exercises, it could be installation of telecommunications cables, though we are usually informed in advance of such things, and have received no advice from our sources that any government or company is doing so. It is currently unexplained activity. Now's your chance to find out if Necro is involved. See if Lord Abzu has found any evidence on the sea floor that Necro has been planning what you suspect, find a way to disable it, and neutralise Necro, if you encounter him. Such pre-emptive action would be far more effective and far less risky than trying to intercept him once he is within reach of, or gains possession of, the Saturnian diamond. If there is no cause for concern, then we can turn our attention to the diamond—even if Nadir is a myth, we certainly do not want Necro in possession of such a power source.'

'How do I get to Abzu? He's at the bottom of the sea!'

'Our Ondan friends can assist,' said Kaito.

'There is an Ondan here in Venice,' said Umiko.

'Find out if they can arrange transport for you. If not, I will contact Chancellor Aroz in Onda and get one of their submersibles sent to collect you, so you can rendezvous with Lord Abzu's ship.'

She ended the call and slumped back in her chair.

'Everything okay?' enquired Quill.

Umiko hadn't been aware that Quill was awake and listening.

'I am not a submariner, and I need transportation to Lord Abzu's vessel,' said Umiko.

She explained to Quill her theory about Necro and Nadir, and how her director had ordered her to pursue Necro and confirm what he was planning.

'I have one of our submersibles docked just outside of the lagoon—I can take you to Abzu,' offered Quill. 'That is, if you're sure about this—we had an encounter with him on the way here, and … well, anything could happen,' he added.

'It might, but it is Lord Abzu who has been scouting the sea floor. He may have some information that can help.'

'Let's set off at dawn then,' suggested Quill.

'Sounds good to me,' yawned Umiko. She curled up on the couch near Quill and powered down into a deep sleep.

Quill could not get back to sleep. Coupled with his own knowledge of Nautilan history and ideology, Umiko's theory about Nadir had been profoundly disturbing.

Though he was aware his regent was liaising with allied Terrans to address climate destabilisation and sea-level rise, he had never heard Queen Cresence or Mabul, the head of Ondan intelligence, mention extraterrestrial superconductors, nor anything like Nadir.

What if Umiko's hunch was correct?

Quill decided he would not only deliver Umiko to Abzu, he would accompany her on her mission, learn as much as he could, and report to Queen Cresence at the earliest opportunity.

Umiko might be wrong, Quill thought, gazing at the sleeping operative. *But if there's a one in a billion chance she's right, none of us can afford those odds.*

He rubbed his palms into his heavy eyes and fell into a fitful sleep.

NEPTUNE'S REVENGE

THROUGH THE GLASS partition, Lord Abzu kept a watchful eye on the young man attached to the game console, seemingly asleep, except for the occasional arm, leg, or facial twitch.

Abzu wolfed down the last of his meal, licked his lips, and then his fingers. He rubbed his stomach, heaved himself out of his chair at the navigation deck, and went into the simulation room.

He sat in the game chair next to Jevon and observed his screen so he could view what Jevon was seeing in the game. If the Terran could beat the game, it would mean a bonus of ten thousand tetzels from his client, which would pay for much-needed repairs to his ship.

The experiment itself was not all that interesting—the creature in Jevon's care kept growing, it ate more rice, Jevon begged the powers that be to understand what this meant for the realm's food supplies, they didn't listen.

Abzu yawned and sat back in the chair. Sometimes,

he wondered about the Terrans, and how they had ever managed to become such a dominant force globally.

He let out a loud belch that reverberated around the game room. His satisfying meal, numerous swigs of rum, and the monotony of watching the experiment on the screen all conspired to send him into a slumber.

✥

Jevon watched in despair as the once-cute creature he was assigned to care for ate its daily quota of rice—double what it had consumed the day before.

Once the portion had fit in the palm of his hand. Now it was bigger than him.

The creature finished its meal, looked at Jevon, wiped its paws across its lips, yawned and stretched, then curled up contentedly.

Jevon could not sleep. He glared at the snoozing creature. Everyone but him was still enamoured with it—how could they not notice what a monster it had become?

It was too big, too demanding, and too selfish. Its downy fur had become matted and mangy, and it badly needed grooming. Its once-adorable face had become conniving and mean, concerned only with getting an ever bigger portion each day. Its sweet nature had given way to bad manners and an attitude.

How he resented the creature.

For days, then weeks, he had been unable to convince the royal ruler that the situation was impossible and could not continue indefinitely, yet the price of not feeding the beast would be his own life.

The hopelessness of being able to see what others could not was paralysing.

Jevon had been formulating various plans for how he might escape this place since the day he realised he was in a no-win situation, but he had dismissed them all as having no chance of success, given the reach of the royal ruler's power.

He gazed out over the balcony into the distance—a stunning vista of forests and mountains, glowing gold. A warm breeze brushed his face. It should have been paradise. The sound of birdsong and then … a jarring noise that didn't fit. An enormous burp? He looked over at the creature, which was now fast asleep after its meal. No one else was around. He shook his head—had he heard right?

As he questioned whether what he heard was real, there was a sudden interruption in his vision. For a minute or so, what he was seeing flickered back and forth between the palace balcony in the late afternoon, and a small, grey room full of equipment that looked vaguely familiar.

It was enough to break the spell.

Jevon wrenched the headset off and gasped. The shock of re-entry into reality hit him, and he staggered as he got up. He struggled to contain his nausea, taking several deep breaths, then wiping the sweat from his face.

He caught his breath as he spotted Lord Abzu, sound

asleep and snoring with his mouth open, in the game chair next to him.

Through the glass partition, he spied a half-empty bottle of rum on the table in the navigation room, along with a plate of food scraps.

At first, he couldn't make sense of where he was and what had happened, but it quickly came rushing back from the recesses of his memory.

Abzu capturing the *Depth Charger*. The experiment. Quill. *Ambra*. Where were they? Had they abandoned him?

Jevon rubbed his palms on his forehead, as if it would help him search his mind, frantically trying to recall the series of events leading up to being plugged into Abzu's machine.

Venice. They had been heading to Venice.

His sister and Quill had gone, apparently ordered off Abzu's vessel. He was trapped. There was no way off *Neptune's Revenge*, certainly not for a Terran.

Unless …

He glanced down at his discarded sensors and headset. His gaze slid up to Abzu, fast asleep in the game chair.

Silently, he moved to pick up the equipment, slowly, slowly, so it did not make any noise that might wake the slumbering submariner.

Jevon attached the sensors to whatever bare flesh he could find on Abzu's armour-clad body, and gingerly placed the headset on his face.

Having affixed the gaming devices to his captor, he stepped back and looked up at the screen above Abzu's head.

The screen flickered to life with a familiar scene. A royal court of another civilisation in another time. A sweet little creature sat, panting, next to a golden throne in an open-air pavilion.

The game had begun anew.

Jevon grinned. He did not know how long the game might run, and *Neptune's Revenge* was nowhere near as fast as the *Depth Charger*, but he calculated that Abzu would not beat the game before the vessel would arrive in Venice.

He slid over to the navigation deck and tried to make sense of the plethora of lights and switches.

Locating the ignition panel, he flinched at the roar of the engines as he brought the ship back to life—surely it would wake Abzu? Jevon held his breath.

Abzu did not stir. The hum of the ship, a familiar background noise to him, coupled with the effects of rum, were not enough of a differentiation in sound to disrupt him from the game.

Jevon breathed out, turning his attention back to the navigation dashboard.

It took him another half an hour before he was able to determine how to use the ship's advanced navigational instruments to plot a course for Venice.

In the black depths of the Pacific, *Neptune's Revenge* rose from the ocean floor and headed for the northern hemisphere.

NAUTILA

NECRO FOUND HIS mother in the vault of the library, a smaller, separate room in the restricted section, where the classified annals of Nautilan history were kept.

There was an acrid smell of smoke, which he only recognised from his trips to Terra, as the use of fire—a form of Terran light—was banned in Nautila. Fire would cause serious injury to pale Nautilan skin just from exposure to flames.

Necro spotted the remnants of around a dozen books that had been recently burnt.

His eyes narrowed. He resolved to discover which books she had burnt and why later, but for the moment decided not to acknowledge what Nefaria had been doing.

Instead, he briefed her on the outcome of his Mumbai trip, including the exchange with The Jeweller, and his impending journey to a remote island in the frozen north.

'She is shrewd,' said Nefaria, with a hint of admiration.

'Yes, so much so that she now has one of our more

valuable assets, whereas I only have a piece of information to find what we need,' said Necro ruefully.

'She will follow her own interests, which will more than serve our purpose,' observed Nefaria.

She motioned to Necro to approach her. 'Now that we have ensured the release of only certain elements of Lightstone's research, we have another, more pressing issue to contend with,' she whispered. 'The Terrans are working on a classified project far to the north, in the polar lands. Our intelligence has yet to confirm exactly what it is. However, it is a device that needs a large—one might say, extraterrestrial—power source.'

Necro grasped his mother's meaning in an instant. 'The Saturnian diamond—it must be! The Jeweller's information is that a superconductor will be used for a project inside the Arctic Circle. Your intelligence says the Terrans have a top secret project in the polar lands to the north, which will likely require the diamond …'

'… and the Terrans almost certainly have it,' finished Nefaria.

'It cannot be a coincidence—but whatever they are up to, it needs the diamond, so it is some competition for our plans,' said Necro.

'Or an opportunity. The superconductor is the last, essential piece to activating Nadir—then our backup plan can become our primary plan, and none of the rest of it will matter,' gloated Nefaria.

'It will be well guarded. I'll need to find a way to get in or otherwise access the diamond.'

'Indeed—though how well guarded can a seed bank be?'

'I think we'll find there's more at that site than a seed bank,' said Necro.

The room fell silent.

'Where is Neven?' asked Necro.

Lately, his brother was almost always in his mother's presence, or never far away.

Nefaria said nothing for a long moment.

Finally, with a gleam of anger in her eyes, she said, 'I have expelled your brother and sister from Nautila.'

'*What!* On what grounds?'

'Treason,' said Nefaria evenly.

Necro saw she was in no mood to discuss it. He felt a momentary pang of remorse for his twin and little sister.

'No great loss,' he said to his mother, though the words caught in his throat. 'They are not supportive of our efforts to restore Nautilan supremacy.'

'I'm glad you see it that way,' said Nefaria.

Necro strode out of the library and headed towards his quarters.

On the way, he passed his brother's now-empty chambers. Little had been left behind. It was like Neven had never even existed.

Necro clenched his jaw and took a deep breath to ease an unusual feeling of discomfort in his chest.

Why couldn't his brother, and his wilful sister, have chosen to be part of securing their family and their nation's future instead of fighting their mother? And no doubt that Ondan princess, a friend of Nemeia, and Neven's former betrothed, had played a part in all this.

He smashed his fist into the door of his brother's quarters and marched on down the corridor.

THE WAY HOME

Ambra was in Thailand.

Warmth, blue sea and sky, the sun glinting off the water.

A swimmer with jet-black hair in trouble. The ocean retreating.

The wave.

Running for her life. Her father's crazed cries.

Tumbling upside down, around and around in black water, filled with all earthly things in its path, the inanimate and the once-living.

She looked for the car stuck in the tree—and the boy she had been unable to save.

Once again, he slipped her grasp and was pulled under the water, which gulped him down greedily.

The car. She was on the car. Safe.

But this time, the water kept coming.

Rising and rising.

Then she was above the world, looking down. She could no longer feel her body. She did not need to gasp for air.

But she could see the horror show unfolding below across the face of the globe.

The water kept rising.

The outlines of continents were changing.

Villages washed away, then towns, then cities. Bridges, buildings, farms and food. Animals, children, the elderly and vulnerable, then those who could run but found they could not outrun the water.

This was not a flood. This was not even a tsunami.

The water kept rising.

Until there was no land left on Earth. There was no Earth. The entire sphere was now blue.

Waves the height of skyscrapers sloshed across vast expanses of ocean.

Everything and everyone had gone.

How could she get home? She wanted to go home.

Where was home? The world—her world—had ceased to exist.

She saw the faces of her parents and brother. The loving brown eyes of her dog.

Then other, more disturbing faces.

A haughty woman dressed in navy silk, with a silver braid coiled around her shoulders. Who was she?

A sinister-looking woman with cat-like eyes and a gold

stud in her nose, holding a shimmering gem in the palm of her hand.

An exquisite-looking man with dark features—though he was beautiful, the sight of him made her afraid.

The faces changed again.

A kindly face with blue eyes peering at her over the top of his glasses—Quill.

He was carrying an umbrella of swirling colours—pale pink, silver, blue, and green.

Quill's features changed.

The Sand Poet?

He reached out and placed his palm over Ambra's heart.

'No afraid,' Ambra heard him murmur.

But despite the calming touch, she was afraid.

She plunged back to earth, though there was no longer any earth, only ocean.

She was under the water.

She could not breathe, but neither could she cry out in fright.

Further into the deep she sank.

She only had moments left. She was out of air. She was going to drown, after all.

She let go, and the water rushed into her lungs.

⤜

Ambra woke with a gasp, thrashing around on her bed in terror.

She remained in the grip of the nightmare for a long, horrible minute, with no idea where she was, before she realised that she had been dreaming. The world rearranged itself back to normal in her consciousness.

Venice. She was in Venice. A city built on water.

Perhaps that explained the nightmare. She concentrated on slowing her breathing to take her mind away from the disturbing visions.

There was only a dim light in her room. She went to the washbasin and rinsed the sweat from her face.

Returning to her bed, she spotted a glowing object on the nightstand.

It looked like a sheet of paper the size of a small paperback book—but it was alive with energy.

Tentatively, she reached out to touch it.

The pearly white artefact did not burn or shock her. Its curious energy settled her.

She picked it up in both hands and turned it over and over.

There were faint markings on it, and on the reverse side, some kind of touch screen with two numerical counters and other buttons to execute a command.

What was this? A type of computer? What were the numbers—did this device require a code in order to work?

'What are you?' whispered Ambra.

The radiant glow brightened in response to her voice, and its markings became more defined.

Ambra peered closely as shapes emerged.

A map?

It was a map of the entire world.

She saw that the counters were labelled 'LAT' and 'LONG' and each had three separate numbers—degrees, minutes, seconds, a button to choose 'N' or 'S' and one to choose 'E' or 'W'.

'T'will only work once,' came a soft voice.

Ambra jumped.

She turned to see The Sand Poet watching her examine the map.

'Only once,' repeated The Sand Poet.

'What is it?' asked Ambra, turning the mother-of-pearl map over in her hands.

'To come home, wherever you are, must use numbers,' Sand Poet pointed at the counters.

Then Ambra understood—she had to use the counters to enter the coordinates of the location she wanted to go to.

'How does it work? How can I be sure it will work?'

The Sand Poet smiled.

'Will work. Only once. To anywhere in Terra. Use at most-needed time. Will bring you and anyone you touch, home.'

Ambra slowly moved one of the counters up and down.

So many questions.

She looked up, but The Sand Poet had vanished.

Ambra toggled from north to south, then set the latitude button to 'south' and the longitude button to 'east'. Turning the map over, she used the interactive map to find and select her coordinates:

34.833° S 138.483° E

NADIR

Ambra was awakened at sunrise by Umiko's and Quill's preparations for departure. She heard Quill downstairs, conversing quietly in Italian with the security guards who were still watching over the apartments. Lillian Lightstone was already at work, managing the rescheduling of her media conference.

Ambra ventured into the dining room overlooking the Grand Canal and found Umiko sitting in an armchair by the window. She was warming herself by the fire, sipping espresso and looking out over the city rooftops and the early morning canal traffic.

'Is everything okay?' murmured Ambra.

Umiko turned to Ambra with a weary gaze.

'He does not believe me,' lamented Umiko.

'Who?'

'My boss, Kaito. I have been telling him for years that Necro—the heir to the Nautilan throne—has been planning for over a decade to unleash a cataclysmic event on this entire planet. Kaito thinks this is a myth, because, in spite of everything I have gathered on Necro, all I have as evidence are a few small pieces of intelligence. But I honestly believe it to be a real danger.'

'What sort of threat? He stole my mother's research. I thought that his use of it through misinformation made him dangerous?'

'That too—propaganda is as much of a weapon. You think we'd be smarter by now, having seen this a few times in recent history,' Umiko said with a wry smile.

Ambra sat down in the chair across from Umiko.

'What exactly do you think this Necro character is planning?'

Umiko hesitated. 'This is going to sound slightly crazy,' she said. 'Necro is building a tsunami-generating device. I don't know exactly what or how, but he intends to develop one that will cause massive events many times the size of any recorded so far. It will kill millions of people, destroy cities, cause global economic breakdown and possibly the collapse of civilisation.'

Ambra's skin prickled, her stomach turned, and her heart rate surged, her body reacting though her mind did not believe it.

'I found this in Piazza San Marco just after Necro dove into the lagoon,' said Umiko, pulling the folded paper with the sketch of Nadir from her pocket.

'How is this possible? Are you sure?'

'I have access to classified records through my work

with the TIA, and I have been able to piece together a picture of Nautilan culture over the years from small amounts of intelligence. Nautilans believe they are superior beings to Terrans, who are fouling the planet—the Terrans take too much from the ocean, upsetting ecosystems and eroding Nautilan food supplies, fouling the ocean with pollution and plastic, changing the chemical composition of the ocean, causing mass loss of species, and so on. And they are right.'

'They are,' said Ambra with a grimace. 'But why flood the whole planet? Won't that make things even more difficult for them?'

'It would, but only temporarily. There would be some Terran waste that could be a problem, but most systems would recover once Terrans are gone and their activities have ceased. Their surface-dwelling counterparts, the Ondans, don't want this at all, because they will wear the worst of the impact and it would bring them close to collapse too.'

Ambra nodded, recalling Quill's story about the conflict between the Sottomaran tribes from when she first arrived in Atlantum.

'And, of course, the Nautilans will have a lot more territory than they currently do,' finished Umiko.

'They have a planet that is three-quarters ocean now!' exclaimed Ambra.

'Much of the ocean's resources they need for food and other requirements are not actually in the depths, but closer to the surface, where they are increasingly in competition with Terran demand on those same resources,' explained Umiko. 'That limits their ability to secure their civilisation's needs, especially when they cannot be exposed to the sun, and have to go to great pains to conceal themselves from Terrans in this era of modern technology. It was easier for them fifty, a hundred years ago, to move up and down the ocean, and access anything they needed.'

Ambra felt an unexpected pang of sympathy for the Nautilans. Umiko caught the look on her face.

'Exactly. They have reasons for doing what they are doing, as extreme and unacceptable as their intended course of action is to others. And Nefaria will not consider coming forth, revealing Nautila, or engaging with the Terrans.'

'Why not? Surely cooperation with the Terrans—I mean, us—is important to Nautilan survival?'

'The father of her children, Nazer, by all accounts a wise and wonderful man, was Terran. He was a one-time oceanographer and ex-navy diver who left his original life years ago to marry a young Nautilan royal—Princess Nefaria. Nazer was the love of her life, and she used her powers as regent to make him King, rather than her consort, so they could rule jointly. Because he was Terran, he could be in Terra with no adverse consequences, so once the Terran supertrawlers, overfishing, and other impacts started to create serious problems, he set off on a mission to negotiate with them. Nefaria did not want him to go. He never returned.'

'What happened to him?'

'Let's just say the Terrans Nazer encountered in his negotiations weren't open to the idea of sharing,' said Umiko. 'They did not recognise his authority as a regent of Nautila and saw him as a threat to their own activities. He did not make it back to Nautila, and though his death looked like it could have been an accident, there is evidence that points to the hand of vested Terran interests in his demise.'

'No wonder she's bitter,' said Ambra.

'Yes, this is a big part of her motivation for vengeance. It is understandable, but it seems grief has poisoned her mind beyond any possibility of reasoning with her. And so, she went down this path of seeking to destroy everything Terran, and now Necro has the means to do it. But there's one thing missing from Necro's plan—an immense energy source to power his device, which he calls Nadir.

'And there is such a source on this planet—a Saturnian diamond, a sample collected by a space probe almost a decade ago. It was stolen from NASA about a year and a half ago, and no one knows what happened to it. If Necro knew, or had tracked it down, we wouldn't be here talking about this. But it's only a matter of time before he does.'

The colour drained from Ambra's face. 'So, it is possible,' she croaked.

'I have also learned that Necro has accessed military archives in New Zealand. The records he viewed give an insight into what he is pursuing. Just before the end of the Second World War, the US and New Zealand governments were doing tests on whether they could create a weapon of mass destruction—a tsunami bomb.'

Ambra stared at Umiko in horror.

'It was called Project Seal. And under certain circumstances, they were able to generate a wave big enough to wipe out a coastal town. But they did not continue with the project, because the Allies had developed a bigger weapon—the atomic bombs dropped on my country, at Hiroshima and Nagasaki.'

As Umiko fell silent, Ambra gathered up her courage.

'I was in Thailand on holiday with my parents and brother when the Boxing Day tsunami hit,' she whispered, as her fingers twisted the leather bracelet on her wrist.

It was a sentence she had learned to utter without emotion many times over the years when an explanation was needed.

Umiko's face contorted at her revelation.

'I was caught in it. Although I survived, I can't … the things I saw …' Ambra's voice trailed off.

Umiko clasped Ambra's hands in hers. 'I am so sorry,' she said, with tears in her eyes. She swallowed. 'I lost my father in the 2011 tsunami that hit Japan. He was in the area for work—my mother and I were in Tokyo. I watched on television as those waves washed over the land. I hoped he had survived, but in my heart, I knew he was gone. He was never found.'

Ambra, now also in tears, was speechless. She squeezed Umiko's hands.

Their eyes locked in an unspoken agreement. They would find Necro. They would prevent him from obtaining the Saturnian diamond. They would eliminate Necro if the opportunity arose. If Nadir existed, they would find a way to destroy it.

'Quill is taking me to one of his contacts, Lord Abzu,' said Umiko, wiping her eyes, 'to see if we can find and disable Nadir—we're leaving shortly.'

'We met *him* on the way here. He still has my brother, Jevon. Quill said it was safe to leave him, but I want him released, so I'm going with you!'

'I thought you were going to be gene-edited during your mother's press conference here later today?' said Umiko.

Ambra sighed. 'I'd planned to. But if this Nadir thing is legit …'

Umiko gripped Ambra's arm. 'Listen to me—my director just conveyed information to me that gives me good reason to believe that a Saturnian diamond is located in, or will soon be headed to, a remote Norwegian island in the Arctic called Svalbard,' she said. 'He just had a meeting with some intelligence agents involved in developing a simulator there, hidden behind a seed vault built into the snow and ice—they need a colossal power source to run the thing. One of those agents was shot and killed during the meeting. There are others aware of that simulator project who don't want it to become operational—and who will be after that diamond. Guess who my money is on?'

'*What?* Then we must warn the people at this Svalbard

simulator about Necro, whether there is a Saturnian diamond already there or not!' cried Ambra.

'Nope. The priority is to determine whether Nadir exists, and, if it does, disable it if we can—and I will need Quill's help to pilot vessels to the ocean floor. If there is no Nadir, or we can disable it, then the diamond doesn't matter.'

'Yeah, but if Nadir *is* real, what happens if Necro gets hold of the diamond before you locate Nadir?'

Umiko exhaled.

'Ambra, you're right. But we need to do both. You might be the only other person in the world who believes this to be a genuine threat. Your mother is about to leave to announce the Rapa Nui Gene findings and demonstrate gene-editing. Quill and I are about to leave in search of Nadir. There's a better than average chance that a Saturnian diamond is on its way to Svalbard as we speak, and Necro may be on the trail of it. Because of the nature and location of the work and the associated security issues, there are no electronic communications in or out of the facility, so someone has to deliver the warning in person. What do you want to do?'

Ambra steeled herself. 'All three. But someone has to cover the Svalbard possibility. So how do I get to Norway? And how do I get inside this simulator project?'

'I'll book you a flight from Marco Polo Airport to Oslo, using my work credit card. You're in the EU, so between Italy and Norway you won't need a passport,' said Umiko, tapping rapidly on her phone. 'Ask at reception for the printed ticket and flight schedule. When you get there, look for my contact who will be holding a sign bearing your name. The island of Svalbard falls outside the Schengen zone, so to avoid awkward questions at customs, passage there will be arranged by high-speed watercraft. From there, a TIA contact by the name of Jostein will meet you and take you to the Svalbard vault.'

Ambra nodded in agreement—she was secretly pleased that her assigned task was mostly on land.

There was a call from Quill below. They stood up, shook hands. Ambra impulsively hugged Umiko. The Japanese agent gave her a grin, and then disappeared down the stairs.

MISSION CRITICAL

DURING THE VOYAGE from Venice back to *Neptune's Revenge*, Umiko filled Quill in on the rest of her research, theories, and ongoing pursuit of Necro over the years.

Quill, mindful of his last unexpected encounter with Nautila, navigated towards *Neptune's Revenge* in a circuitous manner, dimming the lights and reducing the ship's speed as they drew closer to where they had last sighted Abzu's vessel.

Thankfully, there was no sign of Nautila.

Umiko had just finished filling Quill in about Necro's activities in New Zealand, when the *Depth Charger's* radar pinged, and Quill's eyes flicked upward through the ship's bow window.

Still some way off, a string of lights was slowly moving towards the *Depth Charger* just above their location, the faint light illuminating a silver trident on the side of the vessel.

'That's odd,' muttered Quill. 'Abzu is almost always found near the bottom of the ocean. And I thought we still had a way to go before we'd have to dive. I didn't think he'd be on the move yet.'

As they watched, the grey hulk slowed, drifted and then seemed to hang in the ocean—as if it had spotted them and was waiting.

Quill deftly manoeuvred the *Depth Charger* until it was adjacent to the larger ship and secured it to the bigger ship's airlock.

Before Quill could open the door, it was flung open, and a young man with tousled dark hair and wild eyes stared back at him.

'Jevon!' exclaimed Quill.

'Where's Ambra? Is she okay?'

'Ambra is with your mother in Venice,' said Quill, glancing at Umiko, who nodded.

Technically, it had been the truth when he and Umiko had left, and though Quill knew Ambra was on her way to Svalbard, he couldn't afford to have Jevon distracted right now and wanting to leave the ship, when locating Nadir was the urgent priority.

'They are safe,' Quill continued. 'I've given your mother the backup copy of her team's work, and she is rearranging her press conference.'

Jevon breathed a sigh of relief.

'How did you get out of the game? And where is Abzu?' asked Quill.

Jevon's face broke into a grin.

'I'm not exactly sure how I got out—but now Abzu is in his own game!'

'Ha! Well done, lad,' chuckled Quill, as he crossed the threshold into *Neptune's Revenge*, followed by Umiko.

'This is Umiko, a field agent of the TIA, the True Illusion Agency.' Quill gestured at Umiko, who extended her hand to Jevon.

'Hello, Jevon,' said Umiko as the two shook hands. 'I've been in pursuit of Necro, heir to the Nautilan throne, for years. There's been an urgent development. We're here because we need the information Lord Abzu has been gathering for my director concerning mapping tectonic activity occurring on the ocean floor.'

Jevon in the lead, the three made their way to the navigation room, their footsteps echoing off the grey corridor walls.

'Uh—okay, so where would Abzu keep that stuff?' muttered Jevon, as he began rummaging across bench tops and through various drawers. Umiko joined him in the search.

Quill saw Abzu in the next room, hooked up to the game machinery. His facial muscles were twitching, but the rest of his body was still.

'Did you manage to beat the game?' enquired Quill.

Jevon looked up and followed Quill's gaze.

'No. I mean—well, to be honest, I don't know. I didn't *beat* the game, but I got out. It was weird. I was in the game, and it was like there was some interference, which jolted me out of it, once I realised it *was* a game, while I was *in* the game. I tell you what—I felt pretty sick the first few minutes after,' said Jevon.

'Should I disconnect him?' asked Umiko, who had gone over to inspect the apparatus to which Abzu was hooked up.

'No,' Quill answered. 'I don't know enough about this system to say what happens if someone is yanked out of it, as distinct from waking up out of it. In any case, locating Nadir is likely to be an easier task without Lord Abzu awake and interfering—provided we can find and make sense of his surveys.'

'What's Nadir?' asked Jevon.

'Ah, yes—a lot has happened while you've been stuck in Lord Abzu's game,' said Quill. 'Our friend Necro is not only out to cause trouble by ensuring vested interests mis-represent your mother's research, he's been in the process of building some kind of sea-floor apparatus that can trigger earthquakes and subsequent tsunamis.'

Jevon's eyes widened.

'You've gotta be joking,' he gulped.

'I've been tracking his movements for some time,' said Umiko. 'Based on intelligence gathered, we know that it is his intent, we know he's been building *something*, but he's not yet able to unleash the full power of Nadir—as he calls it—without a super-powerful source of energy, one that he can't obtain on Earth.'

'So, he's built this weapon, but can't activate it?'

'Not yet, but we know he is in pursuit of the means to. That's another story, and a much vaguer lead. Right now, we need to find this device he has built and disable or destroy it,' said Umiko.

'Okay, here,' said Quill, who had been rifling through a pile of maps that looked similar to topographical maps of Earth.

'See this?' Quill pointed to a cluster of markings, located along a deep fissure in the sea floor. 'This is where Abzu has noted tectonic activity, right where the plates meet. This is part of the "Ring of Fire", which runs most of the way around the east coast of Asia, and the west coast of the Americas …'

'… but it may not be Mother Nature doing all of the moving and shaking this time,' finished Umiko.

'That's about three hours from here in this leviathan, but only one hour from here in the *Depth Charger*,' calculated Quill. He drummed his fingers on the map, thinking. 'But—we may need the far nimbler submersibles on *Neptune's Revenge* to get close to whatever Necro has built and disable it.'

'What's the point in disabling it? He's built it once—he can do it again,' said Jevon.

'But he's too close to being able to activate it, and we now know he is hot on the trail of the final piece which will allow him to do so,' countered Umiko.

'Assuming it exists, finding and disabling Nadir will

buy us time, and we've now got a much clearer idea of where to search for Necro.'

Quill went to the navigation dashboard and, punching various buttons, plotted a new course. *Neptune's Revenge* shuddered, gave a gentle groan, and headed towards the cluster of markings on Lord Abzu's map, at the bottom of the North Pacific.

THE DOOMSDAY VAULT

THE HATCH TO the aquapod flung open.

A rush of icy air hit Ambra as she reclined in the passenger seat, a cold like she had never experienced before. It was the polar night in the Arctic Circle, though at this time of the year it was not complete darkness, but an ethereal blue glow.

The flight from Venice to Oslo had been uneventful. She had arrived and rendezvoused with Umiko's contact, who took her to a coastal site just out of the Norwegian capital and placed her in an aquapod, then launched her into the water.

In spite of her fears, Ambra had enjoyed her journey in the aquapod, which sped its way north just underneath the surface of the water so there was no turbulence. The craft had taken care of the navigating, and the pod's heating had kept her warm despite the freezing cold water in which she was travelling.

To conceal Ambra's arrival in Svalbard, Umiko's TIA contact had programmed the submersible to arrive north-west of Adventfjorden, instead of at the island's largest settlement and main port of Longyearbyen.

She stared up at the sky, the stars a thousand times brighter away from civilisation. In the middle of the megawatt smile of the stars, a friendly face appeared. A fair-featured man greeted her from under the black, fur-lined hood of his yellow jacket.

'Hello, Ambra, welcome to Norway. My name is Jostein.'

Ambra unbuckled herself from her seat, grasping the man's outstretched hand as he helped her out of the aqua-pod and onto the ice.

'Thank you for meeting me,' replied Ambra, as she followed Jostein a short distance, stumbling in the snow.

He stopped to help steady her.

'I've never seen snow before,' she explained.

Jostein looked at her quizzically.

'Australian,' she said.

'Oh! I wasn't sure of your accent. Well, this will be a new treat for you!'

He led her to a two-person sled, drawn by six Alaskan huskies who were patiently waiting. As Jostein approached, they began leaping and yelping with excitement.

Ambra climbed into the sled, and Jostein bundled heavy woollen blankets around her.

He handed her a navy beanie with the Svalbard Global Seed Vault logo on it, which she pulled down over her ears.

Jostein slung a shotgun over his shoulder, leapt onto the back of the sled, and cried 'Hike!'

The dogs began to pull the sled, and soon they were gliding swiftly away from the water's edge.

Ambra smiled, then laughed at the dogs racing forward as they pulled the sled. She thought of Casper with a pang of longing—when would she see him again?

Her destination was only a brief ride from her landing spot, and it wasn't long before Jostein ordered the dogs to stop.

The sled came to a halt outside a narrow metal structure jutting out of the snow and rock. The height of a two-storey house, the silvery-grey building was accessible over a short steel footbridge.

On the side of the structure was a circular logo, the same as the one on her beanie, and the name: 'Svalbard Global Seed Vault'. Ambra and Jostein disembarked from the sled and made their way to the vault entrance.

'Welcome to the Global Seed Vault, and of course, to MAGE,' said Jostein with a flourish of his red-gloved hand.

'MAGE?'

'The simulator.'

'Oh. Nobody told me its name. What does it mean?'

'You know, I'm not quite sure. I've always just heard it called MAGE.'

Jostein began the process of opening the vault.

'Why build it all the way out here?'

'MAGE has been co-located with the Global Seed Vault, or as the media like to call it, the "Doomsday Vault". This remote location was chosen to ensure both the security and stability of the seeds—isolated, geologically stable, with constant cold temperatures—and was selected as ideal for MAGE for the same reasons,' explained Jostein.

He removed one glove to retrieve a set of keys from inside his jacket.

'This vault is one of the safest places in the world. Anyone trying to enter must pass through several locked doors, and all the keys are coded to allow different levels of access—no single key unlocks all of them. It is also protected by a range of security cameras and sensors and kept under constant surveillance by the Norwegian government's property manager.'

Ambra narrowed her eyes. 'How is it that they will look the other way from someone you let in, not to mention give you the keys?'

Jostein smiled. 'The TIA has friends who trust them in many places.'

As Jostein grappled with chipping ice away from the lock on the vault, Ambra looked up at the sparkling array that adorned the top half and roof of the vault, creating a blue, green, silver, and gold beacon in the white wilderness surrounding it.

'It is called *Perpetual Repercussion*,' said Jostein, nodding upward as he worked. 'Its reflective beauty is created by polished stainless steel, mirrors, and prisms, which refract sunlight during our summer months, and are illuminated by fibre optic lights at this time of the year.'

Ambra was enchanted watching the light play in the sky and on the snow around her.

'Is there anyone in the vault?'

'Oh no. No one lives or works there. It's only opened a few times a year, to make deposits—or on rare occasions, withdrawals—of seeds,' said Jostein.

'There is someone at MAGE itself though, right?'

'The MAGE team is there. That's another reason for this isolated location. It is difficult to get to, and no one expects anyone to be here. Yet it is close enough to a good-sized human settlement, electricity, supplies, and an airstrip.'

Jostein inserted a key and opened the main door to the vault, his gloved hand wresting with the handle until it broke free from the remaining ice.

'I will show you in as far as the MAGE entrance, and then call back to collect you this time tomorrow. In the meantime, please do not attempt to go anywhere outside the vault unescorted by someone with a firearm. Everyone on Svalbard is required to own a gun and be trained in its use.'

'Are you serious?' said Ambra, as they stepped into the vault, Jostein closing the heavy steel door behind them.

'Oh yes. Polar bears outnumber people on Svalbard,' said Jostein cheerfully.

ENTERING THE MAZE

ONCE THEY HAD made their way down a metal tunnel and through the security doors, Jostein gave Ambra a brief tour of the Seed Vault.

The vault consisted of three storage chambers carved out of the permafrost.

Jostein led Ambra into the middle chamber, the only one currently in use, lined with shelving and stacked with hundreds of plastic boxes, all labelled and barcoded.

'This facility took two years to build. It was opened in 2008 and paid for entirely by the Norwegian government. It contains over a million different packets of seeds of nearly 6,000 different species, each an important variety of a crop, stored at a constant temperature of -18C,' explained Jostein.

'Are these seeds only food crops, or all kinds of plants?' asked Ambra, craning her neck to read the labels on the boxes that identified the seeds' countries of origin.

Algeria. Brazil. China. Syria. Zimbabwe.

'Just food. This facility has the most diverse collection of food crop seeds on Earth. These seeds come from almost every country in the world, many from national seed banks. There are over 1,500 seed banks around the world.'

'Countries with their own seed banks send seeds here? What for?'

'They send copies of what is stored in their own banks. It's like a remote backup in case a human-made or natural disaster—disease, war, climate change—threatens the food supply or even the seed bank itself in their own country.'

'So—like a safe deposit box for the world's food supplies?'

'Exactly! And, one could say, preserving the foundation of agriculture is an insurance policy for humanity. In an ideal world, these seeds will never be needed.'

Jostein led Ambra to a door in the far end of the chamber, which was almost camouflaged with permafrost.

Chipping away the ice, he used yet another key to open the door, then led Ambra along a long tunnel that bore downward, gently sloping deep into the earth.

The tunnel was dimly lit with tiny, faint golden lights, which brightened as they approached, and dimmed behind them as they trudged onward.

Eventually, the tunnel widened into a small room, which featured a steel circular door embedded into the rocky wall directly opposite the tunnel.

Above the door was a single embellishment—an upright silver trident.

Jostein indicated the silver fork.

'The trident is the symbol of Neptune—in both Greek and Roman mythology, Poseidon, or Neptune, was the god of the sea, who used his trident to cause mighty earthquakes, and to stir up tsunamis and sea storms.'

Neptune? Earthquakes? Tsunamis?

Ambra looked at Jostein in astonishment. Unaware of her recent encounter with *Neptune's Revenge*, or her quest in relation to Nadir and the Saturnian diamond, Jostein beamed at Ambra's interest.

'The planet Neptune is named after the Roman god, and in esoteric schools, Neptune is the planet associated with illusion. Also, the Greek capital letter "psi", which resembles a trident, is used to represent psychology. So, it is an apt choice for MAGE, as you will soon learn.'

The heavy metal door was framed with red LED light. The door did not appear to have any lock, security system, or even a handle. Curious, she pushed on it, but nothing happened.

Jostein smiled at Ambra.

'It is deceiving. The way into MAGE is through the mind. It has no conventional locks—the entrance to MAGE is protected by a maze comprising seven virtual challenges. And the mazes themselves are not conventional mazes, like those you find your way through physically— they are mazes you navigate your way out of by observing when the human mind must evolve in response to changing circumstances that become progressively more complex.'

Ambra was completely befuddled. What could *that* possibly mean?

Jostein caught the look on her face.

'How can I explain it? There will be a point in each maze where your response to what you experience around you changes, when you will feel like the existing order of things no longer works, that the problems of your world can't be solved with the way things have been, and that will be how you know it's time to leave. This realisation, this mental leap, will trigger your exit. You will need to find your way out of each level to unlock the next, and successfully complete all of the levels to demonstrate that you are capable of withstanding the experience of MAGE. If you cannot find your way through, I'm afraid there's no other way for me to gain you entrance, and I will collect you tomorrow as planned. No matter what happens, remember that all of the challenges are only illusions. Good luck.'

Without another word, he turned on his heel and began the long walk back up the tunnel.

Ambra took a moment to let all that Jostein had told her sink in.

The three-pronged fork above the door was a silent sentinel, and an indicator of what lay beyond.

She looked at the door.

The way into MAGE is through the mind, Jostein had said.

She moved closer to the door and stared at it, visualising it opening. She held her concentration.

A few moments later, the LED frame of the door changed from red to blue. Ambra heard a faint click. With a grating noise that set Ambra's teeth on edge, the door slid sideways into the rock. She took a tentative step through the open doorway into a pitch-black space.

It was completely silent.

Out of the darkness, a soft low light began to illuminate her surroundings. She was in a small cave-like room. The only thing in the room was a series of lamps set into the rocky walls of the cave. She looked behind her but could no longer see the door.

'My name is Clare. Welcome to MAGE,' came a metallic, too-polite female voice over a PA system.

'Entrants will face seven challenges, each more complex than the previous,' continued the voice, in a BBC-perfect accent. You may experience many emotions, but please remember they will all be illusions. They are intended to test your capacity for entering MAGE. Prepare to enter level one.'

The voice went silent.

Ambra was confused—how was she supposed to start? Did she have to say or do something?

As Ambra wondered, she realised the glowing lamps were changing colour, dimming.

Now the lamps were emanating a soft beige colour, swathing the cave in camel-coloured light.

Then the world around her dissolved.

FIRST MAZE: BEIGE

WITHOUT WARNING, **A**MBRA'S mind regressed.

However, she was unaware it had, as she had no memory of her life, and little in the way of capacity for language or abstract thinking.

She heard a rushing river, engorged with meltwater from the snow around it. She was in a forest clearing, surrounded by enormous trees and boulders, the river nearby.

She shivered and pulled the thick fur she was wearing closer around her body. There was no one else about.

Feeling thirst, she took water from the river.

Feeling hunger, she gathered and ate what looked edible in the environment around her, meagre as it was.

Suddenly, a fearsome beast crashed into her clearing.

Responding on instinct, Ambra stood stock-still, though her heart was pounding. It was many, many times bigger than her, with a thick shaggy coat and enormous curved tusks.

Across the clearing, Ambra spied a narrow opening in

a low cliff. She made a run for it, leaping over a fallen tree, knowing that she would draw the attention of the beast.

It trumpeted and came lumbering after her. Ambra dove into the cave entrance head-first, beating the beast by seconds. It snorted into the cave entrance but could not enter or get at her. She moved to the far end of the cave and waited for it to leave.

At last, silence. Water dripped from somewhere in the cave's depths.

Ambra caught her breath. As the adrenalin subsided, and her eyes adjusted, she noticed some markings on the cave wall at the entrance.

She inched her way forward and peered at the now-clear cave entrance. There was no sign of the beast.

Turning her attention to the markings, she saw a series of images depicting human-like figures, in small groups, but many more people than her immediate clan. Together, they were fighting a beast not unlike the one she had just encountered.

The last picture in the series caught her attention—it showed a defeated beast, a human tribe of greater numbers triumphant over their much bigger predator.

A sudden sensation of being watched made her whirl around, and she saw the huge eye of the beast looking at her in her cave. She backed away and hoped it would leave before dark.

Then, the cave lost all light—the beast's entire mouth was over the cave entrance, as it tried to force its way in.

It roared, its hot, foul breath hitting Ambra's nostrils. She watched, petrified, as the beast began to smash away parts of the cave entrance. There was nowhere to run.

There was no way she could defeat the beast and survive in this world on her own, or in her small clan.

Just as the entire front of the cave collapsed, with the beast's head above her, backlit by the late afternoon sun, the world dissolved again.

She was back in the empty cave, with its beige lanterns glowing.

Ambra gasped and inhaled lungfuls of air.

Shaking her head, she began grasping at the corners of her mind to recall what had happened, like trying to remember a dream she'd woken from.

Sitting in the quiet, dark cave, she tried to gather her thoughts and calm her nerves.

Not since the big wave had she felt in such mortal danger.

The entrance to MAGE is protected by a maze comprising seven virtual challenges, Jostein had said.

Had she just been experiencing, and fighting, an illusion? There were scratches on her hands, though, sustained as she dove to get away from the beast.

The simulations might be just illusions, but it seemed the potential for injury was all too real.

As her eyes adjusted, she looked around. There was a

tunnel leading from the cave that hadn't been there before. There seemed to be no other option but to enter.

After a short time, she emerged into a second, slightly bigger cave, also lit with beige lamps. Then slowly, almost imperceptibly, the lamps illuminating the cave began to change colour. They took on an ochre hue, then deepened to a rich purple.

The world around her dissolved again.

ATLANTUM

'**THE PRINCESS LUMINA,** the Crown Prince Neven of Nautila, and the Princess Nemeia of Nautila to see you, Your Majesty,' announced the Ondan Chancellor, Lord Aroz, as the trio of Sottomaran royals entered the staterooms of Queen Cresence of Atlantum.

'Nemeia?' exclaimed the Queen, rising to embrace the young woman.

Neven hesitated, unsure how his presence would be received.

'And Neven! So long since we have seen you. How have you managed to come here? Isn't Queen Nefaria going to …' Queen Cresence trailed off as she noticed the looks on the faces of all three.

'Mother, we will explain later, but for now you must listen urgently,' began Lumina, waving Neven forward as Lord Aroz looked aghast at the direct tone the princess had taken with her mother.

Neven cleared his throat.

'Your Majesty, my brother Necro is after a rare and powerful diamond—one the Terrans brought back from a space mission some years ago. He's been pursuing this for years. He plans to use it as a superconductor, the only possible means on Earth of generating a colossal quantity of power.'

'A space diamond? What does he intend to do with it? Is he building a spacecraft?'

'No,' said Neven. 'Something more earthly. He is building what he calls 'Nadir'—an earthquake-generating machine, located on the ocean floor, in areas of high tectonic activity.'

He paused.

'Necro intends to use the diamond to finally activate Nadir, with the intent of causing catastrophic damage to Terra, by generating earthquake-induced mega-tsunamis.'

'*What?*' rasped Queen Cresence, hardly able to take in what Neven was saying. 'How did you discover this?'

'Nemeia learned of it looking through one of my brother's journals in the royal reading room of Nautila's library. She had barely a minute after she discovered the journal before our mother caught us, and confiscated it,' said Neven.

'These are serious claims concerning the royal family of Nautila, but there is only one eyewitness account—albeit a member of the royal family—and there is no solid evidence,' said Queen Cresence.

Nemeia produced the journal she had smuggled out

of the restricted section of the Nautilan library, moments before her mother had appeared.

'This is one of Necro's journals, from a year or so ago,' she said, handing it to the Queen. 'I suspect he stored it in the restricted room of the library because it's safer than leaving it in his quarters where a number of people could have accessed it. And he knows Neven and I rarely go to the library, so he would have assumed it was secure.'

'How did you—? Mother *saw* you and took that journal from you,' cried Neven.

'There were *two* journals I tucked into my dress,' said Nemeia. 'I gave only one back to her.'

Neven smiled at the triumphant expression on Nemeia's face as she caught his look of admiration.

Nemeia turned back to the Ondan Queen. 'Unfortunately, this is not Necro's most recent journal. However, it is enough evidence to show what he has been planning.'

Queen Cresence was turning the pages of the journal carefully. It detailed how to build and power Nadir— research, diagrams, calculations, suppliers. 'Is this even possible?' she asked.

'It is if he has a superconductor that generates enough energy to power it,' said Neven, his face grim.

'We've been concerned that he and mother have been planning something like this for some time,' Nemeia said, 'but did not think they would ever have the capability to enact their madness.'

'We must find Necro and stop him,' said Lumina.

'Neven,' said the Queen, turning to the prince, 'I don't know where your brother is, but I suspect I know where he is heading.'

'Where? How do you know this?'

A small, serene face appeared beside Queen Cresence. A bald man with almond eyes, older in years but with the stature of a child. He wore a midnight-blue robe.

With one swift motion, he removed the robe, swirled it inside out, and wrapped it back around his body. This time, the robe was a turquoise robe, stitched with an Ondan pattern of silver waves.

'Saphiro,' breathed Nemeia.

'Your mother thinks he is her spy,' said Queen Cresence, gesturing towards Saphiro. 'However, he is in fact my intelligence source,' she declared.

Neven's eyes narrowed. 'Are you sure?' he said, glancing at the enigmatic man. Was that a smile, barely detectable, playing around Saphiro's mouth? Had he not directed Necro to a meeting with The Jeweller, and knowledge of where to find the Saturnian diamond? And he had apparently not mentioned the diamond to the Queen of Onda.

Neven opened his mouth to say more, but Queen Cresence waved his protests away.

'Neven, you must go to Svalbard at once. If Necro is not on his way there now, he will be as soon as he learns of this. You must stop him. If he has not already arrived, warn the people working there to ensure security is tight, and to be vigilant.'

Neven knew she was right, and that this was not the time to question Saphiro's motives. He made a mental note to have a long talk with the Queen later.

'We will go too,' declared Lumina.

'No, it is too dangerous. You are the sole heir to Atlantum's throne,' said Queen Cresence.

'Come—let us go to the library, where we can make plans. Lord Aroz,' she said, turning to address the Chancellor. 'Will you please see that transportation is arranged so that Neven may travel to Svalbard now?'

'At once, Your Majesty,' responded Lord Aroz, with a bow.

Lumina's eyes lingered on Neven, who returned her gaze, until he turned to follow Lord Aroz.

SECOND MAZE: PURPLE

AMBRA WAS IN a lush, verdant forest, in a village set in a clearing, with a few dozen huts and some common areas all close together. Grey smoke was rising from a fire in the centre of the clearing.

Small groups of people went about their daily lives, speaking a language she could somehow understand, and she knew she was part of this tribe who protected and nurtured each other, who kept danger at bay, and who kept the gods happy.

Her kin began to gather around a fire, feasting on freshly roasted meat, and brightly coloured fruits and berries which were arranged near the fire in clay pots.

After the food, the elders began to discuss an issue facing the tribe.

Earlier that day, Ambra had found an exquisite, bright-blue stone, the size of her palm. She had stumbled across it while searching for medicinal plants. Never before had she seen anything like it—a stone the colour of the sky, threaded with gold. The sunlight made it glitter.

In accordance with tradition, she had brought it to the clan council for the elders to contemplate.

It was not the first time she had yielded a treasured find.

The chief identified her to the whole tribe as the person who had found this unusual item. Yes—*she* had found this important item! She was proud.

After more than an hour's animated conversation about the fate of the stone, it was decided to sacrifice it to the gods by sending a special delegation to the top of the fire-mountain, a few days' walk from her village.

Each full and new moon, the tribe elders conducted rituals with offerings to appease the gods.

Though the last eruption from the fire-mountain had happened before she was born, she had heard stories of what happened when it was enraged. Yet the tribe's precious gifts of appeasement had failed to stop the gods from raining rocks and ash on the village.

Still she watched, simmering with resentment, as the elders bundled up the stone—*her* stone—and made arrangements for a delegation to depart three days prior to the next full moon.

Ambra knew the Law.

Anything any tribe member found belonged to the whole tribe, and it was the role of the elders to decide its fate in a way that would benefit the whole tribe.

Yet Ambra had become frustrated with this aspect of tribal life. She felt it was not fair—she had found the stone. It should be hers!

Wild plans entered her head—she would follow the delegation and ambush them.

No, she would find a way to convince the elders that the gods had *already* shown they favoured the forest tribe by providing them with Blue Stone—it was surely magical. And as a medicinal healer who was learning her craft, she could argue that the stone remain in her custody.

There were other ways to keep the peace, to placate the gods, besides sacrificing things that were precious. Why couldn't the stone at least be traded for what the tribe needed?

Ambra called out in a loud voice—in the unfamiliar tongue she was able to speak.

As she spoke of her ideas, the chief elder's face became darker and darker. She realised the rest of the tribe were looking at her with a sense of unease.

She hesitated. The chief did not speak.

There were dozens of angry eyes looking in her direction. They were moving towards her.

Ambra's nostrils flared. She had had enough of these foolish elders and their stubborn clinging to old ways and rituals that were not bringing the tribe any advantage!

Ambra pulled her weapon, a knife she used for gathering plants and herbs, from its sheath around her waist.

In that moment, the murmur of unrest erupted into a rumble of outrage at the sight of her knife, and just as the angry tribes folk rushed at her, the world dissolved.

She was back in the MAGE cave again, awash now with the purple glow from the lanterns.

Though she had been seconds from an almost certain physical attack at the point in which the world dissolved, she was relieved as she emerged from the forest, and not just because she was out of danger.

She was still tense; her heart rate was up. Or was it only a sensation she was having, as the purple lanterns faded to a soft pink, then turned blood red?

Again, the world dissolved.

THIRD MAZE: RED

AMBRA WAS HIDING, waiting, watching. Any minute now.

Behind her, on one side of the dusty road below, were T'ien Shan, the soaring Celestial Mountains. On the other, the steppe led to the vast Taklamakan Desert in the distance.

She surveyed her surroundings. It was the perfect place for her gang to ambush the traders who traversed the road between the lands to the east and the west.

Ambra's gang of marauding thieves had been relieving the wealthy merchants of their wares along this part of the road for a long time.

Silks, spices, gold, and precious gems, all traded for food, weapons, horses, and the power of being the most feared robber-gang of their domain, which it was rumoured had the favour of the local warlord. A tithe of the gang's bounty was a small price to pay for being left to carry out their raids without interference.

The sound of hooves heralded the awaited caravan, which rounded a bend and came into view.

Ambra's body tensed. Her role, given her small frame, was to dive in and look for any strongbox or valuables, while the physically powerful members of the gang dealt with the traveling party, particularly the armed escorts.

Ambra had heard, in various public houses, that people thought her gang were men—of course they would assume that, as all members' faces were hidden under scarves and various head coverings. People had no idea that they were all women, led by the strongly built Rona, who had come from lands far to the west.

The caravan drew closer. The cool mountain air swept down from the snow-capped peaks behind, breathing down the back of Ambra's neck. She glanced along the foot of the mountain where her comrades were lying in wait, behind various rocky outcrops. The gang's horses were quietly grazing out on the steppe, invisible from the road.

The caravan was in range. With only a hand signal, Rona initiated the attack.

Instant pandemonium. Horses rearing, people screaming, weapons hacking at flesh.

Ambra saw the lead driver of the caravan battling Rona, shouting and protesting.

A fountain of red spurted from the man's neck—Rona had slit his throat, and the corpse slithered onto the dirt track. Ambra's stomach churned as she watched.

The other gang members set about slaying and chasing away all the other travellers.

But before Ambra's gang could ransack the caravan, there came the sound of hooves approaching from the steppe.

Caught unaware, the mountain dwellers were themselves set on by another gang of thieves—the desert dwellers.

In minutes, the desert gang had fought their way to seize the treasures the caravan was transporting, their task made easier because half the job had already been done for them.

With a flourish of sand-coloured robes and horses' tails, they were gone as swiftly as they had arrived, taking the valuables with them.

Rona smashed her fist onto the side of one of the carriages.

This was the latest in a long line of skirmishes with the desert thieves that had lost them valuable provisions and equipment, including weapons.

'They must be stopped! This is *our* hunting ground!' thundered Rona.

Ambra's heart sank.

For months, she had tried to talk with Rona about this, to no avail.

Each time the mountain gang had been ambushed, Rona would plot a retaliatory raid on the desert dwellers. Each time, both gangs lost members. Each time, nothing was ever truly gained by either gang—just stolen, stolen back, and stolen again.

It was complete chaos. There was no sense of order.

Ambra wished there was one big boss to keep them all in line—maybe even work together.

In that moment, she made up her mind. She would take a horse and flee to the nearest citadel, find work—anything to have some stability, some peace, some greater purpose.

She turned, ready to escape, only to find a figure in a sand-coloured robe holding a knife pointed at her throat, the jewelled hilt gleaming in the rays of the setting sun.

She barely had time to determine whether the crazed eyes of the knife-wielding bandit belonged to a man or a woman, when the figure thrust the knife at her throat.

Once again, the world dissolved.

Ambra was gasping, clutching at her throat.

The red light cleared from her vision. She was back in the MAGE cave.

She looked at her shaking hands. There was no blood.

Placing her hand over her heart, she felt it pounding until her breathing eventually returned to normal.

The lanterns lost their red bite, faded to lavender, and slowly transformed to a deep royal blue.

THE DEVIL AND THE DEEP BLUE SEA

Neptune's Revenge **HAD** made its way to the location identified on Lord Abzu's maps.

'Now, to get out there and investigate,' declared Umiko.

'I'll go,' offered Jevon.

'No way. You've been entrusted to the safekeeping of the Ondans,' she said, jabbing a finger at Jevon.

'Then let Quill go,' said Jevon.

'Quill has to maintain command of *Neptune's Revenge*—especially if there's a chance we may encounter Nautila again. And not only is it too dangerous, but I've been tracking this character for almost a decade, and I want to be the one to end his insane plans. I need you to be eyes, ears, and support for me in this submersible. Can you do that?'

Jevon nodded.

'Good! Then let's go!'

The three made their way down into the belly of the ship, where they found three small deep-sea submersibles at the ready. Each was named, in bold black letters along their sides: *Allum, Cameron, Nemo.*

Umiko climbed into the *Allum*, securing herself and checking the controls and equipment.

'Jevon, one more thing—there should be a way to capture footage of this exercise somewhere on Abzu's navigation deck. Make sure you record what we're about to do—if there is anything here, my director might believe me, but no one will believe him.'

'Sure—when I was first trying to work out how to move this thing, I found where the AV systems were,' said Jevon.

'Good. Now, if anything happens to me, get this ship to the surface ASAP, and call my director, Kaito,' she said, tossing her phone to Jevon.

'Just investigate first,' cautioned Quill, as Jevon left to go back to the navigation deck. 'If you see anything suspicious, we can call in more support. No need to take any unnecessary risks.'

'Don't worry—I'm only going to prod around,' said Umiko.

'That's what I was afrai …' but Quill's words were drowned out by the roar of the submersible engine turning over.

He watched as Umiko sealed the clear hatch and gave him the thumbs up.

Quill slowly lowered the submersible into the

lock, closed it, and then released the *Allum* from *Neptune's Revenge*.

He hurried back up to the navigation deck to join Jevon, glancing into the adjacent room. Abzu was still deep in the game.

The cameras within the submersible were transmitting to Quill and Jevon the same view Umiko was receiving. While the searchlights were powerful, they were no match for the scale of towering undersea castles of rock and sediment.

Quill and Jevon watched as the lights played over the rocky formations, as Umiko edged along the rift.

'Nothing yet,' crackled Umiko's voice over the comms.

'There's another cluster of markings about a mile further along,' said Jevon, tracing a finger along Abzu's map.

'Okay—keep pace with me.'

Quill nudged *Neptune's Revenge* along behind Umiko's speck of light in an endless blackness. It was a delicate task—letting Umiko stray far from the mothership was risky, but it was dangerous to move quickly or to be too close to her.

'Oh! Are you seeing this?'

Umiko used the cameras on the nose of the submersible to zoom in, and trained the lights on the side of the rift.

There was an extensive, gleaming array of metal constructed along the rift, affixed to what appeared to be a series of tubes about a foot each in width that were embedded in the ocean floor.

'How, *how*—did he get this rig set up down here?' mused Umiko, more to herself than Quill and Jevon.

'There are no shortage of mercenaries and owners of deep-sea drill ships who will do such work, no questions asked,' answered Quill.

Umiko moved the angle of the submersible's camera.

'I don't know how far those things go down into the seabed,' she called, as Jevon and Quill strained to make sense of the structure.

'It's safe to say that this is something out of the ordinary, and enough evidence to warrant further investigation,' said Quill. 'We can surface, contact the TIA, and engage Terran naval experts to safely and properly remove this.'

'That'll take too long—we can't risk it,' insisted Umiko. 'Necro may be close to obtaining what he needs—for all we know, he could be on his way here now.'

'You can't possibly remove that whole apparatus with the submersible arm,' protested Quill. 'And you don't even know what this is, or what will happen if you try. It's too dangerous!'

'Don't worry, I'm not going to try to remove it—just cause some damage in the hope that will disable it and buy us time.'

Quill and Jevon watched anxiously as Umiko extended the *Allum's* mechanical arm, typically used to do minor repairs on the hull of Abzu's ship. She tested her ability to move and manipulate the arm clear of the metal structure, then inched her way towards it.

There was a muffled sound of crunching metal over the comms.

'Ha! I've managed to wrench part of the first section off!'

Jevon exhaled.

Before Quill could again try to coax Umiko back to the ship, bright red light illuminated the ocean depths.

For a few seconds, they could see the extent of Nadir, along the rift on the sea floor.

Then a brilliant white light rocked their ship.

'Oh no,' gasped Quill, trying to manoeuvre the ship clear of the blast, while not losing sight of the submersible.

'What's happening! Has Nadir been set off?' panicked Jevon.

'It can't be—but Necro has clearly laid traps for those who would interfere with his plans.'

One of the rock formations, shattered by the blast, had fallen on Umiko's craft, crushing it to the sea floor. A slow-motion cloud of sediment obscured their vision.

When the silt settled, they saw the submersible on the sea floor. It had been cracked in half.

'Oh God,' whispered Jevon.

Quill closed his eyes.

'We have to go get her!' cried Jevon. 'We have two other submersibles!'

Jevon leapt up from the navigation deck, but Quill held his arm. He looked into Jevon's terror-struck eyes.

'She has already drowned. And even before then, she will have been crushed by the weight of the water.'

Jevon crumpled into a chair, his head in his hands. Quill gazed out at the broken submersible.

'Can we at least see if we can find and recover her body?' croaked Jevon.

'No. It's too dangerous. We can't risk meeting the same fate, and then not getting word back about what is down here,' said Quill. 'There's nothing we can do for Umiko. She's gone. The most critical thing we need to do now is get to the surface. That's what she would do. And that's what she would want.'

FOURTH MAZE: BLUE

THE STEADY RHYTHM of steam, the creaking and grinding of machines.

A metallic taste in the air. The smell of wool.

The activity in the factory provided welcome warmth, as the weather cooled. It would soon be winter.

Ambra pretended to concentrate on her work, all the while keeping a sideways eye on the goings-on in Mr Victor's textile factory.

The boss man was up from London today, inspecting his factory and workforce. With his black top hat perched atop his dark, grey-flecked hair, and his navy cape flourishing around his legs as he strolled along, his presence struck awe in the women who earned their way in the world working for him.

The city was an extraordinary contrast to Ambra's previous life in the village, where her kin worked from sunup to sunset to benefit the lord of the manor. There, the big man not only took the fruits of their labour, but they needed permission from the master to make many decisions about their own lives.

Fed up with life in the country, Ambra had fled to the city looking for adventure and opportunity.

She had found routine and discipline.

Thankfully, she had also found work that yielded her some money in return for her ten-hour days. It was enough to keep her sheltered and fed at the local boarding house for women, week in, week out.

On Sunday mornings, she went to church, and then enjoyed the freedom of one glorious afternoon to do as she pleased. Tomorrow, she might take a simple picnic to a park, or read a book, or walk by the lake.

It was a long and tiring week in between those afternoons, but that precious time was not plagued by worry about where the next meal was coming from, or whether it would be safe to sleep that night. And if she met her quota, sometimes there was a bonus, like a bag of potatoes or some cakes to take home.

It was worth working hard to make sure she could enjoy fresh produce and baked goods.

And it was worth going to church knowing that her work ethic would stand her in good stead in the eyes of God. The church had taught her the way to a blissful afterlife in heaven was through hard work now. Ambra wasn't *entirely* sure about that—but why take the risk? In any case, she had little in the way of other options.

Without warning, a rolled-up newspaper whacked Ambra in the back of the head.

'Lightstone, stop daydreaming and get back to work,' growled the supervisor.

Ambra saw that Mr Victor was drawing nearer to where she was working. She put her head down.

In her hands, threads of blue, red, and orange fibre turned into wonderful, warm, soft wool on the loom.

Over time, as she'd worked, she'd realised that the method of making wool with these machines was inefficient. Ambra had often made woollen garments and clothing in the village, entirely by hand. She had even spun the fibre into thread.

There were four different ways she had determined would make the process quicker—and safer.

The day before, she had tried to raise this with the supervisor, who had yelled at her to mind her own business and get on with the work she was employed to do.

As Mr Victor made his way closer, she gathered her resolve to dare raise her views with the boss man himself. He might like her ideas and adopt them in his factory. It would save him money—she'd fantasised that she might even get a small reward. If she could find a minute to speak to him, without her supervisor within earshot …

She glanced up and caught the eye of her co-worker, Elizabeth, on the other side of the factory floor, and gave her a discreet nod.

Within seconds, Elizabeth had upended the machine she was working on, with a loud crash.

The supervisor excused himself from Mr Victor, and rushed away towards Elizabeth's feigned accident.

Ambra gathered her courage, rose, turned to Mr Victor and gave a small curtsey.

'Sir, if I may have a word …'

Mr Victor looked surprised, but not angry, so she continued on, launching into her ideas for improving production practices.

She was halfway through her spiel, which she'd been practising for the last fortnight ever since learning of the owner's impending visit, when she felt a presence behind her.

She stopped mid-sentence and turned around to see the supervisor glowering at her.

'Lightstone, what the devil do you think you're doing? It's not your place to tell the owner how to run his business! Sit down and get back to work—and no bonus for you this week.'

The whole factory floor seemed to have paused, watching as she was berated.

Face flushed, Ambra slunk back onto her work stool, as Mr Victor and her supervisor walked to the factory exit.

But as her supervisor went outside to hold the door open for Mr Victor, the boss man turned back and looked in her direction momentarily.

Ambra's breath caught in her throat.

Their eyes met. Then he gave her a wink.

A smile played around the corners of Ambra's mouth.

As the door closed, she and several others raced over to the window, and peered out.

Mr Victor had climbed into a grand carriage, drawn by four white horses. Ambra could only see the top of his cane and his hands resting on it, as the carriage drew away.

Her eyes followed the carriage until it was out of sight.

As she went back to her station, she thought, *If only I had the means, I could open my own factory. I'd treat my workforce well, and I know as much or more about wool-making as these men do!*

The entrepreneurial spark caught fire in her head. She resolved to spend tomorrow afternoon in the library.

The supervisor came storming back in, fuming. He strode up to Ambra, continuing his tirade.

Ambra knew she had made an impression on the boss man, and that he would almost certainly adopt some of her ideas—it made no sense not to. Perhaps she had even made an ally?

Her supervisor was threatening her with disciplinary action, eyes popping, spittle flying out of his mouth. Ambra found his face comical and tried—but failed—to suppress her amusement.

The supervisor's face turned apoplectic, and he raised the back of his hand to her. But before he could strike, the world dissolved again, and Ambra was back in the cave, bathed in blue light.

Once again, she felt a sense of relief at having left the world she was in. But where on earth was this mad maze taking her? The lanterns mutated from deep blue to pale aqua, then glowed a vivid orange.

FIFTH MAZE: ORANGE

AMBRA WAS IN a vast room at the top of a skyscraper, with wall-to-ceiling windows all around.

It was the Christmas party of the law firm she'd recently begun working for, and their well-heeled clients.

The room was filled with the blinding light of material wealth and success. Everywhere Ambra turned, she could see only the finest things, on the most beautiful people.

Exquisitely cut suits of gunmetal grey, set off with a splash of colour from a tie or kerchief. Gleaming cufflinks.

Skirts framing long, elegant legs. Manicured nails. Sparkly earrings. Designer handbags.

The scent of exclusive perfumes and colognes, and a slightly acrid but delicious smell of cigar smoke. The late afternoon sun glinting on shiny people and their shiny things, sending dozens of tiny golden beams skimming around the room.

Sunglasses. Watches. Jewels.

Chandeliers, marble. Opulence.

Life's winners.

These achievers had done well, the rewards a result of their own ingenuity—or cunning. And they knew how to enjoy it.

What a time they were having!

Hundreds of people were laughing, dancing, and drinking, swaying to the swing music of a live band.

This place was a blast!

Ambra had always enjoyed a good party. She began to circulate, partaking in the drink and food, revelling in the vibe, noticing she was attracting the attention of fine-looking men of means.

But just as she was beginning to feel comfortable, the atmosphere changed.

There was a loud smash of shattering glass, followed by braying laughter—those who had been building a large pyramid of champagne glasses had consumed a bit too much of the bubbly destined to be poured into it.

The band had finished, and someone turned the music on the stereo system up so loud that it was beyond deafening. It was no longer possible to discern a beat, let alone a melody.

Gradually, the finery of the partygoers themselves began decaying—a torn shirt here, a lost earring there, high heels abandoned. Mussed hair, askew ties, and lipstick stains.

White-powdered nostrils.

Ambra saw the platters and platters of food, hardly touched, which had sat there for hours and were now all the wrong temperature—hot meats now lukewarm; cheeses, seafood and fruits no longer cold and fresh—not appealing to taste, smell, or even look at. A vast, wasteful monument to excess.

Ambra's gaze swept the scene. It was all looking trashy now.

The party had been fun while it lasted, but now the room and its occupants were looking the worse for wear.

She tried to find a quieter corner. Though it was winter, it was warm here, at this height, with these large windows, bathed in the glow of the setting sun.

Looking down at the streets, people seemed so small and distant.

As the streetlights began to blink on in the dark, cold streets below, she could see a queue had begun forming at a nearby soup kitchen. Among the queuers was a small boy holding the hand of an elderly lady, possibly his grandmother.

Outside the window, only a block away, the Chrysler Building lit up, its Art Deco beauty drawing her eye back upwards.

But Ambra couldn't un-see the streets.

She looked around the room. No one else had noticed what she had seen.

Ambra had a lump in her throat.

What was the point of all this? This was not the way

it should be. It would have been easy to stay. But she no longer wanted to be a part of it.

Making for the door, she handed in her entry pass to the concierge. As she crossed the threshold and left the party, the world dissolved, and she was in the MAGE cave once more.

The cave was overwhelmingly quiet after the din of the party. Ambra felt rattled—it had been way too much stimulus. She took a deep breath to calm down. And again. And again. A few breaths later, the cave lamps faded from orange to khaki, then a vibrant green.

TOKYO/NORTH PACIFIC

Kaito's phone screen came alive.

It was Umiko's caller ID.

'Umiko, *hai*?'

It was not Umiko who answered, but a young, distressed male voice.

'Hello, is that Kaito, Director of the TIA?'

'Yes—who is this?'

'My name is Jevon Lightstone. I …' Jevon hesitated, not knowing where to begin.

Lightstone!

'I know who you are. Where is Umiko? Why do you have her phone?'

'I'm on a vessel called *Neptune's Revenge*, commanded by Lord Abzu—we've been at the bottom of the ocean, and we've just surfaced,' Jevon began.

An unexpected pause. Kaito tensed.

'There's been a terrible accident,' Jevon said. 'I'm sorry

to tell you this, but … your agent, Umiko … she's been killed. She was outside the ship in a small submersible, attempting to disable a device on the sea floor.'

Kaito's stomach lurched, and his head fell forward into the palm of his hand.

'Are you sure? What exactly happened?' Kaito tried to stay focused.

'She was trying to use the external arm of the submersible to dislodge the device. Something exploded. It was a big enough blast to rock our ship. When everything settled, we could see the submersible—it had been cracked in half and had sunk to the seabed. There's … there's no way she could have survived.'

'Have you been able to recover her body?'

'No sir—I'm sorry, we were unable to,' said Jevon, his voice breaking.

'Where are you now?'

'I'm not exactly sure—I'm trying to figure out our location now. We are somewhere in the North Pacific.'

'Who else is with you?'

'Just Lord Abzu, but he is currently wired up to a virtual reality machine, and it's not clear to anyone how to safely wake him up.'

'How did you get onto his ship?'

'Quill, the Ondan. He brought me here on a smaller vessel.'

'Where is he now?'

'He's gone to alert the authorities at Atlantum and bring back help. He instructed me to make this call, then dive again, and wait for his return.'

'Alright. When Quill returns, ask him to bring Abzu's vessel to Tokyo.'

'Okay. I'm so sorry about your agent.'

'I'm sorry you were witness to her death,' Kaito said gently. 'She was determined to stop this plot by Necro, and it seems she was right. Umiko is a big loss to the TIA.'

After a moment's silence, Jevon said, 'I don't know if Nadir has been disabled. There was an explosion, but … as I understand it, this thing is intended to trigger massive seismic events.'

Had Necro set traps to keep away vessels and deep-sea creatures—and anyone intent on stopping its use—from interfering with Nadir? wondered Kaito.

'We need to finish it then. We have to completely destroy this device. Dive now, so you won't be spotted by planes or satellites. Wait for Quill's return. I'll see you in Tokyo,' instructed Kaito.

'Yes, sir,' said Jevon.

Kaito's phone screen went dark.

He closed his eyes and swallowed. Wiping cold sweat from his forehead, he fought back a sick feeling in his stomach.

Had he sent his agent to her death?

She had wanted to track down the diamond, and he had ordered her elsewhere.

Though he had genuinely wanted Nadir investigated, in his heart he knew part of his reason for sending her to the depths of the ocean was to conceal his role in the theft of the Saturnian diamonds and protect his position.

And now Umiko lay somewhere at the bottom of the Pacific, the life crushed out of her.

Nadir was still almost certainly real, and intact. And a Saturnian diamond was en route to Svalbard with Adams.

He could only hope that Necro was not yet aware of it.

SIXTH MAZE: GREEN

AMBRA HURTLED DOWN the hill towards the campus on her bike, her friend Mike right behind her.

The previous month, Ambra and Mike had executed a direct action in the North Sea, scaling an oil rig and dropping a four-storey yellow banner that read 'OIL IS FOR FOSSIL FOOLS' in bold, black letters.

As a result of that stunt, which had attracted global media attention, they'd become cult heroes in the green movement and had been invited to address a meeting of The Eco-Crew, a newly formed network of local activists on their college campus.

And they were running late.

Breathless, they entered the appointed room, but instead of an expectant audience, they found a small crowd milling around, enjoying a shared supper.

Ambra and Mike introduced themselves to their host, then helped themselves to the salads, homemade bread, hummus, goat's cheese, organic teas, and vegan brownies.

'Okay, everyone, group check-in!' announced Jim, the network coordinator, clapping his hands several times for attention.

Ambra had done some research on this group after they'd received the invitation. Jim had been a leader in the counterculture movement of Berkeley in the late 1960s and early 1970s, and now lectured part time at the university.

They all settled on piles of cushions in a circle on the floor.

The gathering started with the check-in, which consisted of a brief update from each member as to how they'd been feeling since they'd last met, what they'd done to ensure self-care, and if they needed any help with anything.

Ambra and Mike then gave a brief slide show presentation of their direct action, which drew approving applause from the group.

'This action was the "inciting incident", the first part of our strategy for divestment from fossil fuels,' Mike explained.

'What's divestment?' asked a young woman with a nose ring and sandy dreadlocks.

'It's when we organise to get institutions and individuals to move their money out of investing in companies who are suppliers of, or otherwise involved with, fossil fuels and their supply chains, like oil and coal mining,' responded Ambra.

'Eh heh-heh,' cackled an old-timer, who had been listening intently. 'Y'all never get banks and institutions to un-invest in fossil fuels.'

'We believe we can,' countered Ambra. 'We need to highlight not only the environmental problems, but also demonstrate the *financial* risk—and the insurance companies are already onto this.'

'Juanita has spent most of her life in Mexico and Texas, working for—and fighting against—those kinds of companies,' explained Jim, smiling at the oldest member of the group. The elderly lady winked back at him.

The gathering moved on to the next matter at hand— another guest speaker who had written a profoundly moving book on his incarceration as a political prisoner. He had been wrongly accused of being a spy and imprisoned by the military government ruling his country at the time. His story of how he was tortured for two months until he confessed, and then placed in solitary confinement for thirteen years, brought Ambra to tears.

On his release, he had written a book describing how the simple act of observing the tiniest expressions of life while in jail had helped maintain his spiritual and mental health and had awakened an ecological consciousness within him.

'Are there any questions?' invited Jim.

'Yes!' said a young man wearing a Che Guevara t-shirt. 'How many trees have you planted to compensate for the printing of your book?'

Ambra noticed Mike wincing at her.

All eyes in the room looked to the guest, waiting for a response. Ambra shifted on her cushion, which had suddenly become uncomfortable. There was an awkward silence—but nobody who might have found the question inappropriate raised any concern.

The guest speaker graciously acknowledged that he had some tree-planting to do to offset the paper use associated with printing his book.

The conversation then moved around the circle, where everyone had a chance to speak.

Ambra heard inspiring stories from various members of the group—from the establishment of community gardens and food co-ops, to the development of alternative currencies, and a short lesson about off-grid energy technologies.

The last item on the agenda was a planning session intended to gain consensus around the network's focus and forward strategy.

To Ambra, it seemed like there was a great deal of good intention, but it was all over the place.

After thirty minutes of conversation, the group arrived at a point of agreement.

'So, it's settled then. The Eco-Crew Network is a community of support for people working on ecosystem collapse and issues related to the post-fossil-fuel era.'

An older man wearing a rainbow flag bandana around his head raised his hand.

'Sounds heavy! So, what do we do first?'

'We need to discuss this further—so next week, I'd like

to invite you all to my place for some gardening, yoga, and a group dinner!' said Jim.

From under her eyebrows, Ambra looked at Mike, whose mouth was slightly open. Then he ran his hands through his hair.

Without having to say a word, each knew what the other was thinking:

All these things are so important, but they are not enough. We are up against big money, big power structures. We don't have time. We must organise, at scale, effectively, quickly.

As they rode out of the campus, Mike turned to Ambra and said: 'I'm done with the protesting.'

Ambra breathed a sigh of relief. 'I'm so glad you said that!'

'I have some ideas … for what to do next,' Mike went on. 'Let's go find those people we talked to last week—the ones who helped organise for Civil Rights.'

'That's exactly what I've been thinking!' she exclaimed. 'They orchestrated a recent, effective social movement. But there's a huge opportunity now that they didn't have not so long ago, Mike—how to get information out and organise with the world wide web and email. More and more people have email now. We need to think about how we can use that in our work. If the Civil Rights movement managed to do what they did without digital technology, can you imagine what we can do with it?'

'Sure—you can start by teaching me how to use it.

Then, maybe we can offer a workshop so that others can learn,' suggested Mike.

'You're on—race you to the Bay Bridge!' cried Ambra, kicking her bike into the next gear and getting a head start on Mike.

As the two friends cycled towards the bay, the golden bridge in the distance glinting spectacularly in the evening sun, the fog rolled in.

First it obscured the bridge, rising in ethereal columns, and then it enveloped everything visible, until the world dissolved once more.

Ambra was alone in the MAGE cave. Each time she had returned to the cave before, she'd been relieved to escape a situation that was too much. Now, it was too quiet.

For the first time since she had entered the maze, she was lonely—she missed Mike.

She shook her head. How was that even possible? Mike was a figment of her imagination, an illusion generated in the maze.

As she contemplated this, the green light from the lanterns turned to pale lemon, then a bright yellow.

SEVENTH MAZE: YELLOW

AMBRA SWUNG HER legs over the side of the hammock and padded barefoot into the hut.

Outside, a gentle breeze blew through the palm trees as she opened her laptop and logged in to attend the online meeting that was about to start.

A year before, Ambra had quit her job and relocated to the Antipodes. It had not been a peaceful departure. A wry grin spread across her face as she recalled the stand-up row she'd had with her manager.

Now, anywhere with internet access was an office; anywhere could be home. She liaised with clients, and others she worked with—but no boss.

She stretched and yawned, pleased that she'd been able to have these few days at Kaihoka while the weather was warm, before heading home to Queenstown after a week consulting to a local authority on the North Island.

Working freelance as a creative had its advantages.

Lately, though, she'd realised she only needed to make

enough income to pay for essentials and a few luxuries, and since she was able to set her own hours, had decided to work three days a week.

That freed up time to work on things she cared about, the things that couldn't pay the bills.

And then she'd found a network of likeminded souls—in the online world.

Her screen blinked with activity. One by one, members of the virtual team she was part of appeared in the forum.

They had found each other through common interests. Each of the team had realised they wanted to work together on their shared goals. By using digital skills, they could build things outside formal institutions, and without organisational structures, even across continents and time zones.

It was one of the reasons Ambra had fled the nine-to-five world to become a digital nomad—hierarchies didn't lend themselves as well to creativity, to rapid action, to change. If you had an idea, there was always someone saying you couldn't do something, or that it wasn't in the plan, or that there was no budget. And always someone to ask for permission.

Ambra's passion project involved working with likeminded others to build an open-source platform to coordinate responses to disasters. Instead of directing people to seek help through a centralised entity, it complemented those services by enabling people to both ask for and offer help to each other, enabling direct and more immediate support.

During bushfires in Australia, and hurricanes and flooding along the US east coast, Ambra had observed social media feeds, watching people organising exactly like this, but in a makeshift way, using shared spreadsheets, online groups, and other digital media.

Effective, but rudimentary.

What if they could join up the efforts of everyone, so people could find medical assistance, shelter, transportation, power, help in rescuing animals all in one place?

This work was permission-less and purposeful. And if it took off, they could make their living through their chosen work.

By creating something together that society needed—and all cities and countries needed effective means of responding to disasters, which were becoming more frequent and intense—they could offer training and development in how to use their system, teaching emergency services and relief organisations around the world.

It allowed her to use her strengths, and to work with others whose gifts complemented her own. Ambra was terrible with numbers, great with words. Josh loved handling the business side of things, and actually liked accounting, which was incomprehensible to Ambra, though she was grateful someone did enjoy what she didn't.

'Hey, Ambra,' Sam's voice chirped through her speakers. He was chairing today's meeting.

'How's it going?' Ambra replied, waving at Sam on the screen.

'Great! Hey, we found a new web developer. She's built websites for large organisations and loves what we're doing, so we can now rapidly progress that part of our comms work.'

Among other tasks, Ambra had been contributing some web design to the group's efforts.

'Oh cool! That's great to hear. Pleased to have someone with those skills on board. That'll free me up to do more writing,' she said.

'Yep and we need our best writers focused on producing the things we need to communicate our ideas,' affirmed Sam.

'What else do people have to report?' Sam continued.

'We need to work out how we can track stuff, and as part of that, I have to knuckle down over the next couple of weeks and do this statistical analysis course that MIT have made available online for free,' said Josh.

'Sounds fun,' said Ambra, rolling her eyes, as Josh laughed.

The meeting continued, each member reporting on progress they'd made, barriers encountered, and what was needed to keep the momentum building.

'Alright, I think we're done for today,' said Sam. 'Okay, guys—I'll see you at the retreat in a few months. So exciting!'

Ambra waved goodbye and blew kisses at the faces on the screen.

The faces of her colleagues disappeared, and she was alone in her quiet hut, the distant sound of waves breaking on the shore below.

The day had become overcast, the sky a moody grey.

She opened up a new browser window to check the news, and then she wished she had not.

It was a cacophony of stories about natural and humanitarian disasters all around the world.

The strongest blizzard on record had swept across Europe, with record low temperatures triggering multiple breakdowns in transportation and supply systems that were not designed for such a level of cold. A typhoon had pummelled the Philippines, causing flooding and landslides. In India, extreme heat had killed thousands and destroyed crops.

She opened her email and began typing a message to Sam.

We are all working to create something to help people in need, and that's worth doing. But ...

She paused, chewing her lip. She knew she was risking offending Sam, who had originally proposed the idea.

Then she continued typing:

... we are only fixing the damage. At the rate things are happening, we're not going to keep up.

She pasted the link to the news update she had viewed, and then typed:

We need to be building something that helps people adapt and transition, not just survive.

She finished with: *How can we do this?*

As she hit 'send', the world dissolved, and she was back in the MAGE cave with its lanterns—or at least she assumed so.

The entire cave was filled with brilliant turquoise light. Was she back in Atlantum, under the sea again?

The turquoise light dimmed enough that she could make out a doorway on the other side of the cave.

That was different.

Then she realised that she had made it through the seventh maze

Was this it? Had she finally navigated her way into MAGE?

Ambra took a tentative step towards the doorway.

SVALBARD, NORWAY

AGENT DAVID ADAMS was speeding back towards Svalbard's main town, Longyearbyen, intent on getting out of the freezing bite of the wind, the beams from his snowmobile's headlights slicing through the blue-black darkness.

He had completed his mission of retrieving the Saturnian diamond from Kaito's Swiss bank deposit box, and delivered his precious cargo to MAGE via the hidden supply tunnel that enabled food, equipment, medical supplies, and other essentials to be brought into the facility.

The two-kilometre tunnel, too small for an adult human being to crawl through, had been constructed to conceal MAGE's existence and its regular delivery of supplies provided by Malvern Media. The system was entirely automated, with deliveries placed into a series of wagons that ran along a miniature track into the heart of the mountain.

The main entrance to MAGE via the seed vault, with its physical and virtual security features, need not be breached, and there would be no awkward questions about why supplies were being delivered to the vault, when no one was apparently living or working there.

As Adams rounded a snowy ridge, he spotted a figure standing in front of the entrance to the vault, his cobalt-blue jacket and black pants standing out against a backdrop of white. He cut the snowmobile's engine and lights.

Fortunately, the howling wind was coming from the direction of the vault towards him, concealing the machine's sound.

The lack of reaction from the figure in the blue jacket revealed he had not been alerted to Adams's presence. He seemed to be looking for a way into the vault.

Adams made his move across the thickly packed snow, the man in blue still oblivious to his approach. He had been briefed by Kaito about other interests in the Saturnian diamond, but had assured the TIA Director that once it was inside MAGE, the diamond would be secure.

He drew closer, slowing his footsteps until he was within range. Blue seemed mesmerised by the light installation on the vault's exterior.

Before his quarry could react, Adams had hastened across the steel bridge, and had a gun held to the side of his target's head.

Blue started slightly but, noticing the gun, did not move.

'The vault's closed to visitors,' quipped Adams.

Blue looked at him sideways. In an instant, Adams recognised who it was.

Before leaving Osaka, Kaito had supplied him with the only available image of a character called Necro and provided intelligence about his possible interest in the Saturnian diamond.

'Necro. You move pretty fast,' said Adams.

'I'm not Necro,' protested his captive. 'Necro's my twin brother. I am Neven, and I'm here to stop him stealing the Saturnian diamond.'

Adams grinned. 'Sure you are. Kaito told me you were cunning, adept at switching personas. There is no record of Necro having a brother, let alone an identical twin.'

'There's no record because I've never visited Terra before,' said Blue. 'If you don't believe me, wait and see. He's after a superconductor and he knows it is en route to this place. I'm surprised he's not already here.'

Adams considered this for a moment, but on balance, decided it was too risky. This figure was a positive ID on the individual he'd been warned about, and there had been no intelligence about a brother, let alone a twin brother. Necro was, however, a calculating, devious sort who would not hesitate to claim to be his own twin.

'If you are who you say you are, and your brother shows up, then I'll know whether you are speaking the truth soon enough. In the meantime …'

Adams reached inside his red jacket and produced another device, a mini tranquilliser gun with a clear liquid in it. He held it to Blue's neck and fired.

'No! I'm telling the truth! You'll need me to talk to him, convince …'

Neven's words were lost on the wind as he slid to the frozen ground, unconscious.

Adams went to retrieve his snowmobile, and then returned to the vault entrance, heaving Neven up and folding him face down over the rear of the machine.

There was a group of abandoned buildings a short distance away. He set off, the steady snowfall rapidly concealing his tracks.

Adams dragged the drugged Nautilan inside one of the old wooden buildings, covered him with a thick woollen blanket from the snowmobile's storage compartment, and then rode back to the vault.

Adams calculated he had at least a few hours before the tranquilliser wore off. If his captive was telling the truth, it would become apparent before then. If he was not, then he had Necro immobilised.

He parked a few hundred metres from the vault entrance and turned the snowmobile's engine and head-lights off. He let his eyes adjust to the dim, blue darkness, and settled in to wait, his gaze fixed on the glittering beacon in the side of the mountain.

THE BRAINS TRUST

AMBRA EMERGED FROM her turquoise haze into a large cave filled with golden light.

Is this another challenge? Jostein had said there were only seven.

As her eyes adjusted to the light, she drew in her breath. She was not alone.

Facing her were three not-quite-human figures, at least twice her size, sitting side by side on intricately carved wooden thrones.

Ambra did not breathe or move.

Each had the body of a human, but the head and tail of a different creature—the first, that of a lizard, or perhaps a small dinosaur. The second, a lioness. The third, a silver-grey wolf.

Looking at them, Ambra's mind spun back to tales of mythology she had read as a child—minotaurs and werewolves, Egyptian goddesses, and dragon lore.

Are they a threat?

She finally exhaled when she realised that, though they had seen her, they had not moved to attack her.

The first creature spoke, his raspy voice like gravel.

'We are the Brains Trust. My name is Rex. I represent the reptilian part of the brain, the oldest layer, that which is related to survival. I am Instinct.'

The golden light glinted off his bronze scales as he blinked slowly and scraped his heavy tail around the base of his throne.

The second creature spoke, her silky voice soothing Ambra's jangled nerves.

'My name is Lex. I represent the limbic mind, the layer of the brain that is related to relationships and bonding. I am Emotion.'

Her tawny fur was set off beautifully by a halo of light as she switched her tail back and forth.

The third creature spoke. Ambra couldn't tell if the voice was male or female.

'My name is Tex. I represent the neocortex, the part of the brain that has higher functions such as consciousness, abstract thought, reason, planning. I am Cognition.'

Ambra gazed at Tex's copper eyes, and lush silver fur tail.

'Lovely to meet you all, but I suspect you're an illusion too,' said Ambra.

Rex snorted, Lex smiled, Tex's expression did not change.

'You found your way through the MAGE maze,' said Rex.

'I'm still not entirely sure how,' admitted Ambra. 'I mean - how could I have *flunked* the maze?'

'You could have become stuck, at any level,' said Tex. 'And if you had, while you would eventually have been brought out of the maze on Jostein's return, you would not have gained entry to MAGE.'

'Okay - so how did I succeed?'

'What did you notice about each level?'

'I'm not sure what you mean,' said Ambra. 'Do you mean the colours? Or the time and place?'

'How did you get out of each level, back to the cave and ready for the next level?' elaborated Lex.

Ambra thought back through her experiences—was there even a common theme? Beige, purple, red, blue, orange, green, yellow … they had all been radically different times, places, and scenarios.

She cast her mind back and thought about how the illusions on each level had ended.

'I … I guess I saw that things weren't working for me. The world was changing, and I wanted to change, to move beyond what was happening in the life I was in.'

'What else?' grunted Rex.

Ambra thought for a moment.

'I noticed that the further I went into the maze, the

more complex the world, and the life in each world, became.'

'You are close to discovering the nature of MAGE,' intoned Tex.

'Human beings have collectively terra-formed a world that cannot be sustained for all its people, indefinitely,' said Lex.

'You humans wonder why it is hard to change this,' rumbled Rex. 'You think you operate from your rational mind, but you are also still captive to your instinct and emotion.'

'More so than knowledge, more so than the rational mind, it is beliefs that shape behaviour, and that internal mindscape manifests as the world we see around us,' said Lex.

'MAGE was created to influence that mindscape, and the entrance to MAGE you have conquered is an initial screening process to determine if you are ready to experience MAGE,' said Tex.

'So—all those challenges … those illusions. They really *were* all in my mind?' Ambra rubbed her temples.

'They were manifestations of the collective human psyche as it has evolved through the ages,' said Lex.

'Over millennia, the world and how people live in it gradually became more complex. Then that complexity began to evolve at a faster and faster rate, and the minds of human beings had to adapt faster in response,' added Rex.

'But human civilisation is now facing its greatest challenge, at a scale and pace that is unprecedented—and a way to speed up the response, to adapt accordingly, must be developed,' said Tex.

'Huh? I still don't understand,' said Ambra.

'You will soon. You have shown you are able to handle the different kinds of things you will encounter in MAGE,' said Tex.

The golden light in the cave brightened until it dazzled Ambra so much she had to squint, then cover her eyes.

The light dimmed, and Ambra opened her eyes to see that the three creatures were gone.

Where they had been sitting there was a large stone archway.

She cautiously picked her way across the room and started down the tunnel. Not long into the tunnel, she encountered another heavy door, ringed in red LED light. Recalling how she'd opened the first door, she turned her focus on it until the light changed to green, and the door grated open. She was in.

MAGE

AMBRA EMERGED FROM the tunnel into a dimly lit, concave room with a low ceiling.

It was filled with electronic equipment—an assortment of screens filled with code, keyboards, and hard drives, gently blinking lights of all colours. Binders and papers were scattered over desks. Cables, screwdrivers, circuit boards, and soldering irons were strewn around the room. Stray coffee cups.

There was no one about.

'Hello?' she called, her voice sounding small.

There was a corridor off to the side, glowing with light.

She made her way over to the entrance and peered around the corner. Voices drifted down the corridor, along with the sound of clanking cutlery and the smell of toasted sandwiches.

Slowly she moved towards the source of the sound. She was able to distinguish three different voices, all male. Her jaw clenched.

Why didn't I think to ask Jostein about how many people are in the MAGE team, and who they are?

She inhaled, walked in—and her mouth fell open as her eyes met those of someone unexpected.

'Ambra!'

'Dad?'

Robert Lightstone leapt up from his seat to greet his daughter.

In her father's embrace, Ambra felt safe for the first time since she had encountered The Sand Poet.

'What are you doing here?' she cried.

'What are *you* doing here?' he returned. 'Is everything alright? How did you get here? How did you get *in?*'

'I'm okay. Everything else—well, that's a story and a half.'

Ambra filled her father in on the events in Atlantum, *Neptune's Revenge* and Venice, noticing how his face contorted into a different shape with each new revelation about the theft of Lillian Lightstone's work, Jevon being trapped in a virtual reality experiment in the ocean depths, and Umiko's intelligence about MAGE.

'And then I had to find my way through a virtual maze to get in here,' she finished.

'You beat the MAGE maze!' exclaimed one of her father's colleagues, eyes wide.

'Told you it was useless,' sniffed the third man.

'Ambra, this is Professor Wilf Mortlock—he's the engineer of this place, and he designed the maze. And this,' he gestured at his other colleague, 'is John Goyder. He's our head of operations.'

Ambra shook hands with both of them, noting a look of admiration in Mortlock's eyes.

'I'm impressed you found your way in through my maze,' said Mortlock.

A smug look began to spread across Goyder's face.

'It's just as well we did locate this thing in the Seed Vault then, behind additional layers of security,' remarked Goyder.

'Anyway, what is MAGE? All I know is it's a simulator,' said Ambra.

'It is not a word, but an acronym: Mission Assurance Gaia Experiment,' explained Lightstone.

'Oh. So—that's what MAGE stands for, but what does it *mean*?' asked Ambra.

'In aviation, "Mission Assurance" is the ability to safely operate a craft—a metaphor adopted for "Spaceship Earth". This simulator is part of the mission-critical capability for human civilisation,' explained Mortlock.

'And "Gaia" is the ancient Greek name for the goddess of the Earth,' continued Lightstone. 'It's also the name given to the Gaia hypothesis—the idea that the Earth itself is alive and self-regulating. Of course, this simulator is one big experiment.'

'I still don't understand—what is it for, what's the purpose in building it?' pressed Ambra.

'I'm glad you asked!' crowed Mortlock, as Goyder rolled his eyes. 'Right this way.'

They all followed Mortlock back to the main room.

'MAGE is a simulator that was developed after it was realised that the block to our civilisation's challenges—including, but not limited to addressing climate change—was not the *intellectual understanding* of scientific fact, but the *emotional acceptance* of it. Human beings tend to act according to what we *believe* and *feel*, not what we *know*,' said Mortlock.

Ambra recalled Lex's words from only minutes ago: *More so than knowledge, more so than the rational mind, it is beliefs that shape behaviour.*

'Okay. But what does that have to do with this simulator?'

'Every species has two evolutionary tendencies that humans share,' her father responded. 'Firstly, to expand to fill all potential habitats, and secondly, to use all available resources in a habitat. But throughout most of our evolution, we humans have simply not been capable of destroying whole ecosystems. In the absence of massive habitat destruction, there was no selection pressure, no biological inhibition in our evolutionary history for more moderate behaviour, so modern humans still lack instinctive restraints against doing the scale of damage made possible by technology.'

'And now, the same genetic traits that have assured our competitive supremacy have become maladaptive in the very circumstances that our competitive superiority has created,' continued Mortlock.

'So … there are no evolutionary "brakes" in terms of human biology?' clarified Ambra.

'Right, and the consequences have become much more evident in our lifetime,' said Lightstone. 'However, because of uniquely human social and cultural factors, human beings are not only transmitters of genes, but also beliefs, values, assumptions, and ideologies that shape how we see the world.'

'That means human evolution is as much determined by cultural factors as by biological factors,' explained Mortlock, continuing to fiddle with instruments and settings as he spoke 'and to survive, we must understand that while maladaptive *biological* mutations will be "selected out" in an environment for which they are unsuitable, maladaptive *cultural* patterns can also be selected out. Our cultural programming is the key to keeping our biologically determined, but increasingly dangerous behavioural patterns, in check.

'MAGE offers a way to help our cultural programming overcome our biological impetus. The science and intelligence communities may seem unlikely allies, but both have long been aware that humanity is running out of time to avert future scenarios that we are currently trending towards—climate change, crop failure, flooding, extreme weather events, biodiversity loss, total economic collapse, and civil breakdown.'

'But—how does the simulator work? What does it actually *do*?' pressed Ambra.

'This simulator blazes new neural pathways in the brain, so that physical and emotional experience informs and activates the intellectual information we acquire through a virtual reality experience. It brings the consequences of choices closer in both space and time, and lets people *feel* what happens if we don't work consciously to override our genetic code,' said Lightstone.

Override our genetic code!

Ambra thought of her mother's Rapa Nui Gene-editing technology that Necro had stolen and misrepresented.

Lightstone caught the look on his daughter's face.

'Your mother and I have been working on the same problem but with different approaches. And as much as I disagreed with it, now that your mother's work has been compromised, MAGE is even more crucial. If people are fearful of or averse to a gene-editing virus, we need to be able to try a 'meme virus', a way to fast-forward a shift in consciousness and behaviour that overrides our genetic tendencies. Memes - in the sense of memetics, or transmission of culture - can spread across the same generation, as well as between generations, and can create change quickly.'

'We've been running various tests and created prototypes, like the maze you just experienced,' added Mortlock. 'And we have a few others working on extra elements.'

Ambra wondered about Jevon, and if he was still in Lord Abzu's game.

But before she could ask whether Jevon's experience would be similar to MAGE, Mortlock was pointing at an alcove on the far wall, where Ambra had first entered.

'And that,' declared Mortlock, 'is how the magic happens. Until now we've only had the ability to program and test MAGE on a much, much smaller scale. Now we have the power source we need for the full MAGE experience.'

In the alcove was a socket. Fitted in the socket was an uncut, unpolished stone, of the deepest blue. The size of an orange, it sparkled and shone even though there was little light in the room.

The Saturnian diamond.

'The diamond is *here*? Now? Already?'

In response to quizzical looks, Ambra pointed to the diamond.

'We've only had it delivered in the last hour or so by our American partner,' said Lightstone. 'He knew it was out there, but for a long time, no one knew where. This is the big breakthrough we needed.'

'*That's* the reason I am here. The man who stole Mum's work, the same man Umiko was tracking, wants to steal it and use it for something terrible,' said Ambra.

'Won't happen. This thing is failsafe,' said Mortlock. 'We're in one of the most secure locations on Earth.'

Goyder snorted.

'I just got in,' pointed out Ambra, who was beginning to share Goyder's cynicism over the facility's security features.

Mortlock waved away Ambra's concerns. 'Well, yes—but you did have a contact who got you into the vault.'

'How are you going to get people to try this simulator?' asked Ambra. 'You can't coerce them.'

'Not at all. There will be those who are wary, and those who are resistant, but there will be no obligation to try it, and anyone wanting to experience MAGE will be fully informed about what is involved, and what to expect. Humans are inherently curious. They like games, and don't like feeling as if they are missing out on something. We're confident this will become a prestigious experience for some, and a dare or face-saving exercise for others,' said Mortlock.

'Would you like to try MAGE?' Lightstone asked Ambra.

'We've already given it a run, and it's worked exactly as we intended. We're convinced that this is going to have a huge impact,' said Mortlock.

'But it would help us to have someone who hasn't been involved in its development try it, give us some feedback,' added Lightstone.

Ambra hesitated.

Her mind flashed colours and scenarios, ones she'd truly experienced, even though they weren't 'real'.

And she'd survived them all.

She nodded.

SENSING IS BELIEVING

MORTLOCK LED AMBRA to a small door that opened from MAGE's control room, and then stood back to let her inspect the inside of MAGE.

Peering through the door into the simulator, Ambra noticed little more than an ordinary, average-sized, empty, square room, the interior completely black. There were no lights, no controls, not even a chair.

'What? Is this it? It's a black box!'

Mortlock laughed.

'Appearances are deceiving,' he said, raising an eyebrow and motioning for Ambra to enter.

'Oh, come on! It can't be an empty room.'

'You're in that simulator to concentrate the energy, the frequencies that generate the simulation, and also so that those running the simulation don't get caught up in the sequence of events the participant is experiencing.'

He pointed up to a series of cameras around the edges

of the room's ceiling, positioned to cover all possible angles of activity in the simulator.

'We need to be observing participants at all times to safeguard them and bring them out of the simulation, without getting distracted or involved in what the participants are feeling. This is much more advanced than the VR systems we've been able to use thus far. This is total immersion. Participants simply walk into the simulator, and the illusion does the rest—much like those you encountered on the way in, but vastly more sophisticated.'

'How do I get out of it, once it has started? Do I need to do anything?'

'No, we dial down the simulation, at the same time as one of us will come in to touch you, as a way of bringing you back to your body—while in the simulation, you're very much out of your body, as everything is happening in your head,' said Lightstone.

'It works as we envisioned, now we have the diamond,' said Mortlock, punching the air. 'The maze was the best we've been able to achieve so far. But we'd not be able to run a simulation of this complexity without that space diamond. You are about to be the third person in the world to experience this.'

Third?

Ambra looked at Goyder.

'You didn't want to give it a go?'

Goyder sniffed and went back to his paperwork.

'What's it like?' she asked.

'It's hard to describe in words,' said Mortlock. 'This is something you have to *feel*. That's the whole point of MAGE.'

'Okay, let's do it then,' she said, taking a deep breath.

She stepped through the door, Mortlock shutting the door behind her.

Pitch black silence.

Next, a rumble under her feet, then up the sides of the simulator.

Blinding royal-blue light. Saturnian light.

Then she was flying, soaring through the skies. She had a bird's eye view of the world, from a long way up.

It was unrecognisable.

The world's mightiest rivers—the Amazon, the Nile, the Ganges—had all drastically reduced in volume and length. There was almost no white around the poles, and the land surface was now more yellow and brown than green.

The Earth was the wrong colour.

And the continents were the wrong shape.

The sea was where it shouldn't be.

The physical face of the world had changed.

Ambra began to swoop closer to the surface of the planet, gripped by a sense of foreboding.

She was over savannah. Hundreds, thousands, of kilometres. She noticed there were few big animals left to spot. Was there not a single giraffe or elephant left?

She was over the far north, the frozen tundra, now a cesspool of hot gas, inestimable tons of methane that had long been locked up in the ice now released, and cooking the atmosphere with twenty times more intensity than carbon dioxide.

She was over the once-vast northern boreal forests and tropical rainforests, which had been home to the greatest diversity of plants and animals on the globe, but were now decimated by the loss of rainfall from shifting climatic patterns.

Then she was closer.

She was skimming over farmland, the world's food bowls. Drought. Abandoned fields and agricultural equipment. Desolation and despair on the faces of souls toiling to eke out an existence on land that had once fed the world, but which was now too parched and hot to sustain much life.

Closer again.

She was flying through the cities, home to hundreds of millions of people, on all continents.

Trillions worth of infrastructure—buildings, houses, roads, schools, industry—underwater. Abandoned hospitals, shops, zoos, and universities. She could see makeshift encampments stretching in all directions as displaced people were forced into neighbouring territory.

Everyone was a refugee from something.

But there were no aircraft in the skies, anywhere. There was no way for people to get to loved ones across a country, let alone an ocean. There were no telecommunications—phones, internet—nothing, save isolated pockets where she observed a few hackers had managed to cobble together a rudimentary, localised system, using salvaged materials.

Closer still, she was witnessing the effects of rapidly spreading sicknesses affecting areas and populations that had never before encountered them—malaria, yellow fever, dengue fever, tuberculosis, even bubonic plague.

Borne by disease vectors like mosquitos and rats, shaken out of their usual habitats by temperature and rainfall patterns that had changed faster than the usual speed of evolution, they had triggered pandemics.

Aside from such disease, she saw people afflicted with common illnesses and conditions like gastroenteritis and diarrhoea, dehydration and heat stroke, but with little access to treatment or preventive medication. There were few hospitals, and those few were being run in an ad hoc way, poorly supplied and unable to offer much assistance. People were dying in droves from what had been treatable illnesses.

She was on the ground, among people.

There wasn't enough food. The climate had shifted and destabilised faster than people had been able to adapt to the new conditions to plant, cultivate, and harvest the staple foods the world relied on.

She saw conflict over food, fuel, water. Though there were some enclaves where people seemed to be working together, most of her observations were people fighting each other for resources, motivated by pure fear.

Her heart filled with dread as she wondered what had happened to the vulnerable, those who couldn't fend for themselves. Life was tough enough for the strong and healthy—what of the sick, the disabled, the elderly, and the very young?

Across the globe, human civilisation had been plunged into day-to-day survival mode. There was no capacity or capability for anything more that had made life worth living. There was no sense of organisation or order, no structure or safety.

Ambra fell into the depths of despair at the state of the world.

She looked at the barren ground around her, and beyond to a camp of makeshift tents by the river.

'Mum?' came a small voice from behind her.

Ambra spun around to see who had spoken.

A teenage boy, rake-thin, in need of a bath and a haircut, and wearing clothes that wanted mending, was studying her.

'Are you looking for your mother? Is she with that camp over there?' Ambra said, pointing to the river settlement.

'What do you mean? Where have you been?' he said.

Ambra scanned the boy's auburn hair and grey-green eyes. She looked down at her hands. They were the hands of an older woman.

A creeping cold enveloped her.

'What's your name?' she croaked.

'Don't you recognise me?'

'Tell me your name,' she repeated.

'Lewis Lightstone.'

'What's the date today?'

'The fifth of October 2042,' said the boy, with an air of pride at remembering this detail.

'Where's your father?'

'He's dead. From the malaria. You and Uncle Jevon look after me, remember? Come on, let's go and see if there's anything to eat tonight.'

Ambra clapped both of her hands over her mouth.

This was her son's life, in *this* world?

A world where civilisation had been undone.

Her heart broke and her eyes filled with tears as Lewis continued to talk, but her ears seemed filled with a roaring sound and she could no longer hear what he was saying.

A moment later, the world was interrupted.

SENSING IS BELIEVING 2.0

AMBRA SENSED A strong pair of arms around her, though she could not see anyone.

Oh God!

The re-entry sensation was like being jolted out of a nightmare mixed up with jet lag and being on a stomach-churning carnival ride all at once.

A wave of nausea hit her, and she fought to stop herself from retching.

'Impressive!' said Mortlock, as she emerged from MAGE, leaning on her father. 'I know how sick it can make you feel when you come back. You should have seen the mess after …'

He stopped mid-sentence as Lightstone shot him a look.

Ambra sat down on one of the control-room chairs for a few minutes, alternatively sipping water and taking deep breaths until she had recovered.

'So—what did you think?' asked Mortlock.

'Jesus CHRIST! What the *hell* was that? Are you kidding me?' snapped Ambra at her father. 'Why would you put me through that?'

'That is a world that has hit 4C warming, and burnt through its remaining accessible fossil fuel reserves,' said Lightstone, without a hint of surprise at his daughter's reaction.

'Everything else you see—species loss, collapse of food supplies, displacement, conflict and violence, outbreaks of disease and flooding—are all a result of that,' said Mortlock.

Ambra's face crumpled.

'Well, it's dreadful. It's just *awful*. Beyond words. Especially when I saw my …' she gulped, unable to share the encounter with Lewis. 'If only everyone could feel that, they would … the future would be different, right?'

Lightstone placed his hand on his daughter's shoulder.

'Who wants to live in a world without giraffes?' whispered Ambra, almost to herself.

They lapsed into silence, punctuated by Goyder tapping numbers on an old-style calculator.

Ambra looked up at Mortlock.

'You said MAGE can be programmed to test different scenarios,' she said.

'Yep, we can test what happens given all kinds of variables, different system conditions,' said Mortlock. 'We have access to huge amounts of data, from various United Nations agencies like the Food and Agriculture Organization, World Health Organization, also the International Energy Agency—you name it. Thousands of data sets.'

Ambra looked at him, then her father.

'Then I need to know what it feels like when it works out,' she said.

'What do you mean?' asked her father.

'When we work it out. Not when we fail. What's the world like if we sort it out?'

Lightstone scratched his head. 'Huh. We didn't think of that. Of course, we should also run that scenario; in fact, several variations.'

'Yes!' exclaimed Mortlock. 'People have to have something they want to move *to*, not just to get away *from*!'

Lightstone was already hammering away at keyboards and screens, tweaking the system conditions and muttering to himself.

'Less than two degrees ... reduction in material throughput ... all people in upper-left quadrant of UN Human Development Index and Ecological Footprint overlay graph ... permafrost stays intact ... 50 per cent of all ecosystems set aside for other species ... rapid transition to renewable energy ... increase food production in cities ... end extreme inequality ... adjust economic assumptions to fit within biological limits ...'

Once he was satisfied, he waved to Ambra who stepped back into the MAGE simulator, Mortlock closing the door behind her.

The rumble under her feet, the flash of blue Saturnian light.

Again, she was far above Earth, with an astronaut's view.

This time, Ambra could see that, though there were some minor differences, the shape and colour of the world looked mostly as it should—the polar caps intact, the green belts of the tropics and temperate zones ringing the globe. The rivers flowed. Crops flourished. Animals and birds were thriving.

Closer she flew. A brilliant blue sky.

Every building in every city on every continent was a power station, solar arrays dotting the urban landscape, fields of wind turbines beyond the cities, a sea of blades slowly rotating.

She could see that the rooftops were green, that all kinds of produce was being grown in urban farms right in the city. There were even beehives on rooftops, for the precious pollinators of much of the food supply.

She was on the ground.

Here, Ambra felt something more than the physical world had changed, though she couldn't put her finger on exactly what.

Life on Earth was still no utopia, but she sensed that people seemed less frenetic, and more connected to each other. There was no pervading air of fear or apprehension, no overwhelming milieu of conflict or crime—and no pandemics.

She was in the city. The air was clean, birds warbled,

and the streets were alive with people who were walking or on bikes or cargo bikes, no longer forced inside by dangerous, noisy vehicles. Rapid transit moved people safely and effectively within and beyond the city.

'Mum?' came a familiar voice behind her.

She turned to see a very different Lewis Lightstone. He looked healthy and well-nourished, the faint freckles across his nose almost disappearing into his sun-kissed skin. He was rolling up the sleeves of his checked shirt and kicking dirt from his boots.

Lewis laughed, tipping his wide-brimmed hat off, and running his hand through his tousled hair.

'Ha! Why'd you look so surprised, Mum? You know all the cool kids are into urban ag and city farms—well, that, or they're off engineering distributed renewable energy systems,' he jerked his head in the direction of a teenage girl who was approaching.

'How'd it go?' asked Lewis, addressing the girl.

'Hey! Hi, Mum. Yeah, the city's pretty pleased—let's just say the next time anyone wants a citizen-powered energy-trading system, they'll call Jess Lightstone, founder of LightWork Energy,' she beamed, waving a signed contract in the air.

'Good one, sis! Congrats, that's a huge win. And it goes without saying that I'll sign the farm up as your first customer.'

Ambra stared at her daughter, a mirror image of herself at the same age.

'Here, try one of my strawberries.' Lewis dipped his hand into a bag he wore across his body and held out a handful of bright-red fruit.

'You'll be impressed. Dad reckons they're even better than my avocados.'

Ambra's face creased into a smile, her heart overflowing.

He was only a teenager, but already her son was a farmer, a twenty-first century farmer, using time-honoured techniques as well as modern technology to turn soil, seed, sun, and water into food, right in the heart of the city.

Her daughter, barely out of her teens, was running a co-operative, an employee-owned and governed enterprise that literally put the power of energy generation and trading into people's hands.

Ambra's eyes filled with tears of love and pride.

She had so many questions for her Lewis and Jess, but before she could ask, a feeling of disassociation gripped her once again.

A pair of arms around her.

She broke the surface of the illusion, her father catching her as her knees buckled.

Another wave of nausea, but her heart was singing.

Her father led her out of the simulator and gave her a drink of water.

'And?' asked Lightstone after Ambra had had a couple of minutes to recover.

'What's it like?'

Ambra smiled, through tears of relief.

'It's hard to describe in words.'

She wiped her eyes. But before she could say any more, she hit a wall. The experience in MAGE had been emotionally and physically exhausting, even though it had been created entirely by virtual sensations.

Her eyes were heavy. 'Do you see … what I experience in there?' she asked.

'Yes—well, we design some of it, and your conscious and subconscious mind does the rest,' said Mortlock.

'How do you know my future self has a son and a daughter?'

'We don't,' said her father.

'There are too many variables, not the least of which is your free will and choices.'

'So—Lewis and Jess aren't real?' Ambra's face fell.

Lightstone did not answer but stroked his daughter's forehead.

'Ambra, MAGE is an incredible experience, but it does take a significant toll on your body, as well as having a psychological impact. And you've already been through quite an ordeal to arrive here. Go and get some sleep. We'll talk more in the morning.'

GOYDER'S LINE

AMBRA WAS WOKEN a few hours later by a huge commotion from MAGE's laboratory. Still half asleep, she stumbled out of her bunk and hurried down the corridor to the main lab.

She found her father and Mortlock in an uproar, arms waving and bellowing, but she couldn't comprehend what they were saying, or what had happened.

Were they fighting?

John Goyder was nowhere to be seen.

Ambra glanced at the wall of MAGE controls. There was one glaring omission.

The socket in which the Saturnian diamond had been placed was empty.

The gem was gone.

'Half an hour! Half a bloody hour's kip since the diamond arrived, and this happens,' ranted Lightstone, as he and Mortlock began frantically examining CCTV footage from within and at the exit points of MAGE.

'There!' shouted Mortlock.

Lightstone skipped back through the footage.

Barely half an hour ago, the security cameras showed John Goyder sneaking out of MAGE, back through the vault and its series of doors, and out into the white world. In his hand, he held a black-velvet pouch with an object the size of an orange in it.

He left a trail of deep prints in the snow, and then stopped, waiting.

Within a few minutes, the footage showed a snow-mobile emerging from the darkness. The driver's identity could not be determined, his face hidden by a blue-and-black balaclava.

Goyder jumped onto the back of the snowmobile, which then sped off towards the coast of the island.

Mortlock slammed his fist onto the desk, causing Ambra to jump.

'Goyder!' he shouted. 'This time you've really crossed the line!'

'We thought we had screened him so thoroughly,' lamented Robert Lightstone.

Mortlock jammed both his hands into his hair, eyes wild.

'*Now* what are we going to do? MAGE is useless with-out the superconductor!'

'Who could possibly have been riding that snowmo-bile?' said Lightstone.

'Does it matter?' roared Mortlock. 'The diamond is gone!'

'Yes, it matters. Whoever has provided the means of a getaway has an interest in what has been stolen,' said Lightstone.

'I know who it was,' said Ambra quietly.

Both men stared at her.

'What do you mean?' asked her father.

'I wondered if he could make it in here—through the maze—but he didn't need to. He only needed someone to bring the diamond to *him*,' mused Ambra.

'What? How? *Who?*' cried Mortlock.

'I told you, remember? In Venice, I met that intelligence agent called Umiko who had been pursuing someone trying to get his hands on that diamond, the same one who stole Mum's work. His name is Necro, and he's the heir to the throne of an undersea tribe called the Nautilans,' said Ambra.

Her father and Mortlock exchanged glances.

There was a moment's silence.

'Ambra, you've had a frightening experience,' began her father.

'No, Dad! You know this is true!'

She knew her father was aware of her mother's research connection to the Ondans, but had her mother not told her father about the existence of the Nautilans?

'How could whoever stole it possibly have gotten any

communication for Goyder into this facility?' Mortlock pointed out.

'Well, how did the diamond get in?' asked Ambra.

'We have a miniature train system on tracks built into the heart of this mountain, the entrance of which is on the far side of the peak from the vault entrance. Supplies are delivered once a fortnight,' said Lightstone.

'Supplies—and occasional messages,' said Mortlock.

'Who collects the supplies?' asked Ambra.

'Goyder,' groaned Lightstone.

Without warning, MAGE began shaking and shuddering.

'What's happening?' cried Mortlock.

Objects fell off shelves. Glass shattered. Steel equipment bent and twisted. Loud bangs and crashes. Electrical circuits popped and hissed. Everything went dark.

The shaking continued. Ambra fell to the floor and groped her way under the desk she had been standing next to, where she could shelter until whatever this was stopped.

Finally, dark stillness.

'Dad?' called Ambra.

No response.

Seconds later, a generator kicked in, and though the lights of MAGE remained dark, there was enough low light for her to see the aftermath.

Mortlock was lying on the floor in front of MAGE's controls, bleeding from a small cut to his head.

'Professor Mortlock!' she called loudly, attempting to rouse the scientist.

He did not stir. Ambra checked his pulse and breathing. He was injured and out cold, but he seemed to be otherwise okay, and lying on his side.

Ambra rose and looked around the room.

'Dad?'

She saw her father, slumped against the far wall. Scampering over glass fragments, broken fixtures and upturned furniture, she made her way over to him. Like Mortlock, his breathing and pulse seemed fine, but there was a large bump on his forehead.

She gently shook his shoulder and whispered to him.

Robert Lightstone moaned, tried to move, and then lost consciousness again. Ambra gently slid him down the wall and into the recovery position.

There was no one else around. No means of communicating to the outside world.

Aided by Goyder, the Saturnian diamond had been stolen by someone unknown, but Ambra was sure she knew who it was, and he was the most dangerous person who could have it in his possession.

She had to get help. She vaulted over a fallen bookshelf, ran towards the short tunnel, and the room beyond, where she had first entered.

At the tunnel, she stopped—how could she get out? Would she have to go backward through the maze, and its illusions?

There was no door to the antechamber beyond, where she had spoken to The Brains Trust.

Tentatively, she stepped into the small room to see another tunnel leading away from MAGE.

She made for the tunnel and picked up her pace. The tunnel inclined slightly upwards, golden pinpoints of light illuminating her path as she moved along.

Wait—this is the tunnel Jostein led me down on the way in! But where are the mazes?

She looked back.

There was only the antechamber, the dim light from MAGE beyond it making it seem like it was grinning at her in the dark.

Ambra shook her head.

The maze challenges truly had been all in her mind.

Fortunately, the security doors protecting the seed vault had been designed to keep people out, not in, so she was readily able to manually open each door and make her way back to the external door.

As she made her way through the door that led out of the vault, it occurred to her that once each door closed behind her, there was no way for her to open it.

And Jostein was not due back for hours.

She had no choice but to go out into the snow. The

heavy external steel door had swung closed behind her, with a deep *boom*.

Ambra swore under her breath. If only she had thought to take something from MAGE, from the seed vault—any-thing—to prop the doors open with.

Now there was no way back in.

ARCTIC NIGHT

A̲MBRA E̲MERGED F̲ROM the vault, MAGE sealed and completely disabled behind her.

The blizzard had stopped, but the Arctic wind hurled shards of cold into her face.

She had to get help, had to warn Umiko or Quill or her mother about Necro, but the township was a long way off on foot.

Gazing at the far-off specks of light at Longyearbyen, Ambra's only option was to set off through the snow, and hope she could raise the alarm before Necro was able to carry out his plan.

Against the wind, she estimated it would take her a good hour or more in this weather to reach the town.

Just put one foot after the other.

Her adrenalin surged as she recalled Jostein's warning about polar bears; being unarmed, she could only hope luck would be on her side.

Ambra began trudging through the Arctic night, the

aurora borealis sending an occasional flash of green shimmering across the sky.

She struggled to maintain her footing in the snow, and battling the force of the wind was sapping her energy. Every few minutes she had to stop to rest. She scanned her surroundings. Then she saw it.

A white hulk of fur only fifty metres away, silhouetted by the dark blue sky. A polar bear, staring directly at her. It sniffed the air. Her breath caught in her throat.

I have nothing to defend myself with. And there's no way I can outrun this creature in the snow.

Another flash of green. The bear's thick coat rippled in the roaring wind, and its eyes sparkled with the light. Despite the searing cold, she could feel herself starting to sweat.

As another vivid burst of green light spiralled across the sky, Ambra could clearly see the bear's shiny liquorice nose and pink-stained paws and mouth, evidence of a recent meal. She began to feel faint.

Luck was on her side. The bear ambled away from her and disappeared into the snow.

Ambra let out all the breath she had been holding since she had caught sight of the bear, and resolved to pick up her pace.

Ten minutes further into her trek, she made it to the top of a small rise and saw shadows on the snow not far below, just visible in the ethereal blue light.

A white snowmobile. And the black snowmobile last

seen making its escape from the vault, on its side in the snow—an accident? Engine failure?

Then, further beyond the snowmobiles, she saw two men engaged in a fight, spilling towards the frozen coastline. One wore a blue-and-black balaclava.

Necro.

The other, a dark-haired man with a close-cropped beard, wore red snow gear.

A third, smaller man lay motionless in the snow. Goyder. He was out cold.

Red had a black velvet pouch in his hand, which he was using to land heavy blows on Necro.

Just as Ambra thought Red had the upper hand on the Nautilan, Necro delivered a one-two punch to Red's head and ribs, stunning his opponent.

Red struggled to maintain his footing, holding his ribs and wincing. Necro moved in to take him off-balance.

'Don't let him get his face near yours!' screamed Ambra at Red, her warning carried to Red on the wind.

Her shout caught Red's attention, and he aimed his next attack at Necro's solar plexus, throttling him in the midsection. Necro collapsed backwards, winded.

The injured Red turned toward Ambra, clutching his ribs, his breathing laboured.

'Are you from the vault?' he hollered, pointing at her beanie, with its circular grey, ice blue, and green logo.

Was that an American accent?

'Yes!' shouted Ambra. 'Throw it to me!' She gestured for Red to throw her the black pouch.

Emitting a roar of pain, Red hurled the pouch to Ambra in a powerful arc over Necro's head.

Ambra had to move to catch the pouch, almost wobbling over in the snow, but caught it and put it inside her jacket.

Oh God—I have no way of getting back into the vault!

She quickly scanned her surroundings.

Where can I go to keep the diamond safe from Necro?

There was nowhere else for her to go—the barren white snowscape offered no other sanctuary.

The town?

Necro will easily find me there, and even if I can convince people of this crazy story, there's no guarantee he won't find a way to snatch the diamond from me.

The Sand Poet's map?

I could use it to get back inside the vault! But I don't know if I can make the co-ordinates so precise to land me there. Even if I do, I can't communicate with anyone, and when Jostein arrives, he will be ambushed by Necro. Necro will have to go through the maze, but if he doesn't make it, the only way back out is through him. And I'll endanger Dad and Mortlock. Wherever I go, that will only buy me time until Necro finds me, and the diamond. And who, besides Umiko, will believe me?

The aquapod!

If I can get back to the vessel, I can get the diamond to Atlantum. Dad and Mortlock are injured but are safe behind locked doors. Necro's goal is the diamond, not them.

In the seconds that had elapsed while she mentally ran through her options, Necro had launched a counterattack on the distracted Red, poleaxing him into the snow. He lay gasping, as Necro turned and walked away from the island's shore toward Ambra.

Then, having found some breathing room, Necro produced a device. Ambra couldn't tell exactly what it was, but it looked like a small radio transmitter.

He flipped a switch.

As far as the eye could see, a string of orange lights spaced around a hundred metres apart appeared in the snow, like an airport runway at night.

This whole *length of coastline? What is this?*

Necro pressed several more buttons.

Eight of the lights turned red, isolating an area.

He pressed one more button.

An ominous rumbling sensation began, reverberating up through Ambra's body.

She could see Red had noticed it too, but he was struggling to get his footing.

There was an increase in frequency and strength of vibration, followed by numerous cracking and groaning noises.

Before Ambra could even grasp what was unfolding,

a section of land closest to the shore, almost a mile long, began shearing away from the coast.

Red was trapped on the wrong side of an ever-increasing gap in the ice and rock, with no way off—icy water on one side, a widening crevasse filling with freezing seawater on the other.

Ambra held her breath.

The blue-black balaclava-clad figure of Necro remained motionless, watching.

Ambra stared at him.

He planned this. He knew exactly where to lead anyone who pursued him—into a trap he had already laid.

Red seemed to be estimating how and where he could best make a running leap over the chasm.

Before he could attempt a jump, there was a dreadful screeching sound that drowned out the wind.

Then the entire section of ice and rock cleaved away from the mainland, and fell into the sea, completely submerged, taking Red with it.

Stunned, Ambra could not speak, cry, move, think.

Moments later, the chunk of land shot back up above the surface of the sea, a flash of red miraculously still visible. But the geological disruption had displaced an enormous volume of seawater, which then rushed up into the gap, pushing tonnes of earth outward.

Like riding a huge ice surfboard, Red was carried off

on the wave and out of sight, as the earth and sea continued to settle their argument in the violent aftermath.

Ambra's mind could not comprehend what she had witnessed.

Did Necro … cause the ice … the very earth … to crack and fall?

Was Red still alive?

A jolt of adrenalin shook her out of the shock. She had to get the Saturnian diamond as far away from Necro as possible, as fast as possible.

She scrambled towards Red's snowmobile and fumbled with the controls. It wouldn't start.

Argh! Had it been damaged when Red had first tackled Necro?

Frantically, she looked through the snowmobile's storage compartment for anything she could use to get the machine working. There was nothing except a blanket, and two distress flares. Jamming one of the flares inside her jacket, and pointing the other one away from herself, she fired it into the air. A bright starburst of red lit up the sky—surely someone in Longyearbyen would notice and come to investigate.

And it will give Red a chance—if he's still alive.

Heart hammering, she tried to start the snowmobile engine again. This time, it turned over, kicked into life, and she began to accelerate away, back in the direction of where her aquapod had landed, on the shore around the other side of the vault.

She saw the vault twinkling faintly in the distance like a beacon and headed towards it. From there, she could navigate her way back to where her aquapod was waiting.

As she approached the vault, she heard the revving of another engine. Glancing behind her, she saw Necro in pursuit on the black snowmobile, barely three lengths away.

She increased her speed, then banked away from the vault slightly, and set course for the aquapod. But Necro had caught up. Seconds later, she was crashed-tackled from behind, as he leapt onto the back of her snowmobile.

There was a crunch of metal as the riderless black snowmobile hit the side of the steel vault, exploding as it flipped into the air.

An orange fireball lit up the dark behind Ambra as she tried to dislodge the Nautilan, who yelled in pain as the fire pierced the sky. Then, unable to keep the snowmobile steady as it hit a mound of snow, the vehicle overbalanced, toppling both riders off.

The world rolled around and then she was flat on her back, breathless. Dazed, she saw the green light of the *aurora borealis* flash and fade above.

There was a sound of smashing glass and metal as the white snowmobile hit a rock that jutted out from the snow. The engine coughed and died.

She scrambled to her feet and saw Necro, who had been hurled sideways, close by.

He was removing his mask.

His eyes focused, and he fixed Ambra with a look of a shark eyeing its prey.

His features were breathtakingly beautiful—jet-black hair, blue eyes, exquisite lips—but his face was cold. There was an arrogance about his demeanour.

And he was capable of drowning her with a kiss.

SVALBARD, NORWAY

Necro and Ambra faced off outside the vault entrance, each trying to catch their breath.

The Northern Lights were playing along the deep blue backdrop of the polar night, reflecting splinters of light from the illuminated artwork of triangular mirrors and prisms that adorned the vault entrance.

'Hand over that diamond,' ordered Necro. 'You know what the consequences will be if you do not.'

He winced as the blue-black polar sky danced with green.

The Northern Lights are also Terran light!

Ambra realised that the longer she could delay him, the weaker he would become.

'No way in hell. I know what you're going to do with it,' she yelled.

'And what might that be?' Necro sounded amused.

'Use it to power your tsunami machine!'

'A tsunami machine?' Necro laughed. 'You think Nadir is a tsunami machine?'

Ambra was taken aback.

Had Umiko been wrong?

'Oh no,' said Necro in a low, dangerous tone that somehow carried over the wind. 'My research and plans have advanced much further than that.'

He grinned.

'Nadir is a system designed to rupture undersea rift valleys, by using the extraterrestrial power of the diamond to trigger multiple earthquakes that will be too large for the Terran Richter scale to measure. I've managed a few smaller-scale efforts, without a superconductor. But the objective is not just to generate mega-tsunamis.'

Ambra's face wrinkled in confusion.

'What, you have not heard about the inner sea that the Terran scientists have discovered?' Necro taunted. 'Nadir is designed to release it. It will bring a volume of water three times that of all the world's oceans up and across this planet you call Earth. Even Everest will be under water.'

Ambra stared at him in horror.

'I don't believe you!'

'Then it's safe for you to give me the diamond, is it not?'

Ambra didn't know what was true or not—just that she had to keep the jewel from Necro's grasp. Wherever she might go, however far she could run, wherever she might hide, he would surely track down her and the diamond. He must be eliminated.

She had the Sand Poet's mother-of-pearl map tucked into the pocket on the inside of her jacket. With the coordinates already selected to spirit her home, she only had to take it out and hit the button to activate it, *while in contact with Necro.*

Ambra knew she had just one chance at defeating this lunatic who planned to drown the world and every living being on Earth.

She estimated that the leap from cold dark night to the blazing Australian summer sun would kill Necro in under sixty seconds.

All she would have to do was make sure she could elude him for long enough on the other end of the leap, which she figured would be achievable—he would be in immediate pain from the sun and unable to muster the Nerean Kiss.

Her heart was racing so fast she could scarcely discern a beat.

'I'm out of patience,' warned Necro, taking a step towards her. 'Things don't end so well for people who get in my way. Now you're in my way.'

Ambra stood her ground. She wanted to run at him and get this over with, but it would be easier for her to conceal and activate the map at the last moment if he ran at her - she would have to goad him into physically attacking her.

She knitted her eyebrows and tilted her chin at him. 'You're a pathetic excuse for an heir to the throne. Is this all you aspire to? Eliminating all life *you* say is unworthy? And for what? A bizarre ideology that matters to so few. You'll be a pointless ruler of a realm no one knows or cares about.'

Necro's nostrils flared, and his body coiled.

Ambra readied herself.

Necro charged at her.

In the last few feet, he sprang into the air, ready to overpower her and snatch the diamond.

As he did, Ambra pulled the map from inside her jacket, and hit the button to execute her command, just as Necro's body crashed her to the ground.

But the Sand Poet's mother-of-pearl map was not intended for use under such physically vigourous conditions. The coordinates Ambra had so carefully selected nudged slightly on impact.

There was a pearlescent shimmer as both of them vanished from Svalbard.

They would not arrive at Ambra's intended destination.

RED AND BLUE

NEVEN'S EYES HALF opened.

He was inside a dilapidated wooden shack. Someone had bundled him up in a grey woollen blanket, which was warm, but coarse and scratchy.

Where the hell am I? How did I get here?

The shack provided some shelter from the elements, but there were holes in the decayed walls, and entire sections of the structure had been raided, probably for firewood. Unwanted guests, the wind, and snow had invited themselves in. Despite the blanket, his body was an ice-block.

He rubbed his face briskly, to wake up and warm up.

Kicking off the blanket, he tried to stand, but his legs almost gave way.

Neven recalled a sensation of a needle in the neck, and his memory came rushing back. He realised he was still affected by the drug administered by the American in the red jacket.

How long have I been out? Where's Red? And where's my brother right now?

He grunted in exasperation at his uncooperative limbs.

Must get moving.

After a minute, when his legs had begun to function again, he made his way over to the shack entrance.

Yanking open the door, he peered out into the polar night, willing his eyes to focus.

He began to plough his way through the snow back towards the vault, his compromised muscles screaming in protest at every step. Every green flash of the Northern Lights amplified the pain.

He ached his way up a gentle incline and was about to set off in the direction of the vault when a shower of red sparks high in the sky to his left caught his attention. Within a minute, the red had faded, but as he squinted into the distance, his sight groping around in the dim blue light, he sensed that something had changed since he first arrived.

An enormous chunk of the coastline seemed to have disappeared.

He looked out to sea.

An equally enormous chunk of ice-capped rock was floating in the bay.

Has there been an accident or explosion?

As Neven was pondering what could possibly have happened, something caught his eye.

There was a red speck visible on top of the floating chunk of ice and rock.

Red.

The pieces fell into place. He bolted in the direction of his aquapod, which he had left hidden just out of sight further around the peninsula.

He leapt in, slammed the hatch shut, and kicked the engine into gear, setting off towards Red's ice island as fast as was safely possible. As he got closer, he slowed, manoeuvring his way around the edges until he found a spot where he could dock and secure the aquapod.

He found the grappling hook in the pod's toolbox and hurled it up the side of Red's icy resting place, the hook's claws embedding deep into the ice just below the top of the slab. He tested the rope, then began to climb the rock and ice, the task hampered by the remnants of the tranquillising drug in his system.

Scaling the side of the slab, Neven hauled himself over the rim, caught his breath and then carefully picked his way over to where Red was lying on his stomach, saturated and unconscious. Frost clung to his eyelashes and beard, and his lips were blue.

Neven held two fingers to the side of Red's neck.

A faint pulse.

He rolled Red over and grasped him under the arms, dragging him across the ice in the direction of the aquapod. Red was a dead weight, and his waterlogged clothing made the task all the more difficult.

Neven reached the edge of the slab and hesitated as he looked over. It was only a couple of metres down into the open hatch of the aquapod, but his arms were burning.

Can I safely lower us without falling, or dropping Red into the sea?

In his already weakened state, ten seconds in the Arctic waters weighed down by wet clothes would be the end of Red.

Neven took a deep breath, grasped Red under the arm and across his chest with one hand, and with the other, grabbed the hook's line and, half climbing, half slipping, managed to lower both of them into the aquapod.

Neven collapsed on the floor of the pod, Red slithering to the floor with him.

Breathing heavily, Neven closed the aquapod hatch, cranked up the heating, and removed Red's sodden jacket, pants, and shoes. He wrapped Red in the foil blanket from the pod's emergency kit and began working furiously to warm him back to life by rubbing his limbs and face.

It took a few minutes, but Red regained consciousness, and his teeth began chattering uncontrollably. Colour returned to his face.

Neven levelled his eyes with Red's.

'I'm not Necro.'

Red was unable to speak, but Neven saw that his eyes understood.

'Did you see my brother? Did he show up?'

Red nodded.

'The slab of rock and ice I found you on, did he cause that to break from the coast?'

Red nodded again.

'Do you have the Saturnian diamond?'

Red shook his head.

'Did my brother get away with the diamond?'

Red shrugged. His voice was a rasp, as he struggled to speak through his cracked, swollen lips.

Neven offered him some water.

'He might have,' croaked Red. 'I caught him and his accomplice as they were getting away. We fought. I took the diamond from him, but he landed a couple of good blows and I was in trouble.'

'You said you had the diamond—did he take it from you?'

'No. There was a girl ... I threw it to her just before he ...'

Red groaned and clutched his ribs.

'What girl?'

Red exhaled.

'She was from the vault. I don't know who she was, but I was in danger of losing the diamond ... I don't know what happened after that ... whether she made it back into the vault ... or not.'

'If she made it back into the vault, the diamond is

secure,' said Neven. 'If she didn't—we have to assume the worst-case scenario.'

'What do you mean?' mumbled Red.

'My brother is a dangerous character. He wants the diamond for his own purposes, not just to incapacitate MAGE. I'll fill you in en route to Atlantum—we're going to need the help of the Ondans.'

Neven strapped the American agent in, plotted a course for the Ondan capital, and set off at maximum speed.

BUNDA CLIFFS, NULLARBOR PLAIN
REMOTE SOUTH AUSTRALIA

THE SECOND AMBRA rematerialised she knew she'd made two critical errors.

One was that she was not in Adelaide, but somewhere very remote.

Thunderous metal-grey clouds from an approaching storm and a hot northerly wind swept along a wild coastline of sheer cliffs that were a short distance away. Beyond, she could hear a boiling ocean crashing onto rocks at the base of the cliffs.

The second, and more frightening realisation, was that the sun had completely set, leaving only faint light on the horizon.

It hit her like an iron bar. She had not accounted for the change in time zone. The 'night' in Norway was the polar night—*the Arctic winter 'day'*—and she'd set the map to a location in a time zone nine and a half hours ahead, where it was night.

Necro would not be burned to a crisp under the blazing summer sun as she had imagined. She was out here, alone with him, no way of calling for help.

The leap had knocked the breath from her lungs, but she quickly got to her feet to see Necro close by, also shaking off its effects.

I am the only thing preventing him activating Nadir and causing catastrophic loss of life, if not flooding the entire globe, inside twenty-four hours.

But he was physically bigger and stronger than her. And—she blocked out the thought of what had happened to her mother's colleague.

The moon was obscured by clouds. The last remnants of light were about to be extinguished on the horizon. It would soon be completely dark, and there was no artificial light out here. She had no torch, no phone. Nothing on her, or on the ground that she could use as a weapon.

How can I possibly outrun him? And there's nowhere to hide on this flat, treeless plain.

Ambra put her hand in her jacket pocket. She could feel the smooth, unusually cold, hard surface of the Saturnian diamond inside its pouch.

At all costs, she could not let him have it.

I have to fight him, stall him, whatever it takes until the sun rises. For how long? Eight. Hours.

As she watched, she realised that Necro was not moving easily. The heat, the last faint glow of the sun, and the full moon, which had appeared between the storm clouds, was weakening the Nautilan, who had been exposed to it for over a minute now. And he was already weakened by exposure in Svalbard to the light of the moon and the aurora borealis. With a surge of hope, she stood to face him.

His breathing laboured, Necro fixed her with a stare, holding out his hand.

'Give … me … the … diamond.'

Ambra pressed her lips together and shook her head once.

'No.'

'You know what I am capable of,' he warned.

'Yeah, I do. That's why you're not having the diamond.'

Necro's lip curled.

Ambra glanced in the direction of the crashing surf.

Can I outrun him to within throwing distance of the cliff? Then I could hurl the diamond over it.

Though the sea was Necro's familiar environment, he would never find it among the treacherous rocks and surf, even if he could find a safe way to get to the base of the cliffs.

What he would then do to her was another question, but if he got away with the Saturnian superconductor, there would be far greater consequences.

Necro took a step towards her, tapping his fingers on his lips.

'Would you like me to give you a little kiss?' Necro taunted, his eyes taking on a murderous look.

He took another slow step towards her. Ambra stood her ground but tensed all of her muscles.

'You know you can't stop me. Why not just hand it over and save yourself the pain of my taking it from you?'

'Because you are a psychotic maniac who will use it to drown billions of people, including me.'

'I'm getting good at it now. I believe you're familiar with one of my previous efforts?'

Ambra's subconscious clicked two faces together. Her mind flashed back to a beach in Thailand, years before.

A lone swimmer, a young man with jet-black hair, intently watching the coastline. His hand raised, his face ecstatic. Moments later, the sea disappears.

Ambra's body went completely cold with the realisation, though the hot wind was whipping up her hair and clothes. Her skin tingled with terror.

'YOU!'

Necro smiled.

'Early tests of Nadir. That and my Japanese effort some years later.'

The ominous rumble of the storm drew closer.

'YOU DID THAT?'

Ambra wanted to run as far away from him as possible, but the immense shock had frozen her to the spot.

'Now you truly know what I am capable of!' raged Necro. 'With the Saturnian diamond as a superconductor, I can create much bigger quakes, I can unleash tsunamis, and I can release the inner sea that will end the reign of the Terrans!'

'Over my dead body!' screamed Ambra, into the hot wind.

'Nerean Kiss or over the cliff?' roared Necro. 'Either way, you *will* drown!'

Ambra broke into a run, heading for the cliff, intending to throw the diamond into the watery cauldron and robbing Necro of the key to Nadir. Tears of terror stung her cheeks as she tried to outrun death for the second time in her life.

She could hear Necro pounding behind her. About fifty metres short of the cliff, he crash-tackled her.

Ambra fought him, but he was too strong.

He grabbed her by the wrists and sat astride her. There was a faint smell of fuel on his jacket, likely a consequence of the snowmobile rollover.

She knew if he was able to begin the Nerean Kiss, she was finished.

As she threw her head from side to side in a desperate attempt to avoid his mouth, a fork of lightning split the black sky. The storm was almost overhead.

Necro cried out in pain and loosened his grip.

Aha!

He was vulnerable to the bright flash of lightning as well as sunlight, moonlight and the aurora borealis.

Ambra was able to throw him off, get to her feet, and

run a few more metres before he recovered and caught her again. His face was an ugly grimace.

Another echoing boom of thunder. As Ambra struggled, she willed the next fork of lighting to come.

But it took too long.

Necro held Ambra's face in a death grip and forced his lips to hers.

A sob welled up from within her, as she anticipated what had been her worst nightmare since that day on the beach at Khao Lak.

Nothing happened.

There was no torrent of seawater, no suffocating gurgle. Just a salty tang from the lips of a madman.

The lightning forked again, and Necro yelped.

Ambra spat away the taste of his lips.

Though she was still trapped, she laughed in his face.

'Ha! It's weakened you! You can't apply the Kiss!'

Necro's face morphed into a mask of fury. He clenched his fist and punched Ambra hard across the jaw. She gasped, and her body went limp. Her lip and nose began to bleed. She slipped into semi-consciousness.

While she was stunned, Necro held her down by the throat with one hand, and ripped open her jacket with the other, taking the Saturnian diamond from her pocket. He staggered to his feet and stood over Ambra.

Necro slipped the jewel out of its velvet pouch, and held it up, admiring the sparkling stone as he turned it in the faint moonlight emanating from beyond the clouds, the desert wind swirling around him.

'My beauty.'

Ambra tried to get up. What little she could see was shifting in and out of focus, and the sky seemed to be spinning, though she was still. But he was leaving with the stone—the superconductor.

She slumped back to the ground, head pounding.

I must get up. I must get up.

Her heart was desperate, but like a boxer being counted out, her body was unable to respond.

Then, in the middle of her groggy state, Ambra remembered.

She gingerly pulled the remaining distress flare from the inside of her jacket. Rolling over, she propped herself up on one elbow, lined up the device with Necro who was limping inland, away from the cliff, and fired it at him.

Her aim was slightly too high for a direct hit, but a bright red glow and a shower of sparks filled the air above Necro's head. Startled, he turned and looked up. Ambra waited for him to cry out, for the falling sparks to hit their mark, for the flare to hamper his escape, somehow. But the artificial light had no effect—it was not natural Terran light.

Ambra slid back to the ground, defeated. He was going to get away. He'd hitch a lift with a truckie to Port Lincoln, arriving before dawn.

Then out of the corner of her eye, she saw it.

The Sand Poet's map.

Still charged with energy released from the leap, it lay crackling and fizzing not far from her. With renewed hope, she got to her hands and knees, then managed to get herself upright. Would tackling Necro with a second leap, this time to a daylight location, be possible, despite what the Sand Poet had said?

In the red light offered by the flare, she noticed the map was charred, its coordinates no longer visible. Her heart sank. The Sand Poet was right.

Then Ambra noticed faint tendrils of smoke rising. The map had landed on a small pile of dry brush and twigs.

There was little in the way of food for a fire on this treeless plain, but there were some smaller branches that looked like they'd been brought in for use as firewood by campers who had passed through the area.

As the red light faded, Ambra grabbed as much fuel as she could find within reach, including a couple of the small branches, and fanned the smoking pile. She gently blew on it. It crackled and caught alight. She added some of the brush and twigs. The fledgling fire grew bigger. She held her branches to the small fire until they came alive, with a much bigger flame. *Terran light.* She turned and fixed her sights on Necro, now barely visible in the faint moonlight, but still making his way inland.

Ambra moved rapidly on tiptoe, trying to mask her footsteps as much as possible, as she ran Necro down. But before she had gotten within striking distance, he sensed her there, and spun around.

'NO!' he bellowed, his eyes wide with fear as he saw her brandishing her makeshift torch.

Without another word, Ambra ran at him and swung the fire at his torso.

Necro screeched as the fire made contact with his skin, and in an instant the fuel that had spilled onto his jacket in the snowmobile rollover ignited.

Ambra stepped back, watching with a mix of fascination and horror as he burned. There was another enormous crack of thunder, the storm now right overhead. The fire consuming Necro had grown frighteningly large, and Ambra had to move further away again.

He was screaming in agony, the sound whirling around in the hot wind of the desert plain, but he was not burning like a Terran. As the fire died down, and the screaming gave way to silence, Ambra noticed there was no physical body, no charred remains.

Ambra's fire had vanquished Necro, the would-be water conqueror.

But within the embers that remained, she spied the Saturnian diamond, shining bright blue in the dark, charged with the energy of the fire. She reached out to pick it up, but realised it was far too hot to touch. She sank to her knees. With the threat of Necro gone, she would wait for the diamond to cool a bit before picking it up and heading inland, towards the highway.

The wind dropped.

Ambra looked up uneasily. It was quiet. Unnervingly quiet. Eye of the storm quiet.

She became aware of a low, rhythmic vibration. She wasn't sure if she was feeling it or hearing it. As it took hold of her body, her limbs and torso began quivering. The Saturnian diamond had begun to glow a very bright blue though it was pitch black. She struggled to her feet and moved backward, away from the diamond.

Without further warning, there came an unearthly shrieking as the sky was rent by a gargantuan bolt of bright-blue lightning.

In less than the blink of an eye, the blue lightning had found the stone. For a split second, it was illuminated from within by neon blue light. Then there was an incredible explosion of white light, followed by a colossal blue fireball that shot into the sky, to the height of a skyscraper.

Ambra was blown backwards by the force. Her hair, skin, and clothes were singed, but she had been far enough away from the site of the blast to avoid serious injury.

She watched, transfixed, as the fireball dissipated into pale-blue smoke, then faded.

The wind picked up.

As she got to her feet, the white lighting flashed again, this time further off. The storm was passing over. In the instant of light offered, she saw a large area of blackened and burnt ground nearby. There was a smell of hot metal in the air, and a strange metallic taste in her mouth.

There was no sign of the diamond. Like Necro, it had been vapourised.

If I'd picked the diamond up, I'd be dead.

Ambra shook her head.

What the hell had just happened?

Had Saturn, Old Man Chronos, come for his diamond, returning it to the place from where it had been forged?

Ambra's knees were shaking. She was safe from Necro. Everyone was safe from Nadir.

But she had lost the Saturnian diamond. MAGE was now unable to be operationalised. And with Necro's legacy of lies corroding civilisation into a state of despair, MAGE was needed more than ever.

Not knowing what else to do, Ambra began staggering away from the cliffs, crying bitter tears of shock, relief, and regret. Now that the storm front had moved over, the full moon emerged from behind the clouds.

Finding her way by moonlight, starlight, and the occasional, far-off dull boom of thunder and flash of lightning, Ambra hobbled inland until she found the transnational highway in the middle of this nowhere.

She peered up and down the thin strip of grey that stretched out into an inky void beyond the reach of the moonlight. Not a soul. How long would it be until a car or truck approached? She collapsed beside it, aching and completely exhausted.

EYRE HIGHWAY, REMOTE
SOUTH AUSTRALIA

THE SQUEALING GASP of the road train's air brakes barely roused her.

Ambra's eyes squinted as she realised the sun was already high.

Too bright. Head. Ache.

Her mouth tasted of dried blood and dirt.

She heard a crow cawing in the distance.

Her eyes closed again.

A pair of boots hit the dirt edge of the highway. The rapid crunch of gravel as they ran towards her.

A rough hand on her shoulder. She could only manage a weak groan.

The melodic beeping of a mobile phone being dialled.

She heard a gruff male voice, close by but somehow sounding far away.

'G'day, that the Flying Doc? Yeah, ah, I've got a young

girl here, found her lying on the side of the Eyre Highway. Alive. Semiconscious. On her stomach. Haven't moved her.'

'Bruises, burns. She's a bit of a mess but doesn't look seriously injured. Nah, I can't tell … maybe been hit by a car … or attacked. Dunno.'

Ambra tried to raise her head but could not.

'On my way back from Perth, over the border. About four hundred kays out of Ceduna. Yep. Yeah.'

Her throat was sandpaper. She couldn't speak.

'Two hours? Yep. How long does your landing strip need to be? Yeah, I've got some kit in my cab. I can block off the eastern end with my rig and put some markers up at the other. Right-oh.'

A beep signified the end of the call.

Ambra lost consciousness again before the truck driver could offer her water.

She had no recollection of being loaded onto an RFDS Cessna that had landed on the Eyre Highway, or being flown two hours to Adelaide where she was then raced to the Royal Adelaide Hospital.

ROYAL ADELAIDE HOSPITAL

A SOFT, REGULAR beeping sound. The low murmur of voices.

Ambra's eyes flickered and opened. Everything white, a sterile smell.

Blurred shapes began to coalesce into forms. Her mother. Her father.

'Ambra!' she heard her mother exclaim.

Her mother's hand on her cheek. Ambra's eyes focused.

'Mum?'

Her father squeezed her hand.

'Dad? Where's Jevon?' mumbled Ambra through swollen lips.

'He's here at the hospital. He was only transferred here this morning, and he has been sedated. Once he comes out of that, he has to have a check-up, and then he'll be able to come and see you,' said Robert Lightstone.

'How did he … he was stuck in a game … on the bottom of the sea …'

'Yes,' said Robert glancing at Lillian, 'he was, but he managed to break out, take over the ship, and navigate it to the surface. He's safe now.'

The Lightstones had resolved not to tell Ambra about the accident Jevon had witnessed, or Umiko's death, until she'd had more time to recover.

Ambra lay back into her pillow. She squinted, her eyes darting about the room.

'How'd I get here?'

'A truck driver found you in the middle of the Nullarbor, on the side of the Eyre Highway. He called the Royal Flying Doctor Service, who flew you here.'

'Gawd. How long have I been here?'

'A few days. Can you remember what happened, love?'

'Big explosion … blue lightning,' murmured Ambra.

'Mmhmm,' nodded her father, knowingly.

Her chest jumped as she began to remember.

'Is he dead? Is he really gone?' she gasped, as the machine monitoring her heart rate spiked.

'Our Nautilan nemesis, Necro? He is definitely no more,' said her father. 'The police traced your landing spot back from the highway. There was evidence of a catastrophic lightning strike. Those stones are superconductors, and we know what can happen if you are carrying one of them anywhere near an electrical storm.'

Ambra's head echoed with the shrieking, and visions of the otherworldly blue bolt that had obliterated the Saturnian diamond. She was unable to articulate it right then, but resolved to talk to her father later about how it was no ordinary electrical storm.

'He was going to kill me … drown me,' a sob rose in Ambra's throat.

'But he didn't—and you stopped him,' soothed her mother, caressing Ambra's forehead.

In her mind's eye, Ambra saw two men fighting, the land split and fall, a massive chunk of ice carrying a speck of red into the deep blue.

'So did the American, the man in red, in Svalbard. He might be dead, but he might still be out there. Has he been found? Is anyone looking for him?'

'I think you mean Agent Adams,' said Robert Light-stone. 'One of our contacts has operatives investigating on the ground in the Arctic right now.'

'You don't understand … what Necro was going to do … what he could have done,' said Ambra. 'He didn't just want the diamond to stop MAGE. Umiko told me he'd made some sort of … earthquake machine. He was trying it out on the sea floor.'

Her parents were looking at her, not comprehending.

'He needed the Saturnian diamond from MAGE to make it work properly. He needed a superconductor … to make a quake big enough that the world would flood,' said Ambra.

Lillian looked at Robert.

'I'll get the doctor—she might be delirious from the shock and exposure,' she said.

'I am not! He said to me … he said he had been experimenting … trials with some success. Didn't Quill or Umiko tell you about what Necro had been building?' said Ambra.

'Quill has been busy helping the Ondans in removing Nefaria from power in Nautila, and I haven't had a chance to speak to him since Venice,' said Lillian Lightstone. 'We've only spoken to a man who heads an organisation based in Tokyo called the True Illusion Agency that was investigating all of this. He didn't say anything about an earthquake machine, only that Jevon had been affected by … something he'd experienced on Abzu's ship, and that Necro was after the diamond.'

'It's more than that. The Japanese tsunami—that was Necro and his machine. He calls it "Nadir". It's all still down there … on the ocean floor. Umiko and Quill went to look for it. Did they find it? Someone has to get rid of it … please, make it go away …'

'Necro told you that *he* created the 2011 quake and tsunami?' asked Robert.

'That one … and also …'

Ambra swallowed.

'Also … the Boxing Day tsunami,' she rasped.

Her parents' eyes widened.

'Oh Ambra,' said her mother. 'Are you sure you didn't imagine this? You must have been in a state of terror.'

'No … no! He was threatening to drown me … and the world. And he boasted—he *bragged!*—about the disasters he caused … all those people …'

Tears slid down Ambra's face.

'I saw him … in the ocean. In Thailand. I never told you about this boy I saw in the water, just before the … he was a long way out. I thought he was in trouble and waved to him … he saw me, but he was watching the shore, waiting … laughing. He knew what was about to happen. And he knew me. It was him.'

'If he was telling the truth, then we need to alert military and intelligence agencies to this immediately,' said her father. 'They would have the capacity to investigate and dismantle this contraption. The important thing is—he's gone, the Saturnian diamond he stole is destroyed, and no use can be made of his device.'

'Oh Dad—what about MAGE? I'm so sorry … all your hard work … the diamond can't be used for Nadir, but now there's no energy source for MAGE, and Necro's misinformation is still out there,' cried Ambra.

Robert Lightstone stared at his daughter.

'Sorry? You saved us all, and you're *sorry?*'

Ambra gave her father a crooked smile, which faded as quickly as it had appeared.

'Anyway, Necro might have taken the diamond with him back to Saturn, but there's one thing he didn't know.'

'What do you mean?' asked Ambra.

'A few days ago, we learned that the same space mission that went to Saturn brought back more than one diamond,' said Lillian.

Ambra's mouth fell open.

'Mabul, the head of Ondan intelligence in Atlantum, had one safely stored. Not even Queen Cresence knew it was there.' continued Lillian. 'Mabul acquired it from Kaito's rogue agent, who sold most of the diamonds after Kaito sent him on a mission to remove them from NASA.'

'The other night, your mother and I were summoned to an audience with two young Sottomaran royals, the princesses Lumina and Nemeia, who presented us with the diamond.' said Robert. 'We can continue to develop MAGE.'

Through tears of relief, Ambra's face creased into the most radiant smile her parents had seen in a long time. They let her smile, even as she said:

'I can't wait to tell Umiko.'

SEMAPHORE, SOUTH AUSTRALIA

AGENT DAVID ADAMS sat on the outdoor deck of the beachside cafe gazing out at the bright turquoise-blue palette of sea and sky.

He turned the cup of green tea around and around in his hands.

A young woman with wavy auburn hair strode into the cafe, pushed her sunglasses on to her head, and smiled as she recognised him.

She ordered a coffee and made her way over to his table.

'Thanks for meeting me,' said Adams, as he rose from his chair to greet Ambra. She extended her hand but was greeted with a bear hug from Adams.

Adams produced a copy of TIME magazine and waved it at Ambra. The cover story was MAGE.

'How many interviews is that so far?' grinned Adams.

'Too many,' said Ambra wryly, as they both sat down.

Adams looked at her.

'You showed a lot of gumption in making sure Necro didn't get away with that stone,' he said.

The corners of Ambra's mouth turned upwards.

'You probably know, I've made it clear in all my interviews that it was you who gave me the chance. If you hadn't been there, if you hadn't ambushed him, he would have gotten away. I felt so bad I had to leave without being able to go and get help for you … I'm just …'

She twisted the leather bracelet on her wrist with her fingers.

'I'm so glad you survived,' she finished.

'It was a miracle I did. Thank God Neven was there—and that he was still willing to save me after I put him out of action.'

'When I saw you carried away on that ice after going under, I thought you were a goner,' said Ambra.

'I still would have been—we all could have been, if it wasn't for you. You do realise that flare you set off was what attracted Neven's attention, and how he noticed me on the ice?'

Ambra swallowed, trying to clear the sudden lump in her throat, and shook her head.

'No, I didn't know that.'

Adams placed an envelope on the table in front of Ambra.

'The Serious Games Institute intends to set up another

lab in collaboration with Malvern Media, and I want you to run it. That's a job offer,' he said, nodding at the envelope.

Ambra's eyes widened.

'Me? Wow! Are you sure? I haven't even finished my studies and I'm working part time in an ice-cream shop.'

Adams jabbed his finger onto the document.

'Yes. You're one of a few people who has had direct experience with MAGE, aside from also managing to make your way into MAGE through the seven mazes in the first place.'

'Set up a lab—where? In the UK?'

'No, here in Adelaide. Aside from your experiences, there's a significant family connection with both your father's work in designing the simulator, and your mother's research in overriding our genetic predisposition. The role will require some travel, but we want it based here. The work associated with MAGE has to have a presence in all parts of the globe.'

'Oh, my goodness—I would so love to do this. Thank you so much,' beamed Ambra, opening the envelope and flipping through the document.

'Well, I am very happy this appeals to you. I'll have our new office manager Lewis and our project director Jessica get in touch as soon as possible to kick things off,' he said, his face creasing into a smile, blue eyes twinkling at Ambra.

Lewis and Jessica?

Ambra's encounters in MAGE as her future self came rushing back.

'Sorry—who? What did you just say?'

'Lewis and Jessica—they'll be your team to help get this set up here.'

Ambra stared at Adams.

'Everything okay?' he asked, eyebrows raised.

'Uh—yes. Yes. This is going to be amazing,' she exhaled.

'You'll be at the forefront of some groundbreaking work,' declared Adams. 'The human mind is as much uncharted territory as the depths of the ocean.'

Ambra's gaze shifted past Adams, to the blue line on the horizon beyond.

'It sure is,' she whispered.

EPILOGUE: MAGE UNLEASHED

THE CURSOR HOVERED over the half arrow, then clicked the 'play' button of the online video.

It was twenty-four minutes long. Six months after release, it had been viewed over three billion times.

Between the mainstream media frenzy over the sensational revelations of MAGE, the Sottomaran tribes and the interception of Necro's plans for Nadir, along with Lillian Lightstone's mini documentary on the Rapa Nui Gene Project, the whole affair was generating the kinds of discussion normally reserved for celebrities and sports stars.

Nadir had been located and destroyed by the TIA, the Ondans, and a coalition of Terran navies, aided in this task by Lord Abzu and the new Nautilan king, Neven. Fragments of Nadir, along with an exhibit as to its origins and intended use, had been put on display in public institutions around the world.

The technology powering the *Depth Charger* was the subject of an international collaboration as a means of transferring a large percentage of fossil-fuel-dependent air travel to the ocean. Although on a larger scale it was not faster than air, it appealed to travellers as it was much more comfortable, safer, and radically reduced ocean-going travel time compared with conventional methods. Funded by a consortium of governments, along with a number of leaders in both aviation and submarine technology, 'depth charging' was fast overtaking air travel as the hip new way to travel, as more vessels came online.

The wait-list to enter MAGE was already in the millions and there was demand for replicating the world's most incredible simulator on every continent. In order to power them, The Jeweller had been engaged by the TIA to secure, or advise the location of, four missing Saturnian diamonds. A four-hundred-million-dollar fee from the new body commissioning MAGE development had ensured her cooperation and compensated her for any price she would have been able to command for the diamonds as gemstones.

Kaito, director of the True Illusion Agency, who had long concealed his orchestration of the theft of the Saturnian diamonds from NASA, had emerged a hero for his efforts to secure essential superconductors far from the reach of those who would use them for destructive purposes.

MAGE was an international phenomenon, a fixture on every television and radio news show, and had been the headline-trending topic on social media since the initial announcement. It was a barbecue-stopper, a dinner party debate, and a conversation in taxis and hair salons from Bangkok to Buenos Aires.

People who had entered MAGE were not only bearing

witness to the future—they had been immersed in it and had experienced what it felt like, played out in different scenarios, and in ways that were personal to them.

Those who had been vocal climate change deniers were, surprisingly, among the keenest to experience MAGE, though their rationale was to prove that they could withstand its effects by entering the simulator, experiencing - *feeling* - the future, and showing it would not change their views.

On leaving MAGE, their typical response was silence. Some continued to half-heartedly deride the simulator's models and assumptions, but their voices were as unconvincing as their arguments.

People from all walks of life emerged from MAGE feeling stunned, scared, motivated, exultant, amazed, horrified—but all in some way irrevocably transformed.

There was a feeling of agency about what was possible, and what was necessary.

Mission Assurance Gaia Experiment was accomplishing what many had thought was unachievable—it was beginning to unite the world's people in a common purpose of designing, investing in, and creating a world that provided a good life for all, without undermining the life-support systems of Earth.

The creators of MAGE knew that shifting consciousness was only the beginning. There was a long way to go and a lot more work to do.

But finally, the tide had turned.

AUTHOR'S NOTE

The nature and structure of Atlantum was inspired by the many fantastic concept designs of ocean cities.

The idea for the Rapa Nui Gene Project emerged from a paper written by Ecological Footprint creator, Professor William Rees, in the mid-2000s, called *Is humanity fatally successful?* The concept of the Rapa Nui Gene, and the process for editing it, draws on some real elements; but it is a plot device, not science.

The idea for the MAGE simulator emerged from discussions with the late Andrew Wilford, ex-Royal Australian Airforce, ex-Boeing, an engineering lecturer, a colleague and co-conspirator, outlined in his paper *Spaceship Earth Mission Assurance*. Wilf would have loved that a concept he was developing has been woven into a story. I just wish he were here to read it.

The Sand Poet is, of course, a fictional character, but his means of communication is an art form I first saw performed by Kseniya Simonova in a clip from a Ukrainian talent show.

The Clock of the Long Now is real and currently under construction, but it is a vastly more complicated timepiece in size and engineering than the clock in Atlantum.

The calculation of rice in *Jevon's Paradox* is real and derived from calculations made for the wheat and chessboard problem.

Chiiori is a beautifully restored traditional farmhouse in Shikoku's Iya Valley that I have been fascinated with ever since reading Alex Kerr's *Lost Japan,* and I hope to visit it one day.

Project Seal was a real investigation by the US and New Zealand governments during World War II, which sought to discover whether human-initiated explosions could generate tsunamis. The ABC's AM program ran a story on this in 2013: Tsunami bomb.

The Global Seed Vault is a 'seed ark' on the island of Svalbard, Norway. According to my research, all details about the vault are true.

The MAGE Maze and its associated colours and scenarios for each level is based on the concept of Spiral Dynamics—that humanity has evolved not only biologically, but psychologically and socially—and how people respond to the world around them in given circumstances and with their particular coping abilities. It originated from the work of New York psychologist Clare Graves's 'Gravesian Theory' in the 1950s and 60s.

Goyder's Line is a demarcation line drawn between arable and marginal land in South Australia made by Surveyor General George Goyder in 1865. Goyder's Line was embodied in legislation passed in 1872, which prohibited the purchase of land on credit outside of designated agricultural areas. However, the Act was repealed in 1874, after a few seasons of good rain, to allow agricultural development north of the line—only for rainfall patterns to then return to their longer-term average, with Goyder proved right as farmers abandoned properties after extended droughts. Goyder's Line is also a metaphor and South Australian cultural shorthand for nature's limits and what happens if they are breached.

Scientists believe there is an 'inner sea', but not the kind that could flood planet Earth through a rupture.

Nadir is a fictional device—I hope! Whether human explosions can give Mother Nature a nudge in triggering seismic events that generate catastrophic tsunamis is unclear.

The Saturnian diamond may be real—the idea was taken from scientific reports of 'diamond rain' on Saturn and Jupiter. If any ever are collected and brought back to Earth, don't take them outside during a storm.

*For further information and sources, please see the
'Author's Note' section on the website at
www.magethenovel.com*